"Who knew house arrest could be **sexy and fun?**
Not me, at least not until I read *Ms. Demeanor*. Written
with Elinor Lipman's signature **wit and charm**, this
breezy, engrossing novel tells the story of two people
who make the most of their shared confinement."
—TOM PERROTTA, author of *Election*,
The Leftovers, and *Tracy Flick Can't Win*

"Elinor Lipman, she of the lightest touch and quickest
wit, has written a novel to delight even the weariest,
wariest soul of our times. Art, food, real estate—New York
City rises enthusiastically to embrace the reader, and the
characters rise to embrace each other. Lockdowns morph
into charming English villages, and love, as it must, wins
out. **An enchantment** I, for one, really needed."
—CATHLEEN SCHINE, author of *The Three
Weissmanns of Westport* and *The Grammarians*

"Elinor Lipman's *Ms. Demeanor* features a wry and
resourceful heroine who reinvents herself as a TikTok chef
after her career as an attorney is sidelined because of a public
indiscretion. Lipman, a master chef of literary romantic comedy,
cooks up a **deliciously entertaining** story whose ingredients
include **wit, sass, sex,** and **social satire**. *Ms. Demeanor* is
Lipman's fourteenth novel and one of her best."
—WALLY LAMB, author of *She's Come Undone*
and *I Know This Much Is True*

"When a neighbor's complaint about consensual al fresco
sex turns into house arrest and a suspended legal license, Jane's
recipe for survival involves cooking for another home-arrested
tenant (could this be a match made in confinement?) while trying
to figure out the whys and hows of her mysterious accuser.
Filled with food, family, romance, and intrigue, Lipman's novel
cooks up a bounty of delights as **sparkling** as prosecco and
as **deeply satisfying** and delicious as a five-star meal."
—CAROLINE LEAVITT, author of *Cruel Beautiful World*
and *With or Without You*

"DELICIOUSLY ENTERTAINING." —WALLY LAMB

Ms. Demeanor

Also by Elinor Lipman

Rachel to the Rescue

Good Riddance

On Turpentine Lane

The View from Penthouse B

I Can't Complain: (All Too) Personal Essays

The Family Man

My Latest Grievance

The Pursuit of Alice Thrift

The Dearly Departed

The Ladies' Man

The Inn at Lake Devine

Isabel's Bed

The Way Men Act

Then She Found Me

Into Love and Out Again

Ms. Demeanor

A Novel

Elinor Lipman

HARPER PERENNIAL

NEW YORK • LONDON • TORONTO • SYDNEY • NEW DELHI • AUCKLAND

HARPER ⬤ PERENNIAL

HarperCollins books may be purchased for educational, business, or
sales promotional use. For information, please email the Special Markets
Department at SPsales@harpercollins.com.

FIRST EDITION

Library of Congress Cataloging-in-Publication Data has been applied for.

ISBN 978-0-358-67788-8 (pbk.)

23 24 25 26 27   LBC   5 4 3 2 1

To the memory of Mameve Medwed,
beloved best friend and most charitable critic

Contents

Chapter 1   Regrettably 1

Chapter 2   It Begins 6

Chapter 3   Two Distinct Little Girls 13

Chapter 4   Do You Know Mr. Salisbury? 17

Chapter 5   As Opposed to Sing Sing 22

Chapter 6   Not What I Signed Up For. 29

Chapter 7   Let's Get This Over With 33

Chapter 8   I'd Rather Not Go Into It. 39

Chapter 9   Poulet à la Jane 44

Chapter 10   I'll Figure It Out. 51

Chapter 11   Pretend No One's Watching 55

Chapter 12   Scene of the Crime 61

Chapter 13   Dinner Is Served. 68

Contents

Chapter 14 None of My Business 72

Chapter 15 Company 77

Chapter 16 The Lay of the Land 85

Chapter 17 Weird If I Come, Too? 90

Chapter 18 I Only Have Myself to Blame 101

Chapter 19 New Horizons 108

Chapter 20 TMI 116

Chapter 21 It's Tricky, Though 122

Chapter 22 In the Same Boat 126

Chapter 23 The Pros and Cons 131

Chapter 24 As Ready as I'll Ever Be 138

Chapter 25 Are You Sitting Down? 143

Chapter 26 Good Cop/Bad Cop 147

Chapter 27 Count Me In 157

Chapter 28 And the Goal Here Is What? 163

Chapter 29 The Mission Is What? 170

Chapter 30 Holding Me Harmless 174

Chapter 31 The Morning After 183

Chapter 32 Sidelong Glances 191

Chapter 33 You Must Be Mrs. Salisbury 200

Contents

Chapter 34 States of Mind 212

Chapter 35 Christmas Miracle 219

Chapter 36 Case Closed 226

Chapter 37 A Reunion for Sure 239

Chapter 38 Double Date 243

Chapter 39 MEMORANDUM AND ORDER, JUDICIAL
DEPARTMENT, ON MOTION 247

Chapter 40 Window Table 249

Chapter 41 I Suppose It Wouldn't Kill Me to Take a Look 257

Chapter 42 Woman to Woman 266

Chapter 43 Dream Dresses 271

Chapter 44 Thank You, Frances FitzRoy 278

Chapter 45 Ladies' Lunch 281

Chapter 46 We Four 284

Acknowledgments 289

Ms. Demeanor

Chapter 1

Regrettably

Let's say there were two people, a man and a woman, lounging on the rooftop terrace of an apartment building in midtown Manhattan. She is thirty-nine, a lawyer. He, on the neighboring chaise longue, is twenty-seven, a new associate in the same firm who has this night confessed to a crush that was not brushed aside, as workplace guidelines required.

We'll call him Noah, and we'll call her me. It's barely our first date, after a less-than-professional conversation in a long checkout line at Trader Joe's. We have a drink or two at a nearby Mexican restaurant. We return to my building, specifically for me to show off its newest and proudest amenity, our tiled, furnished, and landscaped roof with its view of Central Park one way and Times Square blinking to the south.

It is a June night with ideal seventy-five-ish-degree breezes blowing. Above us was not just a full moon but a blood moon, huge and red.

Man, woman, mojitos. One thing leads to another, just the way Miss Freitas warned in junior high sex ed. It is past the hour at which the building lights automatically go off.

Noah asks, after a long, companionable silence on our separate chaises, "Did you ever skinny-dip?" It is, I assume, a purely academic question, since there is no pool in my building. I say, "Once or twice."

He then asks, "Do other people use the roof this late?"

I tell him I don't know. This is the latest I've ever been up here.

"No pressure," he assures me, "but do you mind if I take my clothes off? The breeze is beautiful. It'll be like moonbathing."

I don't object. Workplace ethics aside, who wouldn't be a little curious, given what sounded like anatomical pride. And who would know?

I could hear the squeak of the chaise as he lifted his butt, presumably to peel off whatever, if any, underwear a twenty-seven-year-old wears.

I say, "If anyone at work ever found out . . ."

"I'm not stupid. No one ever will." And then, "It feels great. It's like the breezes are massaging me. If I fall asleep, wake me when you want me to leave."

What could be more benign than that? No agenda, no pressure, no suggestion that I, too, might enjoy these tickling breezes on parts rarely exposed to the elements.

After a few more minutes, I volunteer, "Maybe just my dress."

"Totally up to you."

What makes my disrobing a bigger leap than I might otherwise have undertaken is that this halter dress is equipped with an interfacing that imparts built-in support. In other words, I am braless.

Why be a prude? The Eagle Scout's eyes aren't even open.

There I lie, my dress bunching around my waist, more suitable for a mammogram than moonbathing. It takes some sashaying in place, but I work everything down and off—*everything*—proving I am just as much a cool and carefree exhibitionist as any overly handsome associate, a dozen years my junior.

Now what? Sit back and mimic his atmospheric gusto?

I hear "Better not look," followed by "Sorry!"

I do look. Even in the dark I can see his two hands trying to conceal a bobbing penis.

Not unflattered, I say, "It's not doing anyone any harm." We are both silent until I ask, "Would you like me to touch it?"

Then we are, now side by side on one narrow chaise, hip to hip. Did I *not* know fully that our kissing would make his condition more acute? I say, "Maybe we should go downstairs to my apartment."

"Are you cold?"

I say no, hardly. I meant it would just be more comfortable. Just for . . . never mind. Don't stop.

The exceedingly polite Noah asks with every advance, "Are you sure?"

* * *

Having broken my own loose rule about no sex until the fifth date—maybe second, third, or fourth, depending—I intended to comply with the firm's sexual harassment guidelines. Tomorrow, first thing, I'd disclose to HR in the strictest confidence that Noah and I had seen each other outside the office. Yes, maybe news of social note delivered ex post facto, but disclosure nonetheless. Easy. No worries.

I was wrong, very. Because across the street, from a comparable elevation, a law-and-order prude of a Mother Superior couldn't take her eyes off us.

She called 9-1-1, sounding frantic over a crime taking place directly opposite her—in public! She was appalled, disgusted, shocked. She was shaking! Send someone!

When the police arrived and asked, "What do you want us to do?," she *could* have said, "Just tell them never to do it again."

But no. She wanted us arrested! She'd seen our private parts! And here, if the officers didn't believe her, the video on her phone! Is this not indecent exposure? Is this not lewd and lascivious behavior?

The officers crossed the street, badged my overnight doorman, asked if he could identify either of these people from the video, now transferred to their phones.

Whatever Andres said—maybe "Hard to tell with them moving. I think it's Miss Morgan in 6-J"—up they went to the roof, knocked on the door, announced, "Police!"

As we scrambled for our clothes, I yelled, "Give us a sec! I'm fine! We're on a date," and when we were both covered and upright, "okay, you can come in now."

They did. A man and a woman, unsmiling, both short, both solid. Noah volunteered, "If you need me to leave so she can confirm that she's safe and this is all consensual—"

Both officers, I thought, were looking more apologetic than constabular. "No," said the male officer. "We're following up on a 9-1-1 call about a crime in progress."

I told them I was a lawyer. What crime?

"Indecent exposure . . ." then, quietly, "exposing genitals to the public."

"This is private property, a co-op! I own shares in this building!"

He looked skyward. "Open air, exposed. The victim was able to videotape you. It's as good as a public place."

I said, "Victim! Isn't being a Peeping Tom a crime? I'll countersue!"

"We're obliged to follow up, ma'am," he said. "It's about the victim's mindset. To her, it was a shock."

"She had palpitations," said his partner.

"Where is she?" I asked, but it was obvious—surveilling us from the terrace directly across Seventh Avenue, with its show-off potted plants and trellises decorated for every stupid holiday.

I might as well have streaked down Fifth Avenue. In the wattage of a full moon we'd committed a lewd public act or two, considered by the traumatized killjoy across the street as gross indecency and "putting on a show."

The summons brought us a day in court. Represented by a senior member of my firm, Noah was fined, but didn't lose his entry-level job. I, a litigator, represented myself, sure that any judge would find that two consenting adults having sex on private property had done no one any harm.

During my allocution, presentencing, I couldn't bring myself to apologize. I suggested that what happened on my terrace happened all over the city, all over the country, weather permitting, between consenting adults.

"Does that make it right?" the judge asked. "Her grandchildren could've been visiting."

For my gross indecency, my apparent lack of remorse, and (unstated) promiscuity; for workplace sexual harassment, not even charged but implied; for the grainy photo published in the *New York Post*, identifying me with the suffix JD, he made an example of lawless me, an officer of the court. He imposed a fine of $2,000 and 180 freaking days of home confinement. Three already-miserable weeks later I received a letter of censure from the Bar Association with a notice that my hard-earned, income-granting, pride-affirming license to practice law had been suspended.

Chapter 2

It Begins

Who *didn't* suggest that I view my sentence as a sabbatical, a much-needed rest from briefs and deadlines and clients? Would *they* like to try six months off without travel or passport, without weekends away, or nights out, with the only fresh air available from the roof that was the scene of their crime?

If I heard a note of disapproval in anyone's helpful hint, I'd nip it in the bud. Bad behavior or just bad luck? Yes, I may have been having sex al fresco with someone—heaven forfend—I wasn't *married* to, but it's not a crime per se until observed by someone with a 9-1-1 trigger-happy finger.

"Doesn't your building have a gym?" was a favorite palliative. It did, but only someone with the whole city at his or her disposal would consider an in-house gym to be a substitute for real life.

I made a list of might-do activities I could perform solo, indoors: read books; watch the TV series that everyone had discussed with passion in the firm's break room; learn to play an instrument; keep a journal; meditate; do jigsaw and crossword puzzles; relearn to knit; hook a rug; needlepoint a pillow; paint; write letters; write a novel; write poems; cook; bake; feed a sourdough starter. The culinary activities were inspired by my state-of-the-art kitchen, no credit to me, but to the previous owner's expensive choices.

Those generous-for-Manhattan hundred square feet of kitchen were what gave my sister ideas on how to keep me busy—the word *sister* not telling the whole story, because we are identical twins, Jane Morgan, JD, and Jackleen Morgan, MD, a dermatologist with a flourishing solo practice on the Upper East Side.

A factor in her efforts to support me was her belief that she was partially responsible for my home confinement. Having attended my hearing for moral support, dressed in a red suit and a feathered black fascinator, sitting directly and identically behind me, glaring at the judge . . . might he have noticed, she asked.

I knew her. I heard her self-blame not as guilt over her courtroom behavior, but as her lifelong belief that she is the center of attention, that the male judge couldn't help but notice her, intuit her judicial animus, and punish the nearest defendant for it.

*   *   *

My parents and I don't know why Jackleen sees herself as the more important, grander twin. Is it nomenclature? Me, Jane; she, Jackleen, "Jacqueline" on her birth certificate, shortened and made cuter in high school? True, she's a doctor, but I'm a lawyer! We earned the same ribbons in high school sports and went to the same college. As to her airs of superiority and her bossiness, when challenged she doesn't know what I'm talking about.

But my bad luck has brought out the best in Jackleen. Without mentioning money, without asking me directly how I was paying my bills, she was finding ways to underwrite my unemployed existence. It wasn't the unvarnished writing of checks, but support both subtle and unsubtle, literal and figurative. She is ambitious on my behalf, and with her practice thriving, she is generous; so generous that I've stopped mentioning things I want or need, her retention so good that the book or earrings or slow cooker I've admired show up within days. I don't love being a charity case, but having turned myself into an unemployed outlaw, I'm in no position to reject her noblesse oblige. And the friends with all the suggestions about how to fill my hours, who might visit or send a note, a book, a bottle of wine? Where are they now?

*   *   *

Since the first week of my confinement, Jackleen and I talked daily, and have a standing Sunday-night dinner, always her treat, a bounty of extras delivered so I'll have leftovers. The day she suggested we forgo our usual takeout, I sensed she was up to something and asked why.

She missed my cooking! Why order in when we could have one of my brilliant meals? More transparent compliments followed: What I produced was creative and delicious. And my gorgeous kitchen! Was I using it to its full capacity? She wished *her* kitchen had that double oven, these six burners, that trash compactor.

I said, "But you never cook. You keep boxes of shoes in your oven. What's really up?"

She said, "I have an idea. I'll tell you over dinner tomorrow! Order anything and everything you want," she said, her Fresh Direct password texted as we spoke.

I was susceptible. I had no income. I paid my maintenance and utilities from savings; didn't want to touch my 401(k) or take handouts from my parents.

Sunday night arrived with the many indulgences I'd ordered, starting with live Maine lobsters. She complimented every morsel—the salad with its radishes and heirloom tomatoes; the corn, the melted butter; the reduced-fat Cape Cod potato chips. She praised not just my culinary expertise and presentation, but also the courage it took to plunge the lobsters into boiling water. Maybe she, too, was a New Englander, but clearly I'd been the one who'd gotten the cooking gene!

She was a doctor. Did I have to point out that we had identical DNA? "What's up—really?" I asked.

She put down her lobster tail, fork embedded for the extrication. I knew, didn't I, that she'd been to a derm conference in LA the previous week? On the second day, she'd heard a Beverly Hills dermatologist rave about his genius hire of a nutritionist for his boutique practice. "Word will get around," he told the breakout session. *Dr. So-and-So's practice comes with food advocacy! The patient leaves, maybe glowing after a chemical peel, with a list of healthy oils and omega-3 fatty acids, guaranteed to increase her collagen production. Her friends think,* Wow, she looks great. *Do any of their friends' doctors offer this service? No! They switch to you!*

"Are you going to follow his advice?" I asked innocently, pretending it wasn't a pitch to me.

She said no, not hiring a nutritionist. Maybe . . . a food adviser and recipe curator?

"Me?"

"You'd be great!"

Zero appeal notwithstanding, I asked, "Are you talking about putting recipes on your website?"

"Or a booklet. Or maybe just a handout, something like 'Eat your way to more beautiful skin.' You'll test the recipes, and of course they'll do double duty as your lunches and dinners."

That part was good, the financing of my meals.

Jackleen continued, "We'll call it Skinutrition. One word. I coined it myself."

"Just recipes, right?"

"We'll see . . . but definitely with a narrative. You'll tell our story— the one that says cooking has been in our DNA for generations."

She knew me so well. She knew how to get my attention. "Great-Aunt Margaret?" I asked.

"Great-Aunt Margaret," she confirmed.

* * *

Great-*Great*-Aunt Margaret, actually. Her time in the sun was, by today's standards, quiet and sweet. Jackleen and I, our mother, and our maternal grandmother had been raised on a short, disarming chapter titled "Father Hires a Cook," in the once-ubiquitous and best-selling 1935 memoir *Life with Father* by Clarence Day, no relation, yet a hand-me-down family favorite.

My mother and I, especially, loved the whole idea of our Margaret, the Days' longtime cook, portrayed in every adaptation—radio, Broadway, movie, TV! Her manner was humble, her devotion legendary, her stews unequaled.

I didn't answer Jackleen right away; didn't tell her that she'd gotten my attention with the mention of our distant relative who'd been played by an unglamorous British silent film star in the movie version. I'd said only "I have to think it over."

I didn't ask the most obvious questions—*Why go to this trouble?*— because I knew she would say, *It'll be a great patient perk*, rather than the truth: Her younger-by-nine-minutes sister needed something to keep her busier than her police procedurals on BritBox.

I kept ordering with her blessing from Fresh Direct and Whole Foods, using her passwords, forwarding the emailed receipts, as if my food bills were accruing to some legitimate business account benefiting Jacqueline Morgan, MD, FAAD, FAACS.

*   *   *

I've left out the biggest credit of all to Jackleen, the highest test of loyalty, which is also the most painful and public thing that my public indecency produced: the black-and-white photo of me in carnal action, in the *New York Post*, under the headline "Lewd & Law-scivious!" True, you couldn't see my face, and there was a black bar over my naked rear end, but I was identified by name and occupation. Potentially embarrassing to her why? Because we were identical twins with alliterative names—which *J* was this one, on top of a supine man, acting out public indecency? Which one was the lawyer and which one was the doctor? Different haircuts notwithstanding, at thirty-nine—unfortunately not my body of ten years ago—and blurry, we remain pretty much identical. I looked up the *Post*'s circulation: 230,634. Did I know one of them? It didn't matter. I had a listed landline, and for two weeks after the picture ran, men called, asking for Attorney Jane Morgan. All claimed impressive physical attributes I'd surely enjoy, had pressing legal problems such as separations and divorces, and all wanted to make evening appointments.

The photograph caused some tension at home with Jackleen's overly protective boyfriend, who bought all the offending copies at their corner newsstand so no one else could. His disapproval and her defense of me started a rent in the fabric of their otherwise harmonious cohabitation. Jane, she argued, had done nothing that any hot-blooded thirtysomething in New York wouldn't have done! A gross miscarriage of justice meets yellow journalism! He'd better not say one word that suggested otherwise! And if she was putting food on my table, tough luck! It wasn't his money *or* his business.

Not that we needed more bonding or a common enemy, but she and I had been awarded one for life: my nemesis, the woman who called 9-1-1 in the first place. Jackleen and I never missed an opportunity to rail, "Did she who lives in a penthouse need the few bucks she'd probably been paid by the *Post* to further grind her deeply offended heel into my neck while zealously recording what she couldn't bear to witness? Hypocrite! What is wrong with people?"

Chapter 3

Two Distinct Little Girls

When Jackleen and I were twelve, our mother went back to work, afternoons, teaching arts and crafts at the Harrow Girls' Club. We were deemed old enough to be home alone and to use the stove unsupervised. Instructions awaited us on the round maple kitchen table: "J or J: Preheat oven to 350° at 5. Chopped beef is in Pyrex bowl. Add egg, ½ cup bread crumbs, mustard, ketchup, salt, pepper. Put in loaf pan. Bake 35–40 mins. Scrub 4 potatoes. Put in at same time."

Meatloaf on Monday, chicken on Tuesday, pork chops with cream of mushroom soup on Wednesday, spaghetti on Thursday, hot dogs and beans on Friday. If not baked potatoes, then mashed, peeled between *One Life to Live* and *General Hospital*.

Back from the bus stop, our mother would rush into the kitchen, tie her apron over her blouse and skirt, round out the meal with a can of peas, a package of frozen broccoli, or supermarket cole slaw.

Despite the "J or J" of the salutation, dinner became my chore alone. Jackleen wasn't willing to swap her table-clearing and dishwashing for the task that took me away from our favorite soaps.

*　*　*

My parents had met mistakenly at her mother's wake, my father offering condolences to a very pretty mourner, unaware till he glanced at the open casket that he was not at his elderly male colleague's memorial service, one flight up.

He was thirty-nine, never married, an associate professor of art history, later the department chairman, admired by many students at the all-women's Macmillan College, famously too decent to seduce or be seduced.

He was a fond and proud father in a distracted way, his head in the clouds and the Renaissance, reading and studying, squinting at slides. When we visited the campus as preschoolers, we'd color or read in his office, a plum corner one under the eaves in the college library. He'd select a book, big enough to span both laps. We'd been shown how to turn pages gingerly, from the corner with our clean hands, because there were masterpieces on every page. Brueghel was our favorite, all those little people!

Occasional lunches in the faculty dining room gave us a taste of celebrity. "Who is Jane and who is Jackie?" was everyone's favorite question. Our father or Jacqueline herself would correct the uncalled-for nicknaming. The woman behind the grill would ask, "The usual, ladies?," which thrilled us. Yes, the usual! Grilled cheese and french fries. And we hadn't been there for weeks!

We were present the day a colleague stopped by our table, tray in hand, and said to our father, "I note that whenever I see your girls, they're dressed identically."

He'd smiled and nodded, processing her observation as a compliment.

"And their names are?" she'd asked.

He'd told her: Jane and Jacqueline.

Wincing, she'd explained that she'd published papers on twins, on independence and selfhood. Monozygotic twins were of special fascination. It was best for them, for their sense of identity, to be treated as individuals, to foster friendships as singletons. To enjoy separate playdates. And very important: He should refer to us as "Jane and Jacqueline" rather than "the twins."

He might have been too polite to say, *Sally and I know all of this. She was a teacher herself; we've read extensively about twins since the first ultrasound. As for the clothing, surely you must know that well-meaning relatives send nothing* but *matching outfits.*

He thanked her; probably repeated the conversation to my mother, who might've asked, *We do, don't we, view them and treat them as two distinct little girls?* We *were* distinct: good soldier versus luminary; secretary-treasurer versus class president. Despite my near-equally good grades, despite the shared, avid hours of TV, Jackleen was the high achiever and I the . . . what? The people-pleaser. The helpmeet; the daughter who not only preheated the oven, but also turned ingredients into suppers.

Appreciated by my parents? Yes. A smile or wink bestowed after saying grace over dinner, as if thanking not only God but also me for these fruits of the table? True. A dividend paid on my weekly allowance as well? Yes.

I'd ask Jackleen in private to stop bragging about my ability to put a pan of Shake 'n Bake drumsticks in the oven. "Jane is a great cook," she'd say to some fifteen-year-old boy for whom "great" or "good" cook or "couldn't boil an egg" figured nowhere on his list of girlfriend prerequisites. I like to think she wasn't purposely undermining me, wasn't putting an unspoken "plain" before the "Jane."

I'd amused various acquaintances over the years by describing the lockstep menu we'd been raised on. "Wait!" my audience would exclaim. "Every week the same exact meals? Pork chops every Wednesday? You're kidding!" Ironically, it was Jackleen who advised me to find a better, more engaging conversational gambit. "Time to retire that story," she said more than once.

I finally did. Being an identical twin was enough to drop into a conversation, especially with men. Besides, who dwells on her after-school chores, especially after reaching adulthood, graduating from law school, clerking for a judge, joining a firm, and passing the bar?

Not me, not for decades.

Chapter 4

Do You Know
Mr. Salisbury?

My home confinement began on July 4th, a date that mocked the concept of liberty and independence. On that holiday night, I avoided my previously favorite building amenity, the landscaped roof with its fig trees and flowering bushes, expecting it to be crowded with neighbors who knew me only as the building's outlaw. So instead of watching the sky bursting with fireworks, I remained downstairs, putting talcum powder between my chafed skin and my ankle monitor.

Were there friends, acquaintances, partners, associates, or clients keeping in touch? Not so far. Shouldn't Noah have found some way to sneak me an apology—written, oral, electronic, parole conditions notwithstanding? When my thoughts ran in that direction, I scolded myself. *Jane! He's twenty-seven! It's his fault! Who in their right mind strips naked on the roof of a midtown Manhattan apartment building in broad moonlight?* And there I was, the reluctant nudist, punished to the maximum extent of the law, one ankle bracelet short of an orange jumpsuit. *Forget Noah! You don't even want to hear from that exhibitionist!*

My monitor allowed me to traverse my entire building, a decent range if I didn't think about the twenty-three square miles of Manhattan beyond my front door. I'd moved into 6-J only nine workaholic weeks before, and had failed to mingle or join the co-op's various boards and committees. If ever there was a time to turn neighbors into friends, it was now. But introducing myself to strangers? I considered making amends, modeled after letters I'd received from old boyfriends in twelve-step programs, along the lines of *You may have heard of my home confinement. I apologize to every one of you, and take full responsibility for my white-collar, nonviolent "crime." Please join me for wine and hors d'oeuvres on Monday night, 6 p.m., apartment 6-J.*

I never wrote or sent such a thing, resentful that not one neighbor had seen fit to extend a hand or a banana bread first.

*   *   *

My parents wanted to help, with anything, any way. They were retired, looking for projects, looking for ways to boost their sorrier daughter's mood. Would I like them to visit? If I couldn't come to Harrow, then they'd be on the next train to New York!

Did I ever think I'd be saying to anyone, let alone my parents, "I'll have to ask my parole officer"?

"There must be a special dispensation for parents," my mother said.

In truth, there was nothing to ask. They certainly could have visited if I'd wanted houseguests, desperate to be helpful, emptying my dishwasher at 7 a.m., refolding the contents of my linen closet, asking if I had Spackle for the tub and WD-40 for the hinges. I said it was too soon. I needed to prove to my parole office that I was—what sounded believable and inoffensive?—adjusting to my new reality.

"Tell us about him or her!"

"A woman. Diane. I've met her only once, a drop-in visit, and random phone calls."

"Is she nice?"

I said, "We don't sit around and chat."

"It breaks my heart," my mother whispered.

I didn't say, *That's exactly why I'd dread a visit—long faces delivering pep talks. I'd be the one doing the cheering up.*

I said, "It's not bad. I'm catching up on sleep. I'm reading. I ordered a yoga mat. And I might be testing recipes for Jackleen's website." Unseen, neither FaceTiming nor Skyping, I curled my lip.

*   *   *

When I asked Parole Officer Diane during her first visit if she'd like coffee or tea or Diet Coke or anything, she looked startled.

"No? Not allowed?"

"The people I usually deal with . . . they don't offer refreshments. I take cream, no sugar."

In case it was she whom I'd be appealing to for an off-premises dentist appointment or haircut, I reminded her that I was an attorney, and so very white-collar and law-abiding that I'd never break a rule or violate my parole—earning me a look that said, *Ya think I don't hear that every day?*

I asked if she knew what my nothing of a crime was. She did. Gross indecency.

"Ridiculous, don't you think? It was pitch-black up there, private property, and one thing leads to another, especially after a long dry spell, socially speaking—"

By that time, her hands were up in surrender, fending off my testimony. "I'm not the judge" were the words she spoke, but what she really meant was *And don't mistake me for a chum.*

* * *

The doorman wanted to help. It wasn't turncoat Andres, the night doorman who hadn't met my eye since turning me over to the cops, but the ever-cheerful and obliging Roland, who asked as I picked up my mail, "Miss Morgan? Do you know Mr. Salisbury?"

"Who?"

"West elevator?" He pointed. "9-C?"

I said I didn't know him. Should I?

I could tell he was already sorry he'd broached the subject. "I thought you might know him," he murmured, then darted to the front door ahead of a returning couple and their two rhinestone-collared dogs.

I hung back until the couple had passed and graced me with a wince of a smile. I joined Roland at the front door and asked, "What did you want to tell me about this Salisbury guy?"

Roland said, "Don't tell him how you know, okay?"

"Know what?"

He lifted his pant leg six inches, pointed to his ankle, then motioned toward mine.

"He has a *monitor*?"

Roland nodded.

"Are you sure?"

"White-collar," he whispered. "I heard embezzlement. But a nice guy."

I asked if he'd told Mr. Salisbury that there was another person in the building . . . in a similar situation.

"He just gets his mail. He doesn't stop by to shoot the breeze."

"Would you consider . . . maybe next time he's picking up his mail, you could say—"

"No way! I'd be in trouble for telling you this much!"

"Young? Old?"

"I don't know . . . forty?"

"Wife? Husband? Partner?"

"Don't know. At least not living here."

* * *

Over the next twenty-four hours I weighed several outreach options: Would a glass of wine with a neighbor constitute "knowingly communicating and interacting with someone convicted of a felony" in violation of my parole? Maybe Mr. Salisbury would welcome a friend in the building, too. What was the big deal, knocking on someone's door with a plate of brownies? I was motivated and I wasn't shy. Given my own rap sheet, might I allow "nice guy" to cancel out the "embezzlement" part of the appraisal? And would two ankle monitors in the same room trigger acoustic feedback?

Chapter 5

As Opposed to Sing Sing

I abandoned the idea of introducing myself via handwritten note because every draft sounded either flirty or like an invitation to recidivism. Instead I called downstairs during Roland's shift and asked if he'd give Mr. Salisbury a ring to tell him I'd be dropping by.

An unhappy pause was followed by "He's gonna ask why."

"Say you don't know. Say you're calling because you don't give out phone numbers."

"We don't."

Sensing that another house rule was about to be invoked or invented, and with December only five months away, I played the Christmas tip card. "Can you do me this one small favor? I won't forget it."

Another pause. "He's always home. Just knock. And maybe don't say how you found out?"

* * *

I'd already googled Perry Salisbury. *Theft in the fourth degree.* It could be another miscarriage of justice, a big nothing, a misunderstanding; something borrowed and not returned, a bogus charge by a jealous co-worker or jilted lover. And if it were, conversely, bad, deserving of his punishment—well, hadn't I gotten an A in criminal law?

I baked my best brownies, the chewy ones, cut them into sixteen squares while still warm, put the whole batch on a plate and myself in a skirt. I wasn't trying to dress up; I'd be baring my legs as a statement, the way a woman undergoing chemotherapy might eschew a wig. My forthrightly exposed ankle monitor would say, *I, too, am a felon under home confinement. May I come in?*

At approximately 5 p.m., I knocked on the brown-paneled door of 9-C. I knew from Google Images that I had the right guy, this pleasant-enough-looking fellow with gray-brown hair, a few days' growth of beard à la mode, and black-framed, fashionably retro eyeglasses. His T-shirt was silkscreened with a likeness of Bob Dylan. Faded jeans covered his telltale ankles.

"Yes?" he asked.

"I'm Jane Morgan. I live on the east side of the building. I made brownies. No nuts."

He said, "Thanks, but maybe you want—" He pointed to the apart-ment across the hall. "They're new. Are you on the hospitality com-mittee?"

I said, "You're Perry Salisbury? I was hoping to talk to you—"

"About?"

I had an answer ready, a deliberately vague ". . . about my situation."

"If you're collecting for something—"

"I'm not. It's social."

When he still held his ground, I repeated, "It's a social call. Two minutes. Then we'll both get on with our busy lives." He opened the door wider and stepped aside. I didn't have to go far to recognize the layout, a reverse of mine: coat closet on the left, kitchen on the right. He took the plate, and with no discernible enthusiasm, set it on the hall table, as if I'd handed him a leaflet he'd never read.

What was I waiting for? I raised my foot a few inches and asked, "Do you know what this is?"

Finally, a reaction. He took his glasses off; actually whipped them off in a satisfying fashion, squinted at my monitor, and asked, "Is that the real thing?"

"Of course it's real . . . and not many people know what it is."

He put his glasses back on and gave me an appraising stare. "What's your name again?"

"Jane Morgan. On home confinement in apartment 6-J."

I couldn't tell whether those two words had been the bomb I'd hoped to drop. I said, "I should've danced around the topic a little longer. Maybe you don't want anyone to know about . . ." I pointed toward his covered ankle.

"No. Sorry. A curveball. Let's start over. . . . Coffee? Tea? Wine?"

"Wine, for sure."

He cocked his head toward the living room. I helped myself to one of the two armchairs, leather, manly, oversize. I heard the pop of a cork, the opening and closing of a cupboard. He returned with two filled, beautiful etched wineglasses, surely antique. I took one, raised it, and said, "Nice to meet you."

"Likewise. Okay to ask what you did?"

"What I *do*?"

"No, what earned you that . . . thing."

I'd had weeks between incident and confinement to coin the least sexually charged nickname for my crime. "Deliberate exposure," I said, with all the regret I could conjure for a made-up legal term.

"Of what?"

I said with some delicacy, "My body."

"That's a *crime*? Was this a roundup on a nude beach or something?"

"A roundup on the roof." I pointed upward. "This one."

"Someone in the building squealed?"

"No, someone across the street, watching from her roof, freaking out. She called 9-1-1. Two cops came and wrote out a summons."

He asked if I'd been sunbathing, because . . . so what? That's against a law?

I said not sunbathing. It was night, very late. I was with someone.

"And the other guy? Or woman? Do they live here, too?"

"No! And no sentence for him, just fined! He was younger, and I was supposed to know better."

"Because?"

I hated this part, so in one prestissimo summary I explained, "I'm a lawyer and he's an associate at my firm. My *ex*-firm. On top of indecent exposure, and despite never making a move, I was committing sexual harassment, having failed to disclose what I didn't know was going to happen after I left the office and ran into said co-worker at the market."

"Harsh," he said.

"Very. And you?"

He asked if I knew what an art handler does. Before I could answer, he launched into a job description. "You move art around. You hang it up. You take it down. You unpack it and eventually repack it, and probably crate it. You wear an apron and gloves. During auctions, if you go to them or watch online, we're the ones in black aprons and white gloves on either side of the lot being sold."

"Which auction house?"

"Fortunately or unfortunately, Gladstone's."

"And something happened there?"

"Such as 'theft by unauthorized taking or transfer'? Yes."

I said, echoing Roland, "I'm thinking it was more white-collar than criminal."

"As opposed to robbing a bank? True."

"So not . . . unauthorized theft of an old master?"

"You mean, was there a big heist? No—the smallest heist you could ever come up with."

Small? I wondered. *Like a coin? A ring? A rare stamp worth a million dollars?*

"I slipped a lid into my pocket."

"Did you say *'lid'*?"

"A teapot lid."

First thought: *Was it an inside job where one thief distracts by taking something of little value while his accomplice grabs a Monet or a Manet?*

No, it wasn't, because Perry was saying, "I thought it would be perfect for my parents' fiftieth wedding anniversary. It was porcelain, decorated with bands of twenty-four-karat gold."

I said I didn't understand. All he wanted was the *lid*?

"It was a baroque tea set. Twelve cups, creamer, sugar, teapot, antique, French." Then, as if it were a fact known to every bum on the street: "A teapot without a lid makes the whole set practically worthless. I thought no one else would bid on it, and with no reserve, I'd get a great deal."

"Did you?"

"Hammer price, two hundred."

"As opposed to?"

"Thousands."

"But you were caught?"

"It was deemed suspicious. Ceramics knew it had arrived as a complete set, and why was one of their art handlers bidding on something no one else wanted?"

"Couldn't you just give it back? Let them keep the money?"

"Zero tolerance. Fired, not to mention arrested and indicted." His voice changed from regretful to sarcastic. "By depriving the heirs of the fair market value, estimate two to three thousand, I'd committed grand larceny in the fourth degree. Larceny by trick. I pled guilty."

"Did you have to pay them the difference?"

"The house finessed a nonreturn, even though I gave back the lid."

Now, with *art handler* on the brain, I took in the beautiful still life above the fireplace, the bronze gladiator on the mantel, the room-size Persian rug, a possible Tiffany lamp.

"Casing the joint?" he asked. "Wondering what's hot?"

I said no, no, of course not. And to follow that up with the most charitable and sympathetic lawyer-worthy question, I asked if his counsel had pointed out that the alleged theft wasn't for blatant financial gain.

"My lawyer didn't, but I did. I told the judge that the tea set would've been for my parents' golden anniversary, and that I took it on impulse, a regrettable moment of reckless stupidity that I'd never repeat."

"And the judge found that redeeming?"

"Well, I'm here as opposed to Sing Sing."

I said, "Me, too: reckless, stupid, and *so* not worth it."

"But I have to live with this: not an impulse, not like a kid grabbing a video game on a run through Walmart. It was calculated: break up the damn tea seat, get it for a song. What an idiot! And for what— guilt at missing previous anniversaries, at skipping Thanksgiving dinners? I could've sent flowers, or—I don't know—just visited them."

Though I had been an officer of the court, sworn to uphold the law, and remained a person with a strong sense of right and wrong, I was finding many aspects of his case exculpatory, and—one could argue before a judge—sweet.

Chapter 6

Not What I Signed Up For

My mother sent me her latest round-robin of family news that she exchanged monthly with her relatives, sharing what used to be bragging about her professional daughters. Other subscribers circulated updates on children, grandchildren, illnesses, surgeries, anniversaries, retirements, and the annual tomato debate, Big Boy versus Big Girl.

I was not happy with her entry, hinting that I was collaborating with my sister on a recipe blog. For relatives who weren't on the maternal side and/or not familiar with the Margaret legend, she reminded them of the relative who made it onto stage and screen, in the latter case, starring William Powell, Irene Dunne, a young Elizabeth Taylor, Zasu Pitts, and Emma Dunn as Margaret.

I suggested she clarify that our Margaret was a cook and not an actress.

"Too obvious to even mention," she said.

The first relative to write back was an elderly cousin I'd never met named Alice, internet-sharp, with a Gmail address to prove it. She said she remembered Aunt Margaret vividly! As a little girl, she'd visited her in New York, and might have played with some of the Clarence Day boys in their grand house. She closed by asking, "Would your daughters like the two cookbooks I inherited from my mother that were Margaret's? I don't need them, hardly cook anymore, and besides, the recipes are from another era."

My mother supplied Alice's phone number, and I called her, introducing myself as Sally's daughter—

"Are you the doctor or the lawyer?"

I didn't think she was asking, *The felon or the favorite?*, so I said unashamedly, "I'm Jane, the lawyer."

"Did your mother tell you about the recipe books?"

"She did, and that you'd be willing to loan them—"

"Loan, no. You can have them. I was really touched that someone, anyone, remembered Margaret. She's been gone a lifetime. I'm ninety-one. I don't need them. I'll have my son mail them as soon as I wrap them up! He's retired. He likes his walks."

A week later, the books arrived, two nearly identical, faded gray-green cloth-covered hardcovers, the size of pocket Bibles. One was titled *Hood's Practical Cook's Book for the Average Household*, published in 1897, held together with a rubber band. The other, *Good Cooking* by S.T. Rorer (Mrs.), had been published in 1896. Above some of the recipes, in beautiful penmanship, surely Margaret's, was the notation "favourite of Clarence Jr." and elsewhere, the occasional stained page and the words "make often." I felt an ancestral, archival shiver.

* * *

At my next weekly dinner with Jackleen, her chopsticks set aside with what looked like resolve, she asked, "Would you consider talking to the nutritionist in the LA immuno-dermatologist's office?"

Do I have to? my expression must've conveyed.

"Not a good idea?"

I said, "I haven't committed to anything. You know that, right?"

I could see from her pained expression and furrowed brow that she'd need another excuse to cover my food, to keep herself as the FDR to me, her WPA project. I said, "I'll be fine. I mean, what are savings for?"

"The gig doesn't have any appeal? I'd give you a byline for the recipes, rather than taking the credit myself. I certainly don't need the limelight."

When I laughed, she asked what was so funny. I said, reaching over to pat her hand, "You are. 'Limelight.'"

"I just think it would be a platform."

"For me or for you?"

"For salmon, for broccoli, for nuts, for leafy green vegetables, for legumes, for avocados! Good for everyone. Good for the skin." She smiled a victorious smile. "And who loves avocados more than you?"

To change the subject, or so I thought, I left the table and came back with my two new ancient but proudest possessions.

Jackleen wiped her fingers on her napkin, then opened the less-tattered *Good Cooking*. She skimmed a few pages, then asked if I was intending to cook from this.

"Sure."

"Not boiled tongue or giblet stew, I assume. Did you find these books online?"

"They belonged to Margaret! That's the whole thing! An elderly cousin sent them. Keep reading."

I waited while she turned pages, shrugged, turned more. I recommended she cut to the advice, in the last half, which she did. Finally she looked up, smiled, and said, "This is so bad it could be good." She read happily, 'Advice for the anemic woman . . . At twelve o'clock sharp the first meal of the day should be taken: Two well-broiled chops, or sweetbreads, or eggs in any form, one slice of well-baked whole wheat bread, buttered and thoroughly masticated...' What year was this written?"

I said, "Late 1800s."

"The tone, the self-righteousness? You know what it reminds me of, in a good way? Like something straight out of *Anne of Green Gables*, like a food diary her adoptive mother would've kept."

We both loved that book and every one of its sequels. Was she using psychology on me again? Always a good distraction, I raised my monitored foot and set it on the closest empty chair with a sigh. Her lips were moving, silently auditioning words, surely of dermatological advice.

I asked what she was thinking.

"Nutrition nostalgia," she pronounced once, then again, run-on. "Are you picturing it as a combined word, with one *n* in the middle?"

I was picturing no such thing.

Jackleen sighed. "I'm trying," she said.

Chapter 7

Let's Get This Over With

Except for our overlapping confinements, I hadn't felt simpatico with Perry; hadn't detected a sense of humor or much in the way of charm, based on his tepid welcome.

But wouldn't an art handler be good at hanging art?

Every picture from my previous apartment was languishing, some still bubble-wrapped, stacked upright, leaning against walls, waiting for my dad to visit or for me to buy the proper hardware.

What did I have to lose? I'd left 9-C with Perry's business card. Though lacking a title or company name, it was bordered with an ornate antique gold frame, suggesting a once or future calling. I emailed him, asking for his help, adding for flattery's sake, "I suspect you're very good at knowing what should go where."

He wrote back without a salutation or closing, "Do you have picture hooks, hammer, measuring tape, pencil?"

"Pencil, but not the other things."

"I can bring. I'm free today. (Ha.) If good, what time?"

I wrote back, "Excellent. How's 5?"

He arrived with more tools than he'd named, including a yardstick app, and wearing paint-stained jeans and a striped dress shirt. I found his sneakers sad. They looked new, unused, though meant for training and running, not for home confinement. He must've seen me staring down at his feet, because he asked if I had a no-shoe rule. I said, "No, sorry. Shoes welcome."

Attempting to do better, conversationally, as he knelt next to my now-unwrapped collection, I asked if I'd ever mentioned that my dad taught art history at Macmillan.

"What's Macmillan?"

"A small liberal arts college in Harrow, Massachusetts. Still all-women. I went there, tuition-free, since he was a full professor. How could we not—two kids at once."

He held up a framed print. "Nice. Reginald Marsh. I'm a big fan."

I said, "My dad knows my taste. He's joining us today for the placement."

"Joining us? You didn't tell me—"

"On FaceTime. He has a great eye."

Perry emitted a hmmphh, which I translated as *Then what am I doing here?*

I added, "He's got too much time on his hands since he retired. I thought this would be fun for him."

Perry got to his feet. "Okay. Where do we start?"

"Living room. I'll give him a heads-up."

Perry made several trips between hallway and living room with his selections. I texted my dad that we were ready. How's now?

A thumbs-up emoji appeared within seconds.

I began by introducing Perry as a neighbor who knew a lot about art.

"Hello, Perry!" my father bellowed. "Thanks for helping Jackleen-I-mean-Jane!"

Perry frowned—*Jackleen? Where did that come from?*—then gave the phone a brief, ironic salute.

"Perry knows what he's doing," I said. "He's in the biz."

"How so?" my dad asked.

"Actually, I'm taking some time off," he said, motioning, *Flip the screen back to you.*

"On sabbatical?" my dad asked.

"No. Not in academia; an auction house," I said, "but let's get these pictures up."

"Which auction house?" my dad asked, earning a vigorous head-shaking from Perry, unseen now that I'd switched back to me.

"Um . . . it's confidential," I said.

"Oh, of course," said my father, as if the commercial side of art had depths one shouldn't plumb.

I said, "Okay. Here's the plan: One of us will hold a picture against a wall, and you'll tell us if we have the right spot."

"Take me around the room first."

I said, "Good idea . . . Okay, these windows look out on Fifty-Seventh, so I only get sun for about an hour in the morning because of the skyscrapers. . . . The couch is new. Do you like the black velvet? It's why I made the walls white-white."

"Will you be doing something about the lighting?" my dad asked.

Perry said, "She'd better."

"Not until I know what's going where, and when I can afford it."

Perry was holding my largest painting, a Maine coastal scene, its rocks convincingly slick with kelp, up to his first choice of walls.

"Absolutely right," said my dad, "unless you want to try it behind that beautiful new sofa."

"Jane?" Perry asked.

"Let's try it behind the sofa," I said, by this time wondering why I'd thought three heads would be better than two. It wasn't long, as we discussed a grouping, before Docent Dad materialized. "See the flatware in the painting, the direction the knife and fork are pointed? . . . Now switch positions with the café scene. Yes, that way! See what a nice conversation those two paintings are having?"

Onward to a vase of poppies I'd found at a flea market. "Is it signed? Get closer. I want to see the signature." And next, "That Cézanne-y landscape—where'd you get that?" And about a bargain from a dusty antiques mall, a full-length portrait of a flapper, whose ruffles and pearls and brunette bob I couldn't resist: "You have to change the frame. It's horrible. Don't hang it."

Was Perry looking happier? He confessed to hating the frame, too. Had I unwittingly supplied him with some missing artistic fellowship?

On it went. When my father asked, "Did we give you that?" about a Hopper-esque bungalow, I said, "Do you miss it? I can send it back."

"Of course not! I have things in the attic I have no room for. Next time you're home . . ." And stopped there.

I said, "It's okay, Dad. Perry knows I can't go anywhere."

Wouldn't that be Perry's cue to say, "Same here/same boat"? He did not. My father noted that it was almost six o'clock and Mother had dinner ready. "You two are doing fine. Remember the biggest one in the middle and, moving out from there on both sides, make the whole wall symmetrical."

"Did you get that?" I asked Perry.

"Of course," he said. *Bang bang bang bang*; another nail went into the wall with four expert raps.

I heard my mother call, "Talk soon, hon. We're having sole, the one with the herb crumb topping. Tell Jackleen we haven't heard from her in a while."

"She's busy. Keep trying."

"Nice meeting you, Jane's dad," Perry called, sounding surprisingly amiable.

"Wine?" I asked, FaceTime over. "It's the least I can do."

After I'd opened a California red, unwrapped some cheddar, plated the crackers, and sat down, Perry asked, "Who's Jacqueline?"

"Jackleen. My twin."

"Twins! That's why the free tuition was so helpful. Is she a lawyer, too?"

"Nope. A doctor."

"What kind?"

"Derm. Dermatology."

I swear he touched his face, an involuntary appraisal, quickly withdrawn. I knew from my initial google that Perry was forty-one, which put him right into the age group of well-groomed professional New York City men who weren't averse to skin care.

I asked if he had siblings.

"Nope. Just me."

"Are your parents doing okay . . . with your situation?"

Another squint from his repertory of puzzled looks.

"The tea set with the gold trim? What that gesture . . . led to?"

"I couldn't bring myself to tell them what their stupid son did, or why."

"Do they think you're still working for the auction house?"

"I told them I was downsized."

"Do they worry how you're getting along?"

"I'm fine," he said.

"They *don't* worry about you supporting yourself?"

Ignoring that, he complimented the cheese, asked where I got it, then said, "A robber baron great-grandfather would be your answer. What about you? Getting by?"

"Almost. The aforementioned sister helps . . . on the promise of some work I might get around to."

"Legal?"

"Perfectly legal!"

"No, I meant, legal as in practicing law?"

"No. She's been after me to write a blog. Well, not exactly a blog: recipes for her website that are skin-friendly. I'm resisting."

Seemingly perked up by the word *recipes*, he asked if I cooked.

I said I did. I started young because my mother worked—

"What's your best dish?"

I said, "Nothing exotic, but I do make a very respectable roast chicken."

"Comfort food, then?"

"Like I have a discipline? No; why would I?"

"I meant do you do it professionally? Any chance, private chefing?"

Did he not grasp that until one rooftop summons ago I was a practicing attorney, working crazy hours, who rarely had the time or energy to boil an egg? "When would I have time to be a private chef?"

I don't remember if his answer escaped without forethought, or after careful consideration. "How about now?" he asked.

Chapter 8

I'd Rather Not
Go Into It

Disinclined to invite questions about Perry's age, looks, job, income, alma maters, and pedigree, I hadn't mentioned the existence of a male neighbor to Jackleen. But my mother wasted no time taking care of that. Less than an hour after Perry's departure, a text from Jackleen arrived: new friend in the building?

I texted back, Not a friend. Someone who knows art.

My phone rang within seconds. I picked up to hear "Mom made it sound pretty meet-the-parents."

"Because I thought Dad would enjoy weighing in on what paintings should go where—"

"What's this neighbor's name?"

"Perry."

"Does he know about your situation?"

I had only one situation these days. "As a matter of fact, he does."

"Good for him," said Jackleen.

I asked why "good for him"? Because he hadn't shunned me?

"Not everybody is going to be keen on . . . your circumstances."

"Jack! I asked him to help hang my artwork because he was an art handler. I don't even own a hammer."

"Art handler? That's a job?"

"Of course it is."

"How'd you meet him?"

Did I need to protect Perry? I did not. I said, "I knocked on his door after I heard there was another shareholder wearing an ankle monitor, okay?"

That elicited the response I was aiming for, a loud *Whaaat?* tinged with disbelief and what could be delight. "Last name?" she asked.

"Salisbury."

I heard tap tap tap. "Here it is. Got it." Then a murmuring skim-read, stopping to accentuate "fired," "arrested," "sentenced." Then: "Tell me you didn't invite a man into your apartment to appraise your artwork who committed"—and this she read with increasing vol-ume—"'theft by unauthorized taking or transfer'? At Gladstone's, no less?"

"They made an example of him. What he took had—"

"It says what he took: 'a porcelain object that was part of a set, its absence rendering the auction lot almost worthless.'"

I said, "It was the lid of a teapot. That's all. Porcelain; not even silver."

"I'm looking at his mug shot," said Jackleen. "He looks a little in-tense. Is he a klepto? I can't believe you handed him a hammer."

I said, "He's filled with remorse. It was going to be a present for his parents' golden anniversary."

"A lid to a teapot? Some gift!"

I explained: The tea set had gold leaf trim. He thought for one regrettable second that if the set were incomplete, and no one else bid on it, he could win it at auction.

"Do Mom and Dad know who he is and what he did?"

I said, "I'm sure they *will* know as soon as you hang up and call them."

That accusation had an effect I didn't expect. "I'm on your side," she said. "I always am. Maybe you don't know the degree to which I take your side! I didn't deserve that."

It wasn't like Jackleen to take offense or even notice such a small dose of sisterly sarcasm. Something was wrong, and I knew it was unrelated to the bad deeds of Perry Salisbury. "Are you okay?" I asked.

Jackleen said clinically, matter-of-factly, "Duncan and I are taking some time off."

Duncan? How was that possible, after two supposedly idyllic years of cohabitation, and what my mother called "an understanding." I said, "I'm stunned. I'm so sorry. Since when?"

"Since yesterday. He went back to his place."

"Did you have a fight?"

"We agreed to disagree."

"About what?"

"I'd rather not go into it."

"Was it his kids?" I asked, the heretofore most common topic of dispute: Duncan's overindulgence of his two divorce-resentful daughters, both preteens, last I heard, living a mere two blocks away with his ex.

"No." She was sounding uncharacteristically tight-lipped. Ordinarily I'd get the time line, the offenses, the he-saids and the she-saids.

"So it was just . . . you needed a break?"

Again, no elaboration, just a subdued "more or less." She said she had to get off. She was running a bath. *Click.*

What was so out of bounds that she couldn't tell me? Was it because she knew I'd never been a big fan of Duncan and expected me to be less than sympathetic about their split? I texted, Is he there? Is that why you can't talk?

No answer. Five minutes, ten, thirty; national news, Netflix, leftover wine and cheese for dinner. I texted, Call if you feel like talking, followed by the two-heart, twin-ish emoji we used when all was well. In bed, I found myself rereading and not processing the same page of a novel before falling into a fretful sleep and a dream where I was walking in Central Park, remembered my ankle monitor, and ran home to find only a Kinko's where my building should've been.

I reached Jackleen in the morning as she was walking to work. I asked if she'd seen my texts of last night.

"I did, thanks. Just didn't feel like talking."

"Do Mom and Dad know about the breakup?"

"It's not a breakup. It's a *break*. It might be nothing."

I then confessed my fear, based on nothing but Duncan's unfunny wisecracking about my situation, that I'd contributed—

Jackleen cut me off with "He doesn't have a sibling! He sees his mother once a year. They're practically estranged. He doesn't have one ounce of sympathy for you getting disbarred or losing your job. Or for me being supportive!"

"I'm sorry—"

"Don't be. It showed me his true self. As *if*!"

"As if what?"

"As if he wouldn't have sex on a roof if he thought he had it to himself and no one would catch him in the act! As if he didn't drool over *that* for a couple of days."

I didn't say, *You're well rid of him.* Or *None of that surprises me.* I said, "Come over tonight. I'll roast a chicken."

There was a pause until a loud siren faded, long enough for me to ask, "You still there?"

"I'm here. You know what would be interesting? Invite him," she said.

"Duncan?"

"No, the thief."

I said, "Absolutely not."

"Would he come if you asked?"

I explained: I'd been a little high-handed when he asked me if I'd ever done private chefing, because he'd pay me to—"

"Wait—chefing? As in catering? He offered you a job?"

"I wouldn't call it a job. I'd call it having to make him dinner a couple of times a week."

"For how much?"

"It didn't get that far."

"Invite him," Jackleen repeated.

"Why? I thought you considered him a menace to society."

"That was before I knew he'd dangled a paying job in front of you. I'm a good judge of character. I'll know in a minute whether you'd be safe delivering meals to him."

What mitigation did I have left? "It's very short notice."

"For a guy on house arrest?"

Well, I did have a good-size roaster in the freezer with enough time for it to thaw. If he accepted, I'd make it clear that this wasn't a dress rehearsal; that I hadn't changed my mind about freelance catering. Besides, why hire an amateur when there were professional chefs all over the city who'd be so happy to commit.

I emailed him, "My sister the dermatologist, another fan of comfort food, requested roast chicken for dinner tonight, chez moi. I have a five-pounder. Why don't you come, too?"

Chapter 9

Poulet à la Jane

It felt and looked as if all three of us were depressed, and why wouldn't we be? My introductions were a mere "Perry, Jackleen. Jackleen, Perry," resulting in her wan wave from the living room couch. Coincidentally, we were both wearing black leggings and white shirts—completely *different* white shirts, I was quick to point out. "Not a twin thing."

"We don't do that," said Jackleen.

"She's had a rough couple of days," I explained. "A breakup."

Perry looked distinctly unhappy to be the recipient of a stranger's personal information.

I took the two bottles of wine he hadn't yet relinquished. "These look great. Shall I open the white now?"

He asked if I had the fixings for a martini—gin, very dry, olives?

I said I did, and Jackleen liked a martini, too. I'd be right back.

When I returned with the drinks, Jackleen was saying, as if it were a lighthearted and charming gambit, "Uncanny, really, that there would be two people under house arrest at the same address."

In tandem, he and I corrected, "Home confinement."

"Besides, this is New York City," Perry said. "I wouldn't be surprised if there were white-collar criminals in every building."

"White-collar or not, I don't like the word *criminal*," she said. She took her first sip, pronounced the martini perfect, then pointed her glass at me. "I mean . . . public *nudity*? Isn't that a contradiction in terms when you're on your own private property? And you! I mean, one minor piece of porcelain! How does that add up to home confinement?"

Perry reacted exactly as he should have, with a look of near-astonishment at such unwelcome bluntness.

"Obviously she googled you," I said.

"And no mercy for what was essentially a son's bighearted act?" Jackleen asked.

"Let's leave it at that," I said. "You've just met." I pointed at my north wall. "That grouping? It's very Dad, don't you think? I was going to put the still life there alone."

"No, you weren't," said Perry. "It's pretty, but it doesn't have enough wall power."

Jackleen said with a coy smile that announced a change in topic, "You must have several older siblings if they've been married that long."

"I don't follow," he said.

"Your parents' fiftieth?"

"She knows the gift would have been for their golden anniversary," I translated, "and you don't look close to fifty, so she's saying your parents probably had kids before you."

"They didn't. And I'm not sure if they meant to have me."

Before Jackleen could inquire about their sex life or infertility or ask what made him think he was an unwanted child, I pointed to the table and said, "Shall we?" The cocktail hour had lasted ten minutes.

Whether dinner was ready, whether the soup was hot or the chicken done, I was getting on with it, regardless.

*　*　*

Everything on the menu came from *Hood's Practical Cook's Book*, a rollout of obsolete fare that wouldn't showcase my talents or impress Perry. "I couldn't resist trying this," I said, ladling portions of soup from the flea market tureen I'd unpacked for the occasion.

"Not bad," said Jackleen. "Not complex, but satisfying."

"It's literally called Poor Man's Soup because its main ingredient is water."

"Water plus . . . ?" asked Jackleen.

"Beef drippings, potatoes, cabbage, a little butter."

"What are beef drippings?" Perry asked.

"Fat at the bottom of a pan you cook beef in. Instead of that I used a bouillon cube."

"This *has* to be from one of Margaret's cookbooks," said Jackleen.

I explained to Perry: I'd inherited two antique cookbooks, copyright 1896 and '97. Very dear to me because—

"Her favorite subject. She's obsessed," said Jackleen, grinding pepper into her bowl.

"Books and Manuscripts was one of my favorite departments," Perry said.

"You worked in different departments? Not just ceramics?" Jackleen asked.

"Art handlers go where they're needed."

Trying for neutral and cheerful, I asked what was the oldest or rarest or record-breaking book that Gladstone's had ever auctioned.

"Easy," he said. "Folios from a Gutenberg Bible."

Lest Jackleen return to Perry's crime, I pivoted to "I picked this soup as a challenge because it ended with 'Chances are you'll wish you'd started with some good stock.'"

"You pulled this off with, like, three ingredients?" asked Jackleen.

"Five, if you count the water. Six with salt."

"Is that a freakishly small number of ingredients?" Perry asked.

"Apparently the cookbook thought so," Jackleen said.

"I added a pinch of thyme," I said.

"See? She's amazing. Do you cook, Perry?" she asked, eyes wide in fake curiosity.

"Never. Not with restaurants on every block."

"Does that mean that your ankle apparatus has a wider radius than Jane's?"

Oh, God, not again. "We've never discussed the radii of our ankle monitors," he said. "I don't go out, obviously. I order in."

"Seven days a week?"

It was hard to listen to her phony inquiry, since I'd filled her in on all that I knew about his culinary habits.

Perry seemed to be catching on to Jackleen's agentry. "Did your sister tell you about my brainstorm?" he asked her.

"Brainstorm? Was it art related?"

"No. About her cooking for me."

"She did *not*! I'd love to hear more."

I considered asking for her help clearing the bowls so I could order her to stop pitching me for an unwanted entry-level catering gig. But it would look exactly like what it was, a sisterly huddle. I said, "I'll be back with the next course," causing Jackleen to crow, "Can't wait! Poulet à la Jane. It's the best."

I said, "Don't get his hopes up."

I'd chosen a recipe from the "Poultry and Game" chapter that told me to "dish the rough pieces"—surely I'd know them when I saw them—in the center of the serving platter, and cross the legs on the front. I didn't garnish it, as suggested, with crescents of fried bread, but made Franconia Potatoes, page 134.

I returned to the table, expecting some oohs and aahs, but instead: "Perry filled me in on his brainstorm—you providing meals a few nights per week. I think it's brilliant."

I asked what was brilliant about it.

"Jane! You love cooking. You're so good at it. And it could inspire you to write about it." Finally she shifted her attention to the platter and enthused, "What have we here?"

"Dead chicken," I said.

Jackleen's smile disappeared. "I didn't deserve that," she said.

She was right. I was being churlish, resentful that she viewed any potential income as a boondoggle, as if freelance part-time cooking was just what a sidelined lawyer would embrace. I said, "I know you want to help. And you do. You *have*. And I know it's been embarrassing for you and maybe for Duncan—"

"Embarrassing for me? And for *Duncan*?"

"What I did. Where it got me. And the picture in the *Post*. Maybe you've had to explain, 'No, I'm Jackleen. I'm not the felon. That's Jane.'" I wasn't yelling, exactly, but I'd caused both guests to go silent.

"So . . . Who wants what of the Brown Fricassee?" I asked, repentantly cheerful.

Jackleen slid the platter a few inches closer. "Your presentation is beautiful. Anyone else want the wings?"

"I'll take some white meat," said Perry. "And all of the potatoes."

A joke. Good; we needed that.

* * *

Why had I made so many courses? I finally said, halfway through my portion of the Asparagus Salad, "Look, she's never giving up until we get to the point. Hypothetically speaking, how many nights?"

Perry smiled and arched a single eyebrow. "Three?"

"More than I was projecting."

Jackleen said, "Word could get around."

I asked what that meant.

"Right here, at The Margate. All these neighbors who pay for take-out every night. What if they were offered a comfort food option?"

"It won't be by me," I said. I finished my salad in silence. I didn't quote the line I'd memorized that said a proper mayonnaise was the aesthetic manifestation of the culinary artist. Finally I said, "Without committing to anything, should we talk about remuneration?"

Perry said, "I assume you'd want me to pay in cash."

That sounded sketchy and off-the-books to me. But before I could remind him that I'd taken an oath to uphold both the U.S. and New York State constitutions, Jackleen asked what he paid every night for his takeout.

"I don't know. I just add ten dollars for the delivery guy. Forty, forty-five bucks total, maybe?"

Jackleen's raised eyebrows were asking me, *Loaded? No money worries?* "Jane?" she prompted.

"What?"

"Do you want to counter, considering the home-cooked factor, and presumably the charming company?"

I said "company" would not be part of any arrangement—of any *unlikely* arrangement that I'd need time to consider.

"I didn't know this was going to be such a big deal," said Perry.

"I'm sure it isn't," said Jackleen. "Jane has a lawyer's brain. She considers every aspect of every case . . . and though I couldn't eat another bite, I bet there's a delicious dessert."

I had to admit there was, from page 283: Apple Pan Dowdy.

Chapter 10

I'll Figure It Out

Two days after my dinner with my agent-manager-bankroller Jackleen and the Man Who Never Cooked, I emailed him.

"Let's say I took you up on your offer to produce a plate of food 3 nights/wk, would Mon-Wed-Fri suppers be agreeable?"

I heard back within minutes.

"Those days good. I eat everything except blue cheese and liver. What about dessert? Is that part of the deal?"

Deal? What deal? As a practicing attorney, I'd had to keep a close record of every minute spent on a particular client's case. I wrote back, "Before we decide on compensation, we should check to make sure two people serving sentences can associate."

"Check with?"

I replied, "My warden."

* * *

Trying my best to sound hypothetical and chatty during my parole officer's next drop-in visit, I asked her if she'd ever been assigned to multiple people under home confinement in the same building.

"Why would I?" she asked.

Why would I? It sounded like the challenge of an inarticulate playground bully. I said, "It seems possible that in some huge building in a bad neighborhood you could have multiple offenders." When she didn't respond, I added, "Just making conversation."

She'd been there only five minutes, having ascertained I hadn't skipped town, when she handed me back the mug of coffee I'd served her, and said, "Have to run."

"Before you go . . . my doorman hinted that I wasn't the only other resident he's seen wearing an ankle monitor . . ."

She frowned. "Not one of mine."

I said, "You'd think, for efficiency's sake, they'd want to kill two birds with one stone."

"Name?"

I didn't give up Perry. I said, "The doormen here are ridiculously discreet, so I couldn't pry that out of him. But I have a question: What if I came into contact with him or her? Would Big Brother know?"

"Big Brother?"

I pointed to my monitor. "Whoever's at the other end of this."

"You're worried about what—saying hello to someone in the hallway who later turns out to be a guy under home confinement?" She expelled a *jeesh*, testifying to the stupidity of such a prim, middle-class concern.

I said, "I'm new at this. I don't know if I'd be punished for consorting—"

"In this place? We're not talking about some halfway house where people who shared a cell arranged to meet on the outside to cook up some monkey business. I mean, this is the kind of building where people have housekeepers and nannies."

I said okay, thanks. But I had another question, involving the geography of the building. Specifically, can I go up to the roof garden?

"Here? Why wouldn't you?"

"Maybe out of range?" I pointed ankle-ward. What I was actually trying to determine was whether she knew that the judge had barked, "And you'd better keep off that roof of yours!"

"If it's part of the building, go for it."

That brought on a wave of relief, causing me to gush, "That's great! There's tables with umbrellas and lounge chairs. It's such a . . . sanctuary."

Would "lounge chairs" ring a bell? Obviously not. She said only a relatively cheerful "If you're planning to jump, don't. It's the last thing I need."

* * *

I drew up a contract, the first thing I'd done in weeks that vaguely resembled the practice of law. Not that I needed anything in writing; it was just something to do. I kept adding sentences, such as "If I produce an excess of a certain entrée, would he agree that serving said leftovers within the same week would be an acceptable practice?" Wait, was that necessary when all I had to do was freeze the leftovers, date the packages, and serve them weeks or even months later, as if de novo. Desserts? Not a given. On Sunday nights, I'd email him two choices for each of the three upcoming dinners. I would deliver the plate or plates at 7 p.m. on my own dishes. I assumed he had salt, pepper, ketchup, mayonnaise, mustard, napkins, knives, forks, and spoons?

With its roman numerals and lettered clauses, the agreement looked stiff. I designed a logo, freehand, using the stylus that came with my iPad. It was a friendly plate of spaghetti and meatballs with steam rising above it. A title? A company name? I looked up "logos." One expert said the designer should start in the subconscious and pick something that is a visual extension of who you are, and at the same time is aspirational. I came up with it while soaking in the tub, listening to a podcast about Watergate and the near-impeachment of Richard Nixon: I'd call my unincorporated service Ms. Demeanor.

Chapter 11

Pretend No One's Watching

The *New York Times* ran a headline on the front page of its Food section, "The Fast Track to Kitchen Fame." It was about getting yourself on TikTok and becoming a food personality. Not in the market for stardom, never having looked at TikTok and intimidated by it, I only skimmed the long article, frowning.

Not surprisingly, the link arrived in my inbox before 7 a.m. the day it appeared. I didn't respond. Jackleen wrote between patients, "Did you read the article I sent?"

"I did. Thanks."

"Any ideas?"

Ideas. No. Only the same sickening feeling of slackerhood. I wrote, "Will give it some thought."

"No, you'll give it a TRY!" she wrote back, along with three varieties of happy-face emoji.

My phone rang: Jackleen. "I only have a minute. Listen, we've been talking blog blog blog, but that's from another decade. It's now vlogs."

I reminded her that she had patients waiting and frown lines to plump, ending with "These TikTok food stars are all kids. I'd have to be way more motivated to be"—I checked the second page of the piece—"a content creator."

"Do one," she said. "Put it on Instagram if TikTok intimidates you. It's not like these kids have a production team. I checked a few of them out. They prop their phone up on the counter like they're FaceTiming. I'll run it by my under-twenty-five staff."

"To what end?"

"To see if they'd give it a 'like'; to see if they'd follow you."

"Believe me, they won't."

Her voice turned impatient. "Then how about doing it for me?"

* * *

I fixed my hair with hot blasts from my blow dryer, achieving some volume. I put on lipstick and blusher and a black tank top. My kitchen was cluttered with the groceries just delivered, left on the counter in an act of noncompliance for a video I was making reluctantly for an audience of one plus her office staff.

Now what? I'd need a recipe I could make or talk about for the recommended length of sixty seconds. Would it kill me to fake a little enthusiasm? I told myself this: *Pretend no one's watching or listening.*

The *Times* article said that having an ethnic angle gave the vloggers traction. I had almost nothing in the realm of ethnic. Then again, with no TikTok ambition, what did it matter? I could prepare scrambled eggs or a tuna fish sandwich. Or why not pick a recipe from one of Margaret's ancient cookbooks? It would serve two purposes: provide a

recipe that was easy to make, nothing chef-y, and something that would
. . . what? Get a laugh? Make a viewer groan? Could Victorian recipes
be a niche? A quick skim brought me to Boiled Onions. Not appetiz-
ing. Surely outdated. A perfect loser.

* * *

Of course, chefs on the Food Network had lackies who peeled the onions in advance, off camera, but I did it myself, six of them. Already
this was taking more time than I wanted to devote to this exercise.

I started narrating by introducing myself in the manner of someone
who'd never be heard: "I'm Jane, my real name, a once-and-future attorney. . . . ," onward to my alleged crime, my unreasonable punishment, my traitorous law partners, leading to "My license to practice
law was suspended, so here I am, about to make boiled onions for your
dining pleasure."

Alternately flipping my phone from me to the burners, I narrated,
"Boil a pot of water with a teaspoon of salt. Add the peeled onions—as
many as you want." I held up the diary-size cookbook, its faded, worn
gray-green cloth cover looking as if it had been unearthed from a time
capsule. "Now I'm going to quote from the recipe, copyright 1897: 'Allow them to boil half an hour, then drain off the water and pour in fresh
boiling water. Boil another half hour.' And then it tells you, 'This is
the way to cook onions for a family who likes onions without the rank
onion taste.'"

I cooked the onions, video off, then returned, reading from the
book, "'When the hour is up, drain off the water, add half a cup of milk
or cream'"—I demonstrated—"'And shake over the fire until the milk
is hot; removed from the fire, season with salt, pepper and a tablespoon
of butter, and serve at once.' Don't you love 'over the fire'?"

I added more butter with a wink, noting that Julia Child lived into her nineties on a diet of butter. The recipe didn't say whether I should serve the onions in their flaccid whole state, separate the leaves, or mash the whole thing, so I let them fall apart on their own accord. "No eye appeal," I said. "So put it in a red bowl. Maybe sprinkle something green on it." I did. Some parsley leaves I plucked and added.

My time was almost up. I tasted it with the camera now on me. My face registered shock. It was divine.

* * *

Jackleen called with her critique. "First of all, the black camisole—"

Before I could say, *Who cares?* or *It was a tank top*, she was saying, "An excellent choice. Your upper arms looked really good. And I think the old-school recipes that no one's ever eaten could be your niche."

How could old-school be a niche? Surely such a recipe would be seen as a parody of TikTok food sincerity.

Jackleen added, "I know my sister, and you looked as if you were enjoying yourself. You were very natural."

I told her that her ambition was misplaced. I'm not a wannabee food star or a performer—

"Neither are those kids who have millions of followers. That's the point."

"But you couldn't have liked the personal stuff I talked about, what happened on the roof, getting disbarred? That's the kind of thing you say when you don't care who's listening."

"It was real," she said. "You were being casual, but anyone could see that your flippancy was masking heartbreak. Record two more. Keep confessing."

"Two more" sounded suspiciously like a formal submission to somewhere or somebody.

"Why two more?"

"Because three is a package, and I know someone I might run them by."

"Who?"

"One of my nurses has a boyfriend who does this professionally. He gets people on all kinds of social media."

"For a goodly fee, no doubt."

"So what?"

My indebtedness grew. Sisterly support could dig a very deep hole.

* * *

I did record two more. This time I wore an organdy ruffled apron, a hand-me-down from my maternal grandmother, circa 1950, that even my mother wore to get a laugh. I began the video by musing aloud, "Today I'm making Cornstarch Pudding because who doesn't have milk, eggs, sugar, and cornstarch lying around?"

I'd forgotten the personal part, so I started over. "Hi, it's Jane. I'm back. You've already heard about my bad judgment, and the resulting professional interruption, so I'm going to tell you something else personal: I'm an identical twin. It's mostly good. For the first three or four months of our lives, we slept in the same crib. They wouldn't do that today for fear of the babies suffocating each other. Now as an adult, my sister and I are very close. Too close? Sometimes. We wear our hair at different lengths, maybe three inches one way or another. But believe me, we have the same face. It's like a mirror. It's like, 'There I am. How do I look? Is that an attractive face?' Spooky, right?"

I had asked Siri to time me. After a glance at my phone, I said, "But where was I, recipe-wise? That's right: Cornstarch Pudding!" (Hold up *Hood's Practical Cook's Book for the Average Household*.) "I quote from my bible: 'This is pronounced a first-rate recipe: A pint of milk, whites of three eggs, two tablespoons of cornstarch, three tablespoons of sugar, and salt to taste.' Are we ready? 'When the milk boils add the sugar, and cornstarch dissolved in a little milk, and boil until it is thick, then remove from fire, add the beaten whites of the eggs, and beat them all thoroughly together and put in a mold,' which of course I don't have, so this is a Pyrex bowl. It says to flavor with lemon, but I'd try coconut, maybe espresso? I assume you chill it. The ladies of 1900 would know that without being told—straight into the icebox. Enjoy!"

The third one was titled A Good White Sauce, chosen because of the editorializing in the body of the recipe: "So valuable and far-reaching are the good qualities of this one recipe that I would like, on entering the houses of all young housekeepers, to see framed upon the wall." And on-brand: more self-flagellation; more righteous HR anger over how I couldn't possibly disclose a meaningless quickie before it happened.

I sent it via WhatsApp to Jackleen.

"Another," she wrote back.

Chapter 12

Scene of the Crime

With an eye toward socializing on the now-sanctioned roof with a neighbor who wasn't Perry, I asked Roland the name of the woman I would see on the elevator as I was headed for work. Or used to be.

"Old? Young?"

"About my age, taller than me, dark hair, carrying a Thermos? An NPR umbrella on rainy days, or maybe it said PBS. I once saw her in red high-tops."

"Dr. Zussman."

"Zussman? With a *Z*?"

He turned back to the wall-mounted computer, where he was constantly inputting who knew what. Without turning around, he spelled "*Z-U-S-S-M-A-N*."

"Do you know where she works?"

"She's a dentist. Across the street."

"Married? Single?"

He shrugged.

I said, "Aren't you guys supposed to know that?"

"It's just her," he allowed.

"Is it a one-bedroom?" I asked, more out of real estate curiosity than any need to know.

He said, "It's on the B-line, so it's a one-bedroom," in a tone signaling *end of conversation*.

*   *   *

What would be my approach? I had to establish immediately that this was a neighborly outreach, the epistolary equivalent of a banana bread, to deflect any worries that I was campaigning, soliciting, or proselytizing. I wrote,

> *Dear Dr. Zussman,*
>
> *Sixth-floor neighbor Jane Morgan here. I wish I'd introduced myself on the elevator those many times when we were heading off to work. Would you like to meet on the roof for a drink or tea at my place (6-J) after work? You could name the best day and time for you. I'm relatively new here and very free.*
>
> > *Sincerely,*
> >
> > *Jane Morgan*

I taped it to the door of 8-B, hoping that the coco welcome mat bearing the words GO AWAY was meant to be ironic.

When she didn't reply in the first twenty-three hours, I thought, *Okay, that's it, good try*. But Roland rang in the morning to tell me I had an envelope at the front door. Hector would bring it upstairs, okay?

Somehow the pink note in a pink envelope with its pastel polka-dot lining seemed like a good omen. Even better was the answer within, accompanied by an email address and a telephone number:

A drink on the roof sounds great. I'll be home by 6 tonight (Wednesday)
if you get this in time. Otherwise tomorrow.

Thanks for asking,
Amanda

I emailed immediately, "Tonight on the roof would be excellent.
6:30? Don't bring a thing!"

* * *

Would red wine be a dental no-no, a stainer of teeth and/or corroder
of enamel? Since I bought wine by the case these days, I chose one of
my favorite whites. I decided to kill some time making cheese straws. If
complimented, I'd say, *Oh, these? I've lately devoted a lot of time to cook-*
ing, a graceful segue to . . . *while I'm on something of a sabbatical. . . .*

I chose a long denim skirt and a plain white T-shirt to neutralize
any possible portrait of me as The Margate's most promiscuous shareholder.

Amanda arrived a few minutes after I did, dressed even more casually, in jeans, a purple tie-dyed jersey, and a necklace of white beads the
size of Ping-Pong balls. Maybe the cheerful getup of a pediatric dentist? Not a conventionally pretty woman, but pleasant-looking, with
dark hair and an intense, diagnostic stare. I beckoned her to the primo
table I'd nabbed, with its view north to the park.

I stood up, extended my hand, shook hers, and said, "I appreciate
this."

With a quizzical smiled she asked, "Appreciate what?"

"This. Accepting a stranger's random invitation."

"Maybe random, but you're pretty famous here. And I need to meet
more people."

Not what I was hoping for. "Would you like to sit?" I asked.

"Wait. Sorry. Was that robotic? I'm not good at warm and fuzzy; don't need much of it to be an endodontist, but I'm working on it."

"And that's what you do—root canals?"

"Mostly, but"—with pride—"more and more implants." She pulled out the other chair, plunked herself down, and asked, as if it were the most logical and congenial opener, "Who's *your* dentist?"

I didn't remember his name, because it was multisyllabic and multivoweled. "He's in a group. On West Twenty-Third, near my office. Well, my *ex*-office."

The "ex-" didn't escape her. She asked if I was with another firm now and needed a more convenient dental practice.

I said, "I assumed you knew that I'm sidelined for a few months." Should I say it? I did. "Not my choice. The New York Bar suspended my license." I pointed to a row of lounge chairs. "Right over there, in my own building, I was arrested for the high crime of indecent exposure."

"I'd heard that, but up *here*? In the common area?"

"It was late, after midnight. My date and I thought we were alone. Which we were, except for a voyeur"—I pointed across the avenue—"who was watching and recording us on her phone."

Amanda asked if I knew who the snitch was. I said I did, an across-the-street unfriendly neighbor.

"He or she saw you from all the way over there?"

"She. With the aid of binoculars. And a full moon."

"Binoculars at night? Sounds fishy to me."

"No kidding! I asked the police if that didn't make her a prima facie Peeping Tom? They said she was a birder."

"At night?"

"She claimed 'nocturnal species.'"

Amanda asked if I owned binoculars.

"No. Why?"

"To spook her. She how *she* likes it, that rat."

I appreciated that. I said, "The cops could've dropped it if she'd said, 'Just tell those people to put some clothes on and never do it again.'"

"The man you were with . . . he's from here, right?" she asked.

"You mean from New York?"

"I meant here, The Margate."

I wasn't following her yet; I said, "No. He was my guest."

"But . . . I thought he was under home confinement, too," Amanda said.

"Not one day of that! All he got was sexual harassment training and a fine. They probably gave him my old office."

She was still looking perplexed, so I asked, "Do you *know* Noah?"

"Noah? Is that Salisbury's first name?"

Wait. Salisbury? It took me a few more seconds to grasp that she'd heard about The Margate's other monitored shareholder, and assumed he'd been my accomplice. I asked how she knew Perry Salisbury.

"I don't. A couple of weeks ago two takeout orders arrived, one for me, one for him. I got his, so I called downstairs."

"And from that you deduced *home confinement*?"

"No, because Timmy, who was on the door, said something like 'Sorry. I should've known the Peking duck was for him. He orders from The Great Wall just about every night.' I said, 'Really? *Every* night?' and he said, 'Well, he can't go out.' That made me wonder if he was disabled—my practice is ADA-compliant. I asked, 'Is he not well?' Timmy said, 'Um. It's a legal thing.' He never said 'home confinement,' but I figured what else could 'legal thing' and 'can't go out' mean?"

Maybe it was my topping off my own glass and not hers that made Amanda say, "I was way off, wasn't I?" She took a cheese straw, tasted it, complimented it. Repenting still, she explained that at work, except for the *hello, how are you, any pain, any sensitivities*, she could go a whole day without having a meaningful, nondental conversation. Her two hygienists, very good at their jobs, smart women—they'd been dentists in Russia, not yet licensed here—were very tight, plus she doesn't speak Russian. She raised her glass. "I hope it doesn't sound patronizing for me to say that you don't have to be embarrassed about your situation. I hope, if I ever have sex up here, I won't be surveilled."

Was that a joke? Not unless she was the best poker face I'd ever met.

She asked if my colleagues were reaching out to me.

"No! I've been forsaken by every single human being I worked with. Every single partner. Even my administrative assistant!"

"But you have friends in the city? Relatives?"

"Parents in Massachusetts, totally devoted, and one sister here."

"Also totally devoted?"

I said yes, mostly . . . totally.

"Older? Younger?"

"We're twins."

"Identical or fraternal?"

"Identical."

"You're lucky. I don't have any siblings. Ever since I saw *The Parent Trap*, I wanted to be an identical twin."

I said the twin thing had its pros and cons, but mostly it was as good as it was cracked up to be. . . . Jackleen and I were very different, but it's a real thing, the glue.

"How often do you see each other?"

"Weekly, but that could increase because her boyfriend moved out, which I think is my fault."

"Because of your situation?"

Though the truth was embarrassing, I told her anyway: "Because she's been helping me out financially since I lost my job. And though it wasn't one penny of his money, he didn't approve."

My new friend of approximately twenty minutes cried, "You'd do it for her. I know you would. Didn't *he* know that? What a dick!"

I managed a shaky "She's too good for him."

After a few sips of wine, she asked, "No one *I'd* want to date . . . right?"

Really? "Correct. He's a dick, remember?"

"Onward, then," she said. She checked her watch, stood up, said she was sorry to abandon her new neighbor who'd been forsaken by too many friends already, but her mother called every night at 7:15. Was it okay if she took the remaining cheese straws?

I said, "Sure. And as for your mother, she doesn't want you to have a life. We'll work on deprogramming her."

She offered me her free hand and I shook it. "I like to be called Mandy," she said.

Chapter 13

Dinner Is Served

Had I embarked on something I'd soon regret? No. I reminded myself that catering for one client was easy money, pocket money, an activity I'd be performing anyway to feed myself and, if niche-y enough, a recipe to demonstrate on what had become weekly TikTok postings.

For my debut delivery, I put extra effort into presentation, decorating the two dull brown slabs of meatloaf with sliced jalapeños, then a pop of red with some pimento I fished out of olives. The mashed sweet potato added color to the plate, and theme-wise, I'd named the grated cabbage and carrots Cancun Slaw. I put the plate on my only tray, a flea market find commemorating the first moon landing.

At promptly 7 p.m., I rang his doorbell. Perry answered, took the tray, said, "Wow!" followed by a downcast "Only one?"

"Only one what?"

"I thought you'd be eating with me."

"We discussed this, that it was catering and not a dinner party."

"What about a glass of wine? Is that allowed?"

Why was I being such a stickler, especially with the prospect of a no-doubt-excellent red? I said, "Okay. One glass while you eat. You'll give me feedback."

"Be right there," he said, pointing toward the living room.

I put his plate at the head of the long, ebonized table and took a chair kitty-corner to his. I studied the room again. Had I noticed last time that one wall was papered? A deep midnight blue, mural-like, of constellations and planets? A minute after I heard the thwop of the freed cork, Perry appeared with a decanter, glasses, knife, fork, napkin. He sat down, unfurled the linen napkin, tasted his first bite of meatloaf, then a second.

"Good?"

"*Really* good."

To make conversation I asked, "When you were growing up, did you and your parents eat dinner together?"

"Hardly ever. Well, maybe when I got older. But pretty much I ate in the nursery."

In the *nursery*? Like in *Mary Poppins*? Or was I thinking of *Peter Pan*? "Are your parents British?"

"No. My father didn't get home till seven. They ate late. And went out a lot."

"And left you with whom?"

"My nanny. An au pair. A babysitter."

Nanny took me straight to the grudge center of my new existence. I said, "This isn't a non sequitur. The woman who called the cops on me? She was a governess."

"How'd you know that?"

"Facebook! A retired governess to a Polish count."

He said he was pretty sure that Poland was a democracy.

"Pretenders to the throne, then."

After a short silence and a few more sips of wine, Perry asked, "And the guy who you were with . . . are you still seeing him?"

"No! And how stupid is this: We weren't even a couple, just two co-workers on a spontaneous date who got carried away."

He said, eyes on his plate, "That can happen."

"If I could have a do-over, I'd say, 'No, not up here on the roof. What if someone sees us?'"

Except that I *had* said that to Noah, had shown a modicum of sense, suggesting we retreat to my bedroom, but then . . . well, we were already undressed. . . .

Perry was shaking his head. I didn't know whether it was in sympathy or disapproval until he said, "I thought they threw the book at *me*, but talk about a punishment that didn't fit the crime. Some nosy bitch calls 9-1-1, the vice squad swoops down, on private property—"

"With a summons! You'd think we were in Saudi Arabia!"

Perry said, "I've heard you can be arrested in Saudi Arabia just for *smelling* like alcohol." He raised his glass. "To America, where even under home confinement you can have a nice pinot noir."

After we clinked glasses, I asked if he knew there was a kind of monitor that constantly checked the offender's blood alcohol level?

"For DUIs, I think."

Though he was still eating, I'd finished my wine. I said I'd better get going. Will see you Wednesday.

"Remind me what I chose?"

"Chicken curry. And salmon loaf on Friday."

"Sounds good. How much do I owe you for tonight?"

Why should that feel so awkward? I told him I was keeping records and receipts, and Ms. Demeanor would email him an invoice eventually . . . maybe semimonthly.

"Want me to throw out a number?"

"Um, no. I have to figure some things out."

Perry said, "I'm no shrink, but here's what I think: You don't know whether to charge the going rate, or to pity-charge the prisoner in his cell because you don't know what he can afford."

I said, "Not at all." I gestured around the room. "This is no cell, my friend. And I happen to know that you order from restaurants every day, or used to, so no charity needed." That would've been a logical time to say, *Will let you know* and leave. But according to our understanding, I'd be taking the unwashed plates back with me, and he hadn't finished. What else to do but agree to a refill?

Chapter 14

None of My Business

Amanda left her binoculars outside my door with a note that said,

I never use. Keep them as long as you want, and have fun.

Mandy

Have fun with binoculars? Though I knew the aim was revenge-rubbernecking, I was more inclined to focus on Times Square and its changing electronic billboards, or to the north, to spy on dogs and tourists in Central Park. Maybe I should rescue a dog—until I remembered I couldn't walk him or her, and even my fellow residents who hired dog-walkers did at least one shift themselves.

Nonetheless, it was a nice day; hot but with a breeze. I'd bring my laptop, my old cookbooks; maybe do some meal planning, either for catering and/or TikTok posting. Thankfully, Jackleen had stopped campaigning for Skinutrition and Nutritionostalgia, somewhat mollified by my having said yes to her other pet project, compensatory cooking.

Amanda's advice was what again? Aim my binoculars at the tattle-tale across the street, hoping to unnerve her? I wasn't going to wait around all day until my enemy appeared. Besides, I'd been weighing the pros and cons of . . . well, not forgiveness, but moving toward moving on. I trained my binoculars across Seventh Avenue anyway. Nothing. I unwrapped the leaking lunch I'd brought, a TikTok tryout named Salad Sandwich (lettuce, cucumber, capers, mayo), and, between bites, checked out windows in other buildings. More nothing. I saw a cat sleeping on a windowsill; I saw a grandfather clock and a grand piano, but no humans. Was there no hope of my own personal, time-consuming *Rear Window*?

Working close by was one of the building's staff, watering the plants and herbs that made our roof the amenity we all bragged about. He nodded and I nodded back. Should I say something horticultural? I didn't have to, because, pointing his trowel at a large bag at his feet, he pinched his nose.

"Smelly? Is it manure?" I asked.

"Bone meal. You mind while eating?"

"Of course not!" I smiled. "The herbs are coming up nicely. "

"Tarragon, mint, and chives are perennials, so always early, sometimes even March. Thyme, sage, rosemary, oregano over there. Mint is all by itself. Two kinds." He pointed at my binoculars and asked if I'd seen the falcon's nest at 909 Seventh. It was kinda famous.

I said I hadn't. I'd been using them to admire the neighbors' gardens. Then, to support my friendly and benign claim: "Boy, that's some farm she's got over there."

"Where?"

"Directly across, in The Gloucester, the terrace with all the trellises."

I looked through the binoculars again. "She might be away, because things are looking a little wilty over there."

"She's not away. She passed."

"Did you say passed? As in dead?"

"Dead. And not so old."

"Over there? The penthouse? How do you know?"

"My brother."

"Your brother knows her?"

"He found her."

"Found?"

"He manages the building."

"Do you know what happened?"

"He hasn't told me." He waved his trowel: *This is what I'm supposed to be doing.*

"He must know *something* if he found her. Like, how she died? Was it an accident?"

"Miss Morgan, I don't know. Joe only told me because I noticed that the wind had knocked over her mini cedars, and no one had picked them up."

I asked if I could have Joe's contact info.

When Anthony didn't answer I said, "I don't know anyone else I could ask how she died or even when." I opened my laptop and said, "His email would be great."

He recited it unhappily, and with caveats: Joe was bad at email. He doesn't check it every minute.

"Could you give him a heads-up? I'll write in the subject line 'chatting with your brother at The Margate.'"

"Don't say 'chatting.' Just put 'Anthony' in the subject line."

I did, then identified myself as a shareholder in the building that so fortunately employed his talented brother. Could he tell me the circumstances of Miss FitzRoy's death?

He wrote back within minutes. "Don't know yet."

"There must've been an autopsy."

"The family hears about that, not me."

"Are they around?"

"Yes."

"Names?"

"Grabowski a sister & brother they own it."

Did he mean they owned the apartment from which I was surveilled? Was she just visiting, not even a genuine neighbor, maybe not even a naturalized American citizen when she dialed 9-1-1? I searched online for an obituary but found nothing, hoping my gumshoe excitement wasn't obvious to Anthony.

Who else would be interested in knowing that my accuser had died? So far it was only my sense of decorum and my grudge that had kept me from communicating with Noah. Unable to resist, I texted merely FYI: the woman who called 9-1-1 on us is dead. BTW, I'm fine.

He wrote back, At work. Sorry. Take care.

What was he sorry for? I knew what "take care" meant. What an asshole.

I sent a PS to Anthony's brother. "Would appreciate knowing any details. She and I have a history."

He didn't answer. Was I hoping she'd died at the hands of someone else whose life she'd ruined? I'd find out. I yelled over to Anthony, now trimming a potted tree, "Do you see your brother often?"

"Like, every night."

"That's nice," I said.

"We're roommates."

I said, "I met the deceased when she was still alive. In court, actually. I'm an attorney. She was on the witness stand."

He didn't have to ask what she was testifying about, because, thanks to the doorman on duty, the entire staff of The Margate knew about my crime. His back was to me now, avoiding conversation under the guise of more pruning.

"That family?" I called over to him. "It says on Facebook that she was a governess to some counts or dukes or people like that."

I'd exhausted him. He said, "Miss Morgan, I don't know nothing." Whether or not he was finished weeding, watering, pruning, pinching back, and fertilizing, he headed for the elevator with all of his tools and supplies. When I called after him, "Thanks, Anthony!" he sent back a weary wave, one that seemed lacking in motivation and collusion.

Chapter 15

Company

B eyond the call of duty, Anthony slipped a notice under my door that had been circulated within his brother's building:

All Residents of The Gloucester and Their Guests
Are Invited to a Memorial Service
For Ms. Frances FitzRoy (PH2)
On Sunday, July 31, at 5:00 p.m.

In the Meeting Room

Clearly, I couldn't attend, but had five days to find a proxy.

I'd been putting off my parents' visit, claiming I needed time to get adjusted to hanging around the apartment without a purpose in life. They'd declined Jackleen's offer to put them up in a hotel near me anytime they came to New York, and I knew why: a *hotel*— proposed by the daughter who had two bedrooms and a study? Or had it been the now-purged Duncan, acting like the lord of a manor that wasn't his?

I knew my mother and father shared my FitzRoy grudge. In court, they'd endured her testimony on the witness stand, tweed-suited, her blouse fastened to the top button, right hand raised to take the oath, then placed over her palpitating heart, describing the trauma I'd exposed her to.

I did my best in cross-examination. I asked if the person she saw allegedly having sex across the room was in the courtroom. She stared, lips pursed and said, "You know it was you."

"But if you saw the back of this naked person but not her face due to her *position*? How can you be sure that naked person was me?"

"If it wasn't, why did your doorman identify you from the video—"

"I'm asking the questions, Miss FitzRoy." Then, "Is it Miss, *M-i-s-s*? Is that the correct title?"

"It is," she said proudly.

I took a stab, in TV defense-attorney fashion, at throwing her off with a shrink-like question. "Have you ever been in love, and so moved, Miss FitzRoy, under a full moon—?," barely squeezed in before the DA's objection.

After my sentence was announced, the furious Sally Morgan followed Frances FitzRoy out of the courtroom, and without introducing herself as my mother, called after her, "I hope you're proud of yourself!" And as an afterthought yelled, "You prude!"

Now, only a month later, why pretend that my sudden invitation was anything but stand-in surveillance for me? We were only one minute into the call when my mother yelled, "David! We're going to New York! We're going to stay with Janie!"

It was only then that I told her that Frances FitzRoy had died. Did being my eyes and ears at her memorial service sound like an interesting and welcome assignment?

"Oh my goodness! That's a shock. Wasn't she around sixty? Was it sudden?"

"I know nothing. I think the memorial service should shed some light on what happened when."

Yes, yes, of course they'd come to New York; of course they'd covertly represent me. "This is when retirement is a good thing," my mother said. "How many days will we be staying?"

I said, "Pack enough for a couple of nights with me, and then maybe the same with Jackleen."

After a pause she said, "I'm not taking anything for granted."

I knew what that meant: the inhospitable Duncan's deciding vote. Had Jackleen not told them about the breakup?

"Do you need anything from Harrow?" my mother asked.

I said, "Can't think of anything."

I heard my dad asking if I wanted the watercolor on my bedroom wall of the campus pond that I'd always loved. "We hardly ever go in there," my mother said. "It'll fit in our suitcase."

I said, "Sure. If you won't miss it. But otherwise don't bring a thing."

* * *

Jackleen asked, "Did they say how long they'd be staying?"

"Arriving Friday. Maybe leaving on Monday; maybe longer if they spend a night or two with you."

"Have they booked their return tickets?"

I said I didn't know. Probably.

"Why the sudden visit?" she asked.

I hadn't told her that FitzRoy had died, so I started there.

"And that's related to Mom and Dad's visit how? Never mind. Email me. Gotta run." Wednesday, she reminded me, was wall-to-wall Mohs surgery. Several patients without clean margins were waiting for another go.

I did email her but just to ask, "You'll come for their welcome dinner, right?" Suspecting she wouldn't approve of me using my parents as moles at a memorial service, I skipped that part.

✳ ✳ ✳

The sight of my ankle monitor made my mother's eyes fill. "It doesn't hurt," I assured her. "It's not like an invisible fence for a dog. There's no jolt."

"It's not that. It just makes it so real." As for "don't bring a thing," they had disobeyed, bringing hot sausages from a local Harrow market, along with a semolina bread they knew I loved. Also a bottle of wine and a hunk of cheese, just in case housebound me wasn't stocked for cocktails upon their arrival.

Yes, of course Jackleen would be there after she finished with her last patient, I assured them. When my mother asked if Duncan would be joining us, I said, carefully, "It sounds like she hasn't updated you."

"On?" my mother asked.

"On their taking a break."

"We didn't know this," said my dad.

"Was it, *is* it, mutual?" my mother asked.

"She says it was, but I think it was his doing."

"Are we supposed to know?" my mother asked.

I said, "Well, we could handle it two ways: You could ask innocently, 'Is Duncan joining us tonight?' Or you could say, 'Jane told us you and Duncan are taking a break.'"

"I don't like subterfuge," said my father. "We asked you if he was coming and you told us the truth."

"Is she heartbroken?" my mother asked.

"She seems fine. I think she's already in the market."

"Do you mean dating?" my mother asked.

"Just a sense I get, that she'd be open to it."

That sense was confirmed, upon her arrival, before greeting my parents. "Anyone else coming?"

"Like who?"

"Your friend from Gladstone's."

That was interesting: the whitewashing of Perry; no longer "your fellow offender" but my friend who was on leave from a prestigious auction house.

"No. Why would he?"

She was saved from answering because my mother was running toward her, arms open. Our dad was on his feet, waiting his turn, looking delighted. Both daughters in the same space! After the hugs and an apology for being late—her last patient had a meltdown over nothing, over a totally foreseeable, postsurgical hematoma—and after we were all seated in the living room with our wine and cheese, Jackleen asked if their visit was spur-of-the-moment.

My father gave me a nod.

I said, "I started to tell you over the phone that Frances FitzRoy died—"

"The snitch who called 9-1-1 on Jane," said my mother.

I said, "There's a memorial service for her on Sunday, across the street."

"So?"

"Obviously, I can't go."

"So *we're* going," said my mother.

"What's the point of that?" Jackleen asked.

I said, "How often does the accused get to attend the funeral of her accuser, by proxy?"

"Benign enough Schadenfreude," said my dad. "Totally understandable."

"I hope you're not encouraging Mom or Dad to grab the mic and say, 'The woman you're gathered to mourn ruined my daughter's life!'"

Besides the illogic of that—my parents being the last two people on earth who'd be hecklers at a funeral—I didn't appreciate anyone but me characterizing my life as ruined.

My mother said, "Jane found out she was a governess. We're wondering if the family she worked for will be there."

"Young children?" Jackleen asked. "Adult children?"

"We'll find out," I said.

"It's just across the street, we understand," said our dad. "Memorial services can be interesting. We don't mind, do we, Sally?"

"Not at all."

I stood up and said I'd be back with takeout menus, thinking we'd order something Mom and Dad don't get in Harrow.

"Our treat, of course," said my dad.

"No, *my* treat," said Jackleen.

When I returned, I sensed a sudden clamming up. "What?" I asked.

Too quickly Jackleen said, "Mom and Dad think you're coping quite beautifully."

My father said, "We're just catching up. Jackleen sees you regularly. And who knows you better?"

"What about friends?" my mother asked. "It seems that as long as you can have visitors . . ."

"I've gone from no friends in the building to two. I think that shows motivation. Dad, you met one of them remotely, the art handler. And the other is Amanda, a dentist, a little quirky, but at least under the same roof. So that's two friends I didn't have before."

Our dad asked Jackleen, "And how are you doing, honey?"

"I told them about you and Duncan taking a break," I said.

My parents were staring diagnostically at Jackleen, causing her to say, "I'm fine. I was in denial about a lot of his behavior. Plus, he had zero sympathy for Jane. None! I got sick of his jokes on the topic."

"Well, then," said our father. "That closes the case for me. Done. *Fini.*"

"He'll be back," said my mother. "I mean, you're you. Does he think he's going to find someone more accomplished, or smarter, or more successful—"

"Or more beautiful!" I said, our identical-twin standby of a joke.

Jackleen said, "Don't count on it."

I said, "It's a pretty great thing that the main reason you don't want him back is because he had no sympathy for me."

"They love each other," my mother said, a catch in her voice. "My two girls."

Our dad handed the menus back to me, looking apologetic. "You know what I'd love? A Reuben. Back in Harrow if I ask for a Reuben you have to explain what it is."

"I don't know when he orders sandwiches," my mother said.

"Maybe professors emeriti occasionally drop by the faculty dining room," he said, grinning.

I called my favorite deli and got Danny, one of the owners, greeting him by name, as if my occasional Cobb salad made me a regular. "Jane Morgan here! Would you believe I want four Reubens?"

"Smart," he said. "They'll be there in . . . where are you again?"

I gave him my address, added an order of full-sour pickles and a pint of cole slaw, then hung up with a victorious "*Et voilà!*"

My dad said, "I just need the name of the deli and the address."

I said, "Sit down and have another glass of wine. They'll be here in a half hour or less."

"Amazing," said my dad.

"Don't be a yokel," said my mom. "You know that everything can get delivered here, even dry cleaning."

"You never have to leave home," I said. "And I should know."

"Honey!" said my mom. "Six months flies by. Think how soon teeth-cleaning appointments roll around."

"She has some chafing," said Jackleen. "A constant reminder. I brought a topical anesthetic to our last dinner."

"Shall Dad and I set the table?" my mother asked.

I said, "No, thanks. You two relax. Jackleen will help."

It wasn't as if I needed a tête-à-tête with my sister or help getting four plates. I just didn't want to leave all three of them alone in the living room, clucking over poor Jane.

Chapter 16

The Lay of the Land

Holding up two different black outfits, my mother asked, "Which is more suitable for a Manhattan memorial service?"

I said, "In the middle of the summer? The dress, obviously. You don't want to wear a wool suit."

After a nod of halfhearted concurrence, she asked what time they should arrive for the five o'clock service.

"At least fifteen minutes early so you can get the lay of the land."

"We're looking for what again? Or whom?"

Did I even know? Whoever would gain from the death of Frances FitzRoy? Her charges? Maybe FitzRoy siblings or an ancient parent she'd predeceased, or a widowed partner? I said, "Figure out who's who. Get a program. Pay attention to the eulogies. See if anyone mentions cause of death."

She asked why I needed to know these things.

I said, "Maybe it's the lawyer in me. I like the *i*'s dotted and the *t*'s crossed. I mean, who *was* she?"

My mother draped her outfits over the back of a dining room chair, sat down beside me on the couch, and touched one of my knees. "Dad and I are happy to go in your place, but we worry that you're obsessed with this woman, and you're turning a memorial service into a Hitchcock plot."

"I'm just curious; just trying to get a read on the woman who ruined my life."

"I hate when you say that! You're young! You have your whole life ahead of you. You'll practice law again!"

"You don't know that. I may have to start from scratch. Like my dentist-friend Mandy told me—her employees were licensed dentists in Russia, but when they came here they could only work as hygienists!"

"Hon. It's fine. We'll go. We'll keep our eyes open for any loved ones or relatives to see if they seem . . . what would you yourself be looking for? Sad mourners?"

With that sounding like the lamest of assignments, I felt obliged to say, "Look, if you don't want to go, you don't have to."

She checked her watch and stood up. "We said we'd go and we're going. I'd better get dressed."

"Take your phone," I said. "Pictures would be great."

"No. You don't take pictures at a funeral."

"I meant surreptitiously."

"I wouldn't know how to do that. And your father's worse than I am. All thumbs."

At 4:45, I bid them good-bye at the building's front door, pointing them around the corner to Seventh Avenue, where the southernmost corner of The Gloucester was visible. "Good luck," I said, not sure myself what that constituted.

* * *

They returned ninety minutes later, my mother proclaiming before I had my door fully opened, "It was a circus!"

"Not the least bit dignified, let alone funereal," said my father. "And it started twenty minutes late!"

"Because everyone was mingling, like it was a cocktail party," my mother said. "Chatting and drinking, the way you read about where the dying person wanted any gathering to be a celebration of her life. No, not like that."

"Then like what?"

"Like a roast," said my father.

We were standing in my foyer. I said, "Sit. Glass of wine? Cocktails? I want to hear everything."

My father said, "Maybe wine later, with dinner."

"They served champagne," my mother explained.

I asked about the size of the crowd.

"No crowd. Twenty or so people if you count us. We felt a little obvious."

"Young people. Friends of the two hosts," said my father. "Danuta and Krzysztof."

"Danuta formally," said my mother, "but here she's Dani, I think with an *i*."

"Go on. Were there actual eulogies?"

My mother closed her eyes. "So-called humorous ones."

My father said, "Someone from the building's board spoke in a civil manner. He said that Miss FitzRoy kept to herself but was always pleasant in passing, which got several snickers, as if he'd meant 'passing' as in dead, as if she was nicer in death than life. He had to correct himself. Very awkward. He added that she'd contributed to a fund for a doorman who was being treated at Sloan Kettering, and gave other residents cuttings from her plants."

"Did anyone ask who you were or how you knew the deceased?"

"One fellow asked," said my mother. "He seemed an outsider; also looked like he wasn't there for a good time. I said, 'My daughter lives across the street,' and that seemed enough."

"At least there was a trio playing appropriate music," said my dad.

"Why have a memorial service at all if there isn't a single tear shed?" my mother asked. "When are eulogies supposed to be stand-up comedy? 'Do you believe we made it into adulthood, ha ha ha.' Or 'Do you believe those two survived Fitzy's reign of terror?' That kind of thing. Apparently, she'd worn out her welcome as their nanny. If we weren't there on assignment, we'd have walked out in protest."

"Anything about how she died?"

"Not a word."

"Anything personal about Frances—married, divorced, widowed, children?"

"Only snickering. We both sensed there's more to it than just 'nanny.'"

I said, "The building manager named the brother and sister who owned the apartment where she died. Do you know if these two are Grabowskis?"

I could see I was wearing her down. She sighed. "Despite their terrible manners, they did form a receiving line. I asked their full names when I introduced myself. It sounded like Grabowski, pronounced in what sounded like a very authentic Polish."

Wishing I could say they'd cured me of my FitzRoy fixation, I came up with "Hearing how she was disrespected makes me think of her as poor, unloved Frances FitzRoy, as opposed to my archenemy. That's new; that's progress, don't you think? Pity rather than loathing?"

"You'll get there," said my mom.

I couldn't help adding, "If I believed in divine retribution, I'd be saying, '*I* might've been sentenced to home confinement but she got the death penalty!'"

Both parents winced. I said, "Don't worry. That was me thinking out loud. I'm going to move on, or at least try."

"Maybe I'll have that drink now," said my dad.

Chapter 17

Weird If I Come, Too?

The farewell dinner for my parents introduced the first social conflict of my confinement: It was a Monday, one of the three days I cooked for Perry. I texted him on Sunday, farewell dinner w/ parents 2morrow nite. Will re-sched.

He texted back, R U cooking?

Haven't decided.

Weird if I come, too?

Well, yes, but before I figured out how to say that, he added, U know how seldom I get out, as in NEVER.

Since my mother had been encouraging me all weekend to branch out, to invite people over, to interact with other humans, I wrote, OK come at 7. I'll see if Mandy is free.

Who?

Amanda Zussman, DMD. Lives here. Jackleen coming too.

He answered with a run-on: doctor dentist lawyer I'm not worthy.

Did I want to be Perry's psychiatrist? I did not. I answered with the meaningless compliment U can hold yr own.

* * *

I called Mandy's office. Her receptionist said the doctor was with a patient.

"Could you ask her if she can have dinner at my place tonight?"

"And you are?"

"A friend, Jane Morgan. I live in her building."

"Hold on."

I heard music, alternating with dental hygiene advice, then "Okay, what time?"

"Seven. One more question: Is she a vegetarian? Or do you know of anything she doesn't eat?"

"Not a vegetarian." After a pause she said, "When I call in orders I tell them 'no onions.'"

After I'd hung up, I found myself wondering if my administrative assistant at Sullivan Schwartz would have been able to inform a caller about my likes and dislikes. I decided yes, she would. We had a standing joke, didn't we?—our saying in tandem "with extra feta" before she called in an order.

So why hasn't that glorified secretary called me? Laziness, lack of empathy, a gag order? Or all of the above?

* * *

My parents food-shopped out in the world, returning to tell me we'd start with deviled eggs and then move on to shrimp salad, perfect for a hot night. "We looked at the avocados but they were hard as rocks, so I'll make a nice salad. Jackleen's bringing dessert from that bakery she loves."

"There's going to be six of us," I told her.

My mother's expression changed from menu gusto to consternation. "Six? When did this happen?"

"While you were out. I thought you'd be happy. They're the two friends from the building."

"Male? Female?"

"One of each."

"A couple?"

"Nope. They haven't even met yet."

"So we'll be six. . . . Are they big eaters?"

"Are you worried? How much shrimp did you get?"

"Two pounds. I can stretch it with celery." With that, she opened my refrigerator and began canvassing my crisper drawer.

I walked over to the kitchen windowsill and held up an avocado. "Voilà! *Not* hard."

"And with the salad and the baguette . . ."

"Plus Jackleen's dessert."

"Call her. Tell her we're now six, in case she was going to get cupcakes."

I said I'd already texted her. "Why don't you and Dad go to MoMA. I can handle deviled eggs and shrimp salad."

"He can go. I've had enough art on this trip. Besides, I want to spend my last afternoon with you."

So we did. We went up to the roof, me in the lead with a pitcher of iced tea and plastic glasses I'd bought just for this destination before I was avoiding it. Once settled and reclining, I said, "I'm trying to desensitize myself, to stop thinking of it as the scene of my crime."

After a long pause she asked, "Remember the trip the Hirshmans took?"

"The Hirshmans? Linda Hirshman's parents?"

"No, her grandparents. They never wanted to return to Europe after what they went through, but then they did, and visited the concentration camp she'd been liberated from."

I said, "Well, that surely gives me perspective."

"It just popped into my head when you said 'crime scene.' Imagine what horrible memories! So brave of them!"

I agreed, yes, for sure. Linda wrote her college essay about that trip.

Sitting up again, she complimented the potted plants, the flowering bushes, the views, then pointed across the street. "Maybe she thought you were being raped over here."

I'd considered that, about giving Frances FitzRoy the benefit of the doubt, reimagining her call to 9-1-1 as an effort to save a stranger's life. I said, "Maybe, if she thought I was being raped, I could forgive her. Except she never said that—not to the cops, not on the witness stand."

"And if yesterday was all about her, it painted a very unsympathetic portrait. You're not the only one who can't forgive her. Not a tear shed, not one positive note sounded, as if they were both holding on to grudges."

She patted my hand and said, "I'm not being helpful, though, am I? Let's change the subject."

I introduced a topic I knew would instantly engage: Jackleen's love life. I said, "I think Jackleen is over Duncan. In fact, I think she's interested in Perry. You'll tell me what you think, watching them together tonight."

"I won't let on," she said. "I'll be cool. Do we approve?"

"Not especially," I said.

*　*　*

Mandy arrived with a bouquet of new toothbrushes tied with a ribbon, saying she just couldn't come empty-handed. She was wearing a tropical-print sundress and dangly Calder-esque earrings. "Love the ensemble," I said.

"Thank you. It's overcompensating for being in a lab coat all day."

My father offered his hand. "David Morgan, Jane's dad . . . Dentistry, we understand. Must be very fulfilling."

"People don't usually think that. But it is. Thank you."

He launched into a description of his own fulfilling career choice, how he'd always loved studying paintings, even as a child; how he'd asked for an easel for his tenth birthday, which some parents might think was odd, but his were rather enlightened people—

I escaped midparagraph when the doorbell rang. It was Perry, ten minutes late. He said he'd almost forgotten, which I found insulting, since he'd only been invited twenty-four hours ago.

"Peace offering," he said, handing an unsmiling me a chilled bottle of white. "Who's here again?"

God, really? "My parents, Sally and David. You met my father on FaceTime. And Amanda Zussman, who lives in the building. I told you this via text yesterday."

"Right. Does she know—" He pointed ankle-ward.

"Yup."

"Because you told her?"

"She already knew."

"From?"

"She once got your order from The Great Wall."

"So?"

"The doorman knew it was yours because you get it a lot."

"And?"

"And . . . he might've said that you get takeout every night as opposed to going out."

"Which doorman?"

I murmured, "Don't know," then called into the living room, "This is Perry, everyone. He's brought a beautiful Sancerre that I'm putting on ice. How's the prosecco holding up?"

"Plenty left," my dad said.

When I rejoined them, my mother was talking about the provenance of the deviled egg dish, how I'd found it at the Brimfield Fair, same visit when she'd found a Queen Elizabeth coronation mug in perfect condition.

"Jackleen's coming, right?" asked my dad.

"Texted from the taxi. Should be here in five."

"I've met her," Perry announced. "Your twin, right?"

"Identical," my mom said. "The psychologists think we did it all wrong."

"Excuse me?" I said.

"Two names beginning with *J*. Plus dressing them alike until they rebelled."

"They were dressed alike when I had dinner here," said Perry.

"Hardly," I said. "White shirts and black leggings, just like the rest of the world. But totally different shirts."

"Jackleen's a doctor," said my dad. "An MD."

"She gave me her card," said Perry. "We had a video appointment."

News to me, I thought.

"Nothing serious, I hope," said my mother.

"Dermatitis. I already knew that but didn't have any refills left on my prescription."

"It's very handy having a dermatologist in the family," said my mother.

"We send her pictures on our phones," my dad added. "Usually it's just a bite."

"We have our own dermatologist at home, but we don't want to bother him every time we have an itch," said my mother.

Mandy volunteered that, similarly, her parents had kept their own dentist when she set up her practice. They lived in New Jersey. Besides, she was a specialist, an endodontist. . . . Please no root canal jokes, that old stigma, because the patient is comfortable during the procedure, et cetera.

That was the tenor of our conversation: *my* parents, *her* parents, their medically professional daughters. I looked around the living room. Had anyone mentioned the placement of the artwork as a collaboration between two of my guests? Would that enliven the conversation? I said, "Speaking of video visits, that's how Dad and Perry met, FaceTiming over which paintings should go where."

"Good job," said Mandy. And to Perry, "Did I hear that you're an artist?"

"Art handler."

"At Gladstone's! No more prestigious auction house than that!" gushed my dad.

"I draw," Mandy said. "I'm just a beginner, but I signed up for a class next door, and I quite like it. How could I not take advantage of that place?"

We all knew that "next door" meant the Art Students League, our most illustrious neighbor, if you didn't count Carnegie Hall. "Good for you," said my dad. "What course?"

"Figure drawing."

Perry said, "I worked there."

"As what?" asked my dad.

"Drawing, long pose. I was a model."

Why would I be struck silent by that? Luckily, Mandy wasn't. She said, "I don't know how you models do it, holding the pose as long as you do. What do you think about?"

Was it possible that Perry Salisbury was blushing? He said, "You try to make your mind go blank. I didn't love it. You think, *What are they staring at?*"

Luckily, I heard a low kick at my front door, which I recognized as Jackleen arriving without a free hand to ring the bell. "She's here," I said. "Carry on."

Jackleen greeted me with a kiss on both cheeks. "Line out the door at the bakery, even just for pickup." I peeked inside the white boxes and saw one chocolate cake with jammy layers, and the other a festival of sprinkles.

"Wow, gorgeous. Do I have to put them in the fridge?"

"They should be fine. Everyone in there? I can introduce myself. Do whatever you have to do."

I was back after finding room for the cakes, and taking both salads out of the refrigerator, tasting them, adding salt, checking the microwave clock to gauge how much time had passed since 7 p.m. Not as much as it felt like.

Jackleen was on the couch next to Perry, a spot my mother had, I guessed, eagerly vacated, and from her new seat was yet again describing the tone of the FitzRoy memorial service. As soon as I entered the room she said, "Jane's heard it all before, but I can't stop thinking about it."

"We've been to more funerals than we can count," said my dad, "but this was one for the books."

"Who died?" asked Perry.

"Jane's Public Enemy Number One," said Jackleen.

"We have the program if anyone wants to see it," said my mom.

I said, "Maybe we've exhausted the topic—"

Perry said, "Now I remember. The whistle-blower."

I gestured toward the dining room table. "I made place cards, so shall we find our seats?"

"Already?" asked Jackleen. "I haven't had a single egg."

I said, "Okay. No hurry."

"Especially on our last night," my mom said. "Plus, the food is cold. I mean, on purpose."

Though I knew Jackleen didn't like practicing dermatology outside the office, I heard her ask Perry, "Just a dab, twice a day, right? Any improvement?"

"A little. I can show you."

"Maybe after dinner," she said. And then to us, "Don't be scandalized. It's just the back of his knees." And again to Perry, "Did I ask you if you had any food allergies?"

"You did. I don't."

My mother repeated, "It sure is handy having a dermatologist in the family,"

"And a lawyer," said my father, with a pat to my forearm.

*　*　*

I wouldn't have called it out-and-out flirting, but Jackleen was at her most charming during dinner. *Well, why not*, I asked myself; *she's single now, and Perry hasn't mentioned a girl- or boyfriend.*

The shrimp salad was a hit. Mandy said the avocado was a surprise, a welcome one. And fresh dill—an excellent pairing.

"All Mom's idea. And I thank them for doing the shopping and most of the cooking."

"Hardly any work," my mother said. "They were already cleaned and deveined."

Jackleen finally remembered her manners and asked Mandy questions about her work, where her practice was, if she had a subspecialty. I was relieved. I wouldn't have enjoyed a future glass of wine with Mandy where I had to defend my sister lavishing attention exclusively on the table's only eligible male.

* * *

The cakes caused a stir, introduced with ceremony, Jackleen and me in a procession, each cake on its own platter. When I asked, "Coffee or tea, anyone?," Perry said, "Not for me, but I'm going to get something upstairs. I should've brought it. Be right back."

During his absence, Jackleen asked, "What did he do again?"

"Art handler," I said.

"No. I meant what did he do that got him fired?"

Because neither my parents nor Mandy knew of the sad piece of ruinous judgment involving a teapot lid, I said, "He was downsized," with a stare for Jackleen that meant *Drop it*.

He was back in what seemed like only minutes. "It's ice wine," he said. "Do you have cordial glasses?"

I didn't. I passed out juice glasses decorated with oranges and tomatoes, a buck apiece on eBay. The wine was cold, sweet, and, we all agreed, delicious. Jackleen as toastmaster said, "To new friends. To our parents, who virtually jumped on the train when Jane needed them. I'm not going to mention the trip's raison d'être—because that woman doesn't even deserve a 'rest in peace.' So this is the opposite: to life!"

She must've seen me grimacing, because she blew me a kiss and added, "And let's not forget our wonderful hostess, to whom I say, 'It's over. Done. In the rearview mirror. She can't hurt you now.'"

Surely she was right. How could Frances FitzRoy hurt me from the grave or urn?

I would soon find out.

Chapter 18

I Only Have
Myself to Blame

Why was it ill-advised to quiz Frances FitzRoy's building manager about the circumstances surrounding her death, or to send Sally and David Morgan to the memorial service, where—I soon found out—a plainclothes police officer was surveilling people who might not belong there, both of whom very conveniently signed the guest book?

Because while still alive, Frances FitzRoy wasn't content with merely turning me over to the police and turning my apartment into a jail but had to hold a permanent grudge, on paper, and notarized.

I found out about the depth of her ill will a few days after my parents left, when Roland called upstairs to tell me that two police officers were in the lobby and wanted to talk to me.

"You mean parole officers?" I asked.

"Not the usual one. Should I send them up?"

"As if I have a choice," I said.

While waiting for their arrival, I wondered or perhaps fantasized that the two officers who'd started this whole thing were returning to apologize for the summons and all that it wrought, and to tell me I was a free woman again, since the complaint was wiped out by the death of the complainant.

No, they were two different detectives, a shaggy-gray-haired skeptic and a skinny younger one, the sides of his head nearly shaved, then a burst of brown hair on top. Neither looked as if he were bringing good news.

"New York City Police. Mind if we come in?" the older one asked.

I said, "I don't want to be the clueless woman who lets two men impersonating police officers into her apartment and gets murdered."

Their IDs were out before I finished my sentence. I checked each one, pronounced each first name, Rene and Terrence, then opened the door wider.

Once seated, the older one took out a notebook. "You knew Frances FitzRoy?" he asked.

I said, "Not personally."

"Any reason she'd be worried about you?"

"If she had a heart, she would be! She's the reason I'm under home confinement—you probably know that. And the reason I've been disbarred—well, suspended—which pretty much means I've lost my identity—"

The younger one cut me off. "We didn't mean worried about your emotional state. We mean any reason she'd be afraid of you?"

I said, "*Me?* No one's afraid of me, especially not her. She had all the power in this nonrelationship. I was *her* victim."

That one, Terrence, took out his phone, tapped the screen, and showed me a photo of a document. I asked if he could enlarge it so I could read it. He did. What I saw was a handwritten note, signed Frances deWinter FitzRoy, consisting of one accusatory sentence:

> If any harm, injury, accident, or untimely death should befall me, and deemed not from natural causes, I am asking the New York City Police to question Jane Ellen Morgan, Esq., of New York City, who will know exactly why I am writing this.

I gasped. "The nerve! The . . . the . . . gall! It's ludicrous!"

"The date on it? Does it have any significance?" asked the phone owner.

It did. It was the day after my court appearance.

"Did you threaten her on the witness stand? Or maybe pass her in the corridor and say something like 'See you in the neighborhood'?"

"Threaten? Just the opposite. I asked if she'd ever been in love!"

"Maybe you embarrassed her," said the older guy.

"Seriously? If that embarrassed her, after what she did to me . . ."

"You must've hated the woman who called the police on you," he tried, offhandedly, eyes averted, just like the inspector detectives on my shows.

I asked, "Do you know why she called the police on me? She was a Peeping Tom with binoculars, posing as a bird-watcher!"

"We'll ask again if you threatened her in any way that would make her fear for her life."

"No! Never!"

"Were members of your family in attendance?"

"Where?"

"In the courtroom."

"They were, but they've never threatened another living soul. My sister's a physician and my father's a retired professor of art history, for God's sake!"

No answer; there was no body language expressing regret or apology for turning me into a suspect when I was so obviously innocent. "Now I know she's officially crazy," I continued. "This letter proves it."

When neither agreed nor disagreed, I asked if they followed up on every if-I'm-found-dead letter that paranoid citizens leave with police.

The older one said, "We judge them on a case-by-case basis."

"Well, I hope this counts as the interview-slash-interrogation, and you're satisfied that I never threatened her, that she was bonkers, and you can rip up that letter when you're back at the nick."

The younger officer said, "Everyone thought she was in perfect health, no meds found to indicate otherwise—"

"Who's 'everyone'?"

"Sorry, not at liberty—"

"The Grabowskis? Danuta and Krzysztof?"

They exchanged looks that I read as *Do we confirm that?* Or maybe it was *Does she ever shut up?*

I volunteered that everyone might've *thought* Frances FitzRoy was healthy, but oh boy—she had to be mentally ill, first calling the police for nothing, then leaving a note like those crazies who imagine the FBI or CIA or Scotland Yard is after them.

"Maybe she didn't think she was calling 9-1-1 for nothing," said the older officer, whom I was now mentally branding the bad cop.

"Would *you* call 9-1-1 like your life was in danger if you saw two people having consensual sex on private property across the street? You knew all that, right?"

"Actually, we didn't," said the younger one, his eyebrows raised just enough to suggest prurient appreciation.

"How'd she die?" I asked, which earned me nothing except a reference to confidential police matters and HIPAA laws.

I said, "I know very well what HIPAA does and doesn't protect. But in a murder case, which is what you're implying, the accused should know—"

"You learned that in law school?" said the bad-cop wise guy.

I asked just the same, "Did she fall? Was there an accident? Did you rule out suicide?"

Notebook owner Rene leafed ahead a page, then back a few. "We were told that you sent several emails asking about cause of death."

Anthony's brother, obviously: another snitch. I pointed out that no murderer would have to badger them about the cause of death. "Was it Joe the super who told you I'd been asking questions?"

The younger guy was shaking his head. "C'mon. Do you think we talk about who came to us?"

I said, "I know you're not asking me, 'Where were you on the night or morning or afternoon of FitzRoy's death?' but may I point out"—and then I was yelling as much as a temperate and innocent person allows herself to yell at two cops—"that I am monitored twenty-four hours a day! I can't go anywhere! I couldn't cross the street to murder my worst *enemy* if I wanted to!"

Big-city police officers are trained in how to deal with the angry and the agitated. The younger one changed his tone to phony-congenial. "We understood that your parents attended the memorial service on your behalf."

"So?"

"Did they know her?"

"My parents are very comfortable attending memorial services. In fact, they met at my grandmother's wake."

"So they go to funerals where they don't know the deceased?" asked the less nice one.

"They went because I couldn't."

"But you hardly knew her. Why'd *you* want to go?"

Should I fake it? I said, "I wanted to rise to the occasion and express my condolences and show I was a bigger person than I might previously have demonstrated. And I thought there would be eulogies that might help me understand her actions better."

"Actions like writing down that she was scared of . . ." He tapped the screen of his phone.

I said, "I'm suing you."

Was the second guy actually smiling? "For what?" he asked. "For taking up some of your billable hours?"

"For accusing me of murder!"

"Is that what you think?" said the first guy. "Interesting."

I said, "She wrote that stupid note *knowing* I was under home confinement."

"Not indefinitely," said the second one. "How many months to go?"

"I resent that! She didn't die sometime in the future when I was back in circulation, but that didn't stop you from paying me a visit and traumatizing me."

"Oh, please," said the first guy. "We politely asked you some relevant questions."

I said, "You know there's a syndrome where parents keep dragging their kids to the pediatrician, making up symptoms, because they're in love with the doctor, or something crazy like that. FitzRoy might have had the 9-1-1 equivalent, calling the police for every little thing." I picked up my phone and googled "Syndrome mother takes kid to doctor just to get attention," then read aloud as if it settled everything:

"'Munchausen syndrome by proxy. Not just a syndrome but a mental illness and a form of child abuse.'"

"Some people . . . ," said the older guy, followed by his most banal and annoying answer yet. "It takes all kinds, doesn't it?" With that he stood up and his partner followed suit.

"Is this the end of it? Or is my picture thumbtacked to a whiteboard in the Incident Room with all the other suspects, and arrows pointing toward me with dry-erase markers?"

"You watch too much television," said the older guy.

"So would you if you couldn't go anywhere," I said.

"Thank you for your time," said the younger one.

In my most trustworthy, off-the-record voice, I asked, "You can't tell me how she died? I took an oath to uphold the laws of the State of New York. I mean, it had to be suspicious if you followed up on that delusional letter of hers."

The older guy said, "Good try. Have a nice day, Miss Morgan."

The younger officer held back when his partner kept walking out the door and toward the elevator, without even a *thanks*. I sensed I'd made a friend, or was this my new normal: Anyone who wasn't snarling at me had ally potential?

But wait. His lips were moving. Was he blowing me a kiss? That couldn't be.

I must've looked startled because it earned me a do-over. This time I got it: He wasn't blowing me a kiss. He was mouthing the word *poison*.

Chapter 19

New Horizons

Poisoned? Was I a suspect? What a ridiculous notion, since I was not free to wreak any havoc beyond my own building. Still, I needed a lawyer who wasn't me so I could . . . what? Sue the dead woman for defamation? No. I'd sit it out, hoping I'd heard all there was to be said on the topic of me being a threat to the life of dead Frances deWinter FitzRoy.

I also knew from my favorite police procedurals that autopsies tell all. Every forensic pathologist was so brilliant that a single fiber from the killer's jumper or mackintosh solved the mystery. Surely real-life American pathologists were equally clever and compulsive as those on BritBox. I needed details if I was going to interview prospective criminal lawyers, who'd surely ask what kind of poison killed the woman who'd put a bull's-eye on my innocent back.

Which poison? was the follow-up question I'd neglected to ask retreating yet quasi-sympathetic Officer Terrence. They'd told me to contact them if I had any insights. I didn't, but I had Sergeant Terrence O'Malley's business card.

*　*　*

"You remembered something?" he asked, minus any preliminary niceties.

I said, "I made that up. I just need to know if I'm in trouble, and what the poison was, and who else has seen the slanderous note that Frances left with the police. If I hire a lawyer, they'll want details."

"Don't rush into any lawyering," he said.

"Is that code for 'We know it was bullshit'?"

When he didn't answer I said, "I just need to know if that note has gotten any traction."

"I don't know that."

"She probably made copies and left them all over her domicile."

When he didn't confirm or deny that, I added, "I think she died of a guilty conscience."

"Good one," he said.

"I don't mean she wasn't poisoned. I mean building up to that, for getting me in trouble, not to mention selling that photo to the *New York Post*! What's lower than that? Have you ruled out suicide?"

There was a pause. Was he hiding something, or writing everything down, or googling my naked picture? I added, "If anyone should be holding a grudge, it's me. But I've made peace with her now."

"Ya. I can tell."

"Suicide?" I tried again.

"Doubtful."

"Because she left that note?"

"Can't talk about an investigation."

Of course I knew that, but I had more to discuss. I said, "Oh, as long as I have you on the phone, could you help me switch parole officers?"

"Sorry, separate system. Is there a problem?"

I said, "No. Just a really boring woman. No chemistry." For good measure I added, "The other person in the building on home confinement likes his parole officer well enough. You'd think they'd want to kill two jailbirds with one stone."

"Can't help," he said.

"One more question about the Grabowskis—"

"Who?"

"Grabowski. Dani and Krzysztof. Who now very conveniently own the apartment. Do you have either of their mobile numbers?"

"What for?"

"I'd like to touch base with them. As a friendly neighbor who didn't kill their nanny."

There was a pause that gave me hope. But what followed was "That other person in your building who's under home confinement? What for?"

I asked, "Are you worried that I'm hanging around with a dangerous element?"

"No. Just curious. What's his name?"

Do I give him up? I asked why he needed to know. He repeated, "Just curious."

"Perry Salisbury."

"For?"

"An extremely white-collar crime."

"Meaning what?"

"He screwed up something at the auction house where he worked, and they prosecuted. Zero tolerance."

"How do you screw up an auction?"

"Not a whole auction. Just one lot, a tea set, porcelain—"

"Fine, fine. I get it. He broke it and is paying the price."

I let him think that; let him think that an auction house's zero tolerance policy made breakage punishable by sacking and prosecuting.

"Anything else?" he asked.

"You told me what the poison was, right?"

"Good try. No. And by the way, you didn't hear 'poison' from me."

"I *literally* didn't hear that from you. You mouthed the word. I could say that on a witness stand and it would be the God's honest truth."

"You're not gonna be on any witness stand," he said.

"Because I'm no longer a person of interest?"

"No, because the defendant in a murder case rarely testifies."

I forced a laugh. Banter? I hoped so.

* * *

Any doorman at The Gloucester and certainly Joe the super would have the penthouse's landline. I emailed Joe, overlooking the grudge I was holding for telling the police I'd been FitzRoy-curious.

I decided on a friendly "Hi, Joe. Can you send me the tel. numbers of the new residents of Penthouse-2? I'd like to pay my condolences. And the *least* I can do is answer any legal questions they might have."

No answer that day or the next. Was he ignoring me, knowing I'd been disbarred and couldn't help a soul? When his answer finally arrived at dawn on day three, it was the predicted "We don't give out tel. numbers."

"Even to lawyers who may be representing them?"

What a bullshit artist I'd become with all this time on my hands. I sent a PS: "Probate, etc. They're foreigners. They may need advice from an American lawyer."

Joe must've squealed to his brother, because my overtures earned me a call from our co-op board's president, advising me to refrain from asking the staff for favors outside their job descriptions. Squelching the impulse to fire back with *Favors such as asking a doorman to take that pony-size dog of yours for a quick pee when you're working late?*, I said, "Noted."

I emailed Joe one last time: "If you can't give me their numbers, please give them mine, and say I'm a lawyer who knew their governess, and to call me if there is anything I could help them with."

It worked. Two days later, Dani called, plunging right in with "The super said you were a lawyer. Is this about our papers?" She had an accent I didn't recognize, not French, not Spanish, not Russian. British nanny-speak on top of Polish?

I said yes, I was a lawyer. What papers, exactly?

"I have a B-2 visa and my brother has a B-1."

I moved over to my laptop and googled "types of visas."

"Are you there?" she asked.

A quick read on travel.state.gov prompted me to answer, "Tourism and business. Do you need extensions?"

"What we *don't* need is ICE kicking down our door and putting us on the next plane."

I said, "It's not my area of expertise, but I can certainly recommend someone."

"You're not the lawyer Krzysztof's friend knows from the gym?"

So that was why she called back. . . . I said, "Sorry, no. I live across the street. My family attended her memorial service," hoping it didn't sound like the lowest form of ambulance-chasing.

"I'm not interested in whatever you're selling."

"Wait! I'm not selling anything!" And then, to test her knowledge of what damage Frances FitzRoy had inflicted on me, I said, "Our buildings' terraces overlook each other."

Because I didn't hear a *So what?* or *I could care less*, as I'd expected from someone characterized as heartless and bratty, I said, "I haven't introduced myself. I'm Jane Morgan."

Did my name ring a bell? Apparently not. It occurred to me that if Dani was the rebel who didn't observe memorial service etiquette, a better approach might be leading with my own bad-girl behavior. I said, "Your ex-governess called the police on me. Thanks to her, I'm under home confinement now for nothing."

Clearly, I'd chosen an excellent tactic, because she answered with a shocked "Whaaattt?" and a breathless "Why?"

"For being naked on my roof."

"Sunbathing?"

"No. It was midnight."

"That was it? For being naked?"

"I wasn't alone. I was with a man. Frances was watching, and claimed to be traumatized and scandalized. She called 9-1-1 and next thing I knew—"

"Were you having sex?"

I said yes, consensual.

"So bloody ironic," I heard. "So fucking ironic."

I managed a constrained "Go on. . . ."

"Her past," said Dani, "her entire . . . ," followed by a long Polish word that sounded both mocking and insulting.

I was afraid to interrupt a potential smear by asking for a translation. "You mean her past before she was hired to be your nanny? Didn't she come with references?" I asked.

"Ha!"

Ha? Was her *ha* more about her parents' cluelessness or their complicity? "They hired her anyway?" I asked.

"You don't know everything about an employee in advance, do you? And then it was too late."

"Because?"

"Because our father enjoyed her."

Would that verb have another context in Polish? "Enjoyed her? As in having sex?"

"Of course!"

For the moment I abandoned all thoughts of autopsy results, which poison killed her, and my own legal jeopardy. I had new horizons. I asked, "What about your mother? Do you have one?"

"I have a mother. Why?"

Why? Seriously? "Wouldn't she fire a nanny who was sleeping with her husband?"

"This is Europe. In my family . . . Look. He's a count. My mother had her own liaisons. They wanted a British nanny, and not every British nanny wants to work in Poland."

How? When? Why? *Her?* I asked, "For how long? I mean the affair?"

"She came when I was a baby in order to make another when my mother couldn't. They tried, but there were no more eggs in there."

I repeated, "Did you say 'to make another baby'?"

"Yes. That would be Krzysztof."

"Are we talking about Frances FitzRoy?"

"Yes. We had only one nanny."

Maybe one of us was lost in translation. I asked, "Did you mean she was there *since* the birth of your brother, or she *gave birth* to your brother?"

"Gave birth. Through my father."

"On purpose?"

Impatiently: "Yes, hopefully to make a son."

I asked if she remembered her nanny being pregnant? A baby brother appearing?

"No. I was a baby myself, so I didn't know what was happening."

"Till when?"

"Till May. When Krzysztof discovered he had not-very-distant cousins in the UK named FitzRoy on 23andMe."

My life was suddenly picking up. I said, "Would you like to come over for coffee? Or a drink? I can't go out."

She said, "I'm on the terrace. Are you?"

When I said no, she asked me to go out on mine and wave.

I told her I'd have to take the elevator up. Could she hold for two minutes?

"Fine."

She was just inside the terra-cotta half-wall overlooking Seventh Avenue, in an orange caftan, her gold hair sprouting from a high, lop-sided ponytail. I waved and she waved back. Was there a point to this? None that I could think of. Our phones were still up to our respective ears. I said, "Okay, so that's established."

"I wanted to make sure you're who you said you were, from across the street, and not from some bureau that deports people. When should I come over?"

"Now?"

"I'll put some clothes on," she said.

Chapter 20

TMI

Dani seemed puzzled by my apartment, as if she'd experienced nothing less grand than penthouses and palaces. I volunteered, "A two-bedroom is considered good-size for a New York apartment."

Now dressed in a gauzy shirt, her black undergarments visible, and loose linen pants, she'd brought me a droopy potted plant. "Do you know how to take care of these things?" she asked. "There are too many for us, and we've already killed several."

I said yes, thank you. I'll water it. Drinks on the roof?

She asked if I had vodka, and I said yes, of course. Martini or straight up?

"On rocks with twist," pointing to the bowl of lemons on the counter.

Drinks in hand, we took the elevator to the twelfth floor. She seemed to be studying the walls and ceiling before asking if it was for my private use. Rather than educate her on how ridiculous a concept that was for the proletariat, I said only "No. In fact, it's the service elevator, the only one that goes up to the roof."

It was a balmier night than August usually delivered. A mild breeze, pink sky, pears and crabapples on the potted trees. I led her to a table with the best view of her own terrace, in case the subject of my recent ignominious past and her nanny's role in it came back up. Raising my glass, I asked what a Polish toast might be.

"*Na zdrowie*! 'To your health!'"

I repeated the phrase as best I could, and she tweaked my pronunciation.

"Your English is perfect—*British* English," I said.

"By accident."

I asked what that meant.

"Full-time British nanny. Absent Polish-speaking parents."

"Literally absent?"

"Absent if they visit once or twice a day, no? If I didn't go to school in Warsaw, I might not speak the language at all."

"Are your parents still alive?" I asked.

"Yes. Both—and not understanding why we'd rather be in New York City than Warsaw. How is that thinking possible?"

I made a mental note to get back to the whys of their ongoing NYC visit, but sensing Dani might leave as soon as she finished her drink, I went straight to "Your brother and Frances FitzRoy . . . can we talk about that?"

"About her dying?"

A curious leap, I thought. "No. About her being his mother."

"I told you that already."

"You told me he didn't find out about it until he had a DNA test. But did *you* know? I mean, growing up?"

"No! I was a baby, not even two when he came along. Babies don't think about such things, or whether the nanny is big." She pantomimed a protuberant belly.

117

"Did he ever suspect, maybe by some withholding by your mother, or the way Frances favored him—"

"No, never! It's why he was shocked when he found out—no sign, ever. Nothing like . . ." She adopted a sympathetic face, a quivering lip, approximating maternal tenderness.

When I asked if she knew how long her father and Frances had carried on their affair, she said, "An affair? More like an arrangement. My parents had separate bedrooms, and my father had permission."

"For?"

Dani's furrowed brow was asking *Was I thick? Was it not abundantly clear?* "To have sex with her. They flew to London to interview the candidates, and he chose her."

What century was this happening in? Was there a statute of limitations on trafficking? "Chose her to be your nanny or his mistress?" I asked.

"Officially, nanny. But by the time the interview was over, she knew what she was applying for."

So odd; so Frances-incongruous. Indulging my shallowest curiosity, I asked, "Was she pretty?"

"She *had* to be, didn't she?"

Did she? "Wouldn't your mother want the least attractive au pair living under the same roof?"

More obtuseness and naivete on my part, obviously. She said impatiently, "They weren't going to pick someone unattractive or short or stupid or uneducated, were they? First, you don't want a baby who grows up to be a short, homely count. And second, he needed to feel an attraction, because Tata was going to make a baby the normal way, in bed. I mean, it could've taken several tries over several months." Dani smiled. "And it worked. They got their male heir, and—have you seen Krzysztof? He's pretty hot."

Trying not to look astonished, I asked, "Was Frances duped into taking this job? Did she know what she was being hired for?"

"I asked her when we found out: What did she think she was being hired for? She took great offense! She was brought over for language immersion! She was an au pair, an equal. She and my father fell in love—her story—got pregnant, had his baby, stayed."

"And kept it up?"

"The sex?" She shrugged the shrug of the casually bedded.

Sex. Love. A love child, no less, from the loins of the incorrigible prude who had me virtually locked up for consensual sex.

"But none of this was known until Krzysztof did the DNA test?"

"By us, correct. A birthday present. He emailed the results to our father."

"Did he deny it?"

"He said, 'So what? What difference does it make now?' He denied it was an affair. It wasn't adultery. It wasn't cheating. It was about a male heir and a title." Dani gestured grandly in the direction of The Gloucester.

"A title to the penthouse?" I asked.

"No, to be a count. But as it turned out . . . ," followed with a wink that I interpreted to mean *until she conveniently died*.

"A lot to unpack," I said.

"For Krzysztof maybe. I know who I am . . . who my parents are."

Would it be rude to point out how feudal those parents had been, needing a son and heir, discounting a daughter? Instead I asked what made Krzysztof take the 23andMe test in the first place? Were there suspicions?

"Ironically, yes, but they were the wrong kind. My mother had liaisons. Both of us wondered if she'd gotten pregnant from someone other than Tata. But no. The 23andMe tests were presents."

"From?"

It seemed to be the question she'd been waiting for, judging by a slight uptick in her conversational energy. "Take one guess!"

"Frances?"

"Of course. She knew what would happen. She wanted the cat to be let out of the bag. The romance was over. She'd gotten her reward."

I felt, for the first time, a ripple of sympathy for Frances FitzRoy. "At least she knew before she died that Krzysztof had learned the truth."

"It wasn't nice," she murmured.

"What wasn't?"

"The fight! He was furious! It was all 'You were my mother but I got nothing from you!'"

I prompted, "No affection? No love? Even on the sly?"

"That was only for our father. For us, always strict. I don't know how we became normal adults."

"She couldn't have been happy," I said.

"I don't think about that," said Dani. "I don't want to."

I reached for the bottle of vodka, hoping another pour would deliver more intel, more drama, more Frances. Plus means, motive, opportunity.

"No. I have to run." She turned the bottle around so the label faced her. "It's quite good for American vodka."

"You should come back and bring your brother."

"Why?"

To use my disbarred legal wits to find out who or what poisoned Frances. I said, "She messed up my life, too. I think he'd relate to that."

"He won't care. He doesn't know you."

I said, "You're forgetting that I'm an attorney. And I know you're worried about your visas. I'll find out more about"—what was the shiniest object to dangle?—"what you'd have to do to live and work in New York legally." Then, out of nowhere except visions of the refrigerated cases at Wozniak's Market in Harrow, I asked if Krzysztof favored meat, cheese, or potato pierogi.

Chapter 21

It's Tricky, Though

I started labeling phone calls from my sister "professional development," usually starting with a TikTok metric such as "Your 'likes' are holding steady."

I asked if she'd noticed that I'd added "hashtag Skinutrition" when talking about a fatty fish or green leafy vegetables.

"Thanks. Maybe you could add 'hashtag MorganDerm' to those posts?"

I said sure, no problem; just right for an upcoming Sardine Salad.

"How's the catering going?" she asked. "Are you finding the commitment too much? Just right? Are you enjoying his company enough?"

"Enough for what?"

"Enough to up the ante."

Though I knew exactly what she meant, I asked for a translation.

"Well, you spend three nights a week up there—"

I said, "You keep insisting that it's a dinner date. It's not. I drop off the plates and occasionally stay for a glass of wine." Unspoken: *or two. Plus the occasional entrée.*

"Is he seeing anyone?"

"Not that I know of."

"He's straight, right?"

I said, "He's had girlfriends."

"So you *do* talk."

Yes, we did. He'd had a girlfriend at Gladstone's, but she, like the rest of the world, like anyone we two personae non gratae had ever worked alongside, disappeared.

"Do you sense he's open to dating someone else?"

"Do you mean me?"

A pause, and finally "Or your twin sister? Is that okay? I mean, you have first dibs."

Did I really say "Go for it," as if endorsing a reasonable idea?

"Promise you'd tell me if you were getting a vibe from him?"

"No detectable vibes."

"It's tricky, though," she said.

"What part is?" I asked, thinking, *Every part is*.

"If he hasn't shown any interest in *you* . . ."

I knew what she meant: If she and I were essentially the same being, and he hadn't manifested interest in me, what were her chances? I countered by asking, "When has any potential boyfriend ever thought, 'Hmmm, I can't decide which sister I like so I'll toss a coin'?" What I didn't cite was the hundreds of times, in the halls of Harrow High, that we'd been hailed as the other twin.

Because she was my benefactor, my sponsor, my paycheck, I said, "You'll come with me one of these nights when I'm delivering his dinner."

"Unannounced? Or you'd give him a heads-up?"

"You could just show up with me, and if you're enjoying yourself, you'll give me a nod and I'll say, 'I've got a course online, live, starting in five minutes. Gotta run.'"

"A course online would be great for you," Jackleen enthused. "My front desk people are doing one on positivity. The sessions are under five minutes apiece."

Positivity? How long had she been waiting to spring that one on me? I said, "I didn't mean it literally about a course. It just flew into my head as a plausible excuse to leave."

"Do we think asking for Friday looks too date-nightish?" she mused.

"I thought that was the goal."

"Let's let him decide. If he chooses Friday, it'll mean something. Call him."

"Now?"

"Call him on your landline, on speaker, so I can hear the conversation."

I tried to beg off. Perry and I never made arrangements by phone. I said I'd text him, per usual—day, time, menu choices.

"But I want to hear how he responds."

Obediently, I called. When he picked up, I plunged right in with "My sister is coming along when I bring dinner on Friday? She'll probably stay and eat with you."

Even though she wasn't on speaker, I heard Jackleen call sharply, disapprovingly, "Jane!"

Perry asked, "Wouldn't it be easier if I came to your place?"

Yes, much easier, but not if I was going to play matchmaker and leave. I was out of practice thinking on my feet and didn't know what to say with Jackleen listening via my cell. After burying it beneath a couch cushion, I whispered to Perry, "She likes you, okay? If you don't want to have dinner with her, tell me now. We won't waste anyone's time."

"Didn't she just break up with someone?" he asked.

124

"That was a while ago," I said, and repeated, "How's Friday?"

"Friday's okay. But we're still on for tomorrow, right? This doesn't change our regular schedule?"

His questions sounded more plaintive than I was expecting, particularly seconds after I'd declared him the object of Jackleen's romantic ambition. I said, "Yup, tomorrow, per usual."

"Do you know what you're making?"

"Not yet. Any preference?"

"I bought more of that Sancerre you like."

I said, okay, I could probably stay for a glass. I'd bring fish.

"Looking forward to it," he said.

He was? Maybe his sounding friendlier than usual was just a reflex, just good landline manners, not a vibe. After saying good-bye, see you tomorrow, I unearthed my cell. "All set for Friday," I told Jackleen.

"What happened? I lost you."

"Dead spot, I guess. He said okay."

"Just okay?"

"He's not Mr. Personality, especially on the phone."

"You didn't sound too charismatic yourself. No small talk, just straight to 'Hello, my sister's coming with me when I next feed you.' I wish he'd sounded more animated."

"In the dropped part of the call he was more enthusiastic . . . even . . . flirtatious." What made me confess that? Contrariness? Unspent sibling rivalry?

But Jackleen didn't question who or what triggered Perry's change in tone. "Flirtatious when you told him I'd be joining you? Really? That came through even though he didn't know I was listening, and he could've said anything, including 'no, thanks'?"

Oh, to have such exalted self-esteem. "Loud and clear," I said.

Chapter 22

In the Same Boat

Next night, the promised Monday, I made Shrimp de Jonghe, enough for two, a vintage dish that sent me online for its provenance. Thanks to the James Beard Foundation's website, I learned that the de Jonghe brothers, Belgian immigrants, introduced it at their Chicago restaurant at the turn of the twentieth century. Good; that would give me something to discourse on, should the conversation over wine go cold.

It didn't. Even before I lifted the lid of the shrimp en casserole, Perry introduced a topic that can only be described as The Two of Us. It wasn't romantic. It was clinical, The Margate equivalent of a questionnaire in a Masters & Johnson lab: Would I be willing, totally willing, interested in/ever inclined . . . to have relations with him? But wait; let him explain!

Before I recovered, he said he'd made an outline. Could he read it?

Startled but curious to hear what someone with Perry's heretofore limited emotional range would use to enlist a sex partner, I said, "Okay, shoot."

"It's on my iPad," a reach away on a kitchen counter. He cleared his throat with a stagey *ahem*, and smiled. "I don't want you to expect a love letter. It's a list, not an essay, not a brief."

The words *love letter* were so far removed from anything that had passed between us that I wondered if I'd heard him right. "Got it, an outline," I murmured. "Proceed."

He straightened himself in his chair. "Okay, number one: We're both single." He looked up. "I assume it would've come up if you were currently with someone."

"Correct."

"And straight." He looked up again. "It was a guy on the roof, right? The other defendant?"

"Right."

"Three: home confinement times two."

Like a good debater I said, "True. But we can have guests. And I could make a case for going online."

"*Are* you going online?"

"Not at the present time."

Next, with less conviction, "Four: We'd be consenting adults, both consenting in advance and . . . when the time came."

"For sure. Okay, number five?"

"We're already friends." He looked up. "Right?"

"Friendly acquaintances maybe; friendly more-or-less business acquaintances."

"Except we don't have to answer to an HR department. We can cross certain lines without, as you would point out, disclosing."

I found myself listening with unexpected attention. I asked how he pictured such a thing moving forward. Where would we start, theoretically speaking?

"Here. Unless you wanted me to come to your place."

"Not geographically, procedurally. Is it your understanding that we'd just go straight from"—I pointed to the wine and the shrimp—"to bed?"

"Not good? Because that would feel . . . procedural? Abrupt?"

How to answer? I said, "Hardly abrupt, since we're talking it through. It's not like you suddenly grabbed a breast."

He said, "Exactly! I thought the logical approach might appeal to you."

I wanted to ask if I appeared to be all-logic, but that might be fishing for a compliment. I asked, "Is it—I don't know—subjective or just 'need a woman/any woman'?"

Without elaborating he said, "It's subjective. Quite."

I walked to a cabinet and got two plates. Back at the table I said, "What number are we up to on your outline? Because I could add this: We wouldn't have to explain, the way we would with a new sexual partner, 'Oh, it's an ankle monitor, can't take it off. Have I not mentioned I'm under home confinement?'"

"Very true."

"I assume you're not enlisting anyone else?"

"I am not."

"The girlfriend at Gladstone's—still haven't heard from her?"

"Radio silence."

"Likewise," by which I meant overall nothingness except for the creepy yet identical crank calls from *Post* hopefuls, who were all well-endowed and suggesting an evening consultation.

"Look," Perry said. "You're already coming up here three nights a week. No one has to know. You'll still bring the picnic basket. No one will notice."

"People noticing is the least of my worries."

"Then what's the *most* of your worries?"

That question was ten times more psychiatric than any he'd ever posed before. I said, "Here's a big one: Let's say we proceed for the same bird-in-hand reason that made you think of me. But I don't enjoy it? I want out."

It was, I admit, a coy question along the lines of *Give your technique a letter grade.* Wouldn't most men come back with *Oh, trust me, little lady, you're going to enjoy it.* But this one said, "No questions asked. In fact"—he read from his iPad—"for only as long as both parties want to participate."

I allowed, "It's not crazy. Everyone's heard of 'friends with benefits.'"

Perry said, "Sleeping with someone you're not involved with isn't exactly a revolutionary notion. It's been known to happen . . . pretty spontaneously, every night in every borough."

"That thing that my college roommate used to call 'a fucking accident'? Like *boom!*"

"Except this would be the opposite of that, wouldn't it? Not an accident. Almost like a date." He read aloud the last item on his screen: "Questions? Comments?"

I said the shrimp needed reheating, maybe sixty seconds in the microwave. When I returned with our plates I said, "If I agreed, and we scheduled a test run, we wouldn't have to flirt over dinner, okay? We'd just—" I gestured in the direction of his bedroom.

"If that's what you want. It can even be a night other than Monday, Wednesday, or Friday. No food required."

I said, "But if the sex doesn't work out, the catering would be very awkward."

"We've covered that. We'd get over it and go back to our original agreement. Food only."

I said, "I'd probably still stay for a glass of wine."

With a smile that seemed fonder than the usual one accompanying his compliments, he said the shrimp was delicious and I should make it again.

I said, "I'll put Shrimp de Jonghe in the rotation. And with respect to the personal stuff, what's your time line?"

"No hurry," he said on this Monday night. "It's a lot to think about."

"How about Wednesday?" I asked.

Chapter 23

The Pros and Cons

Whom to confide in, whom to consult? I ruled out my usual first stop, Jackleen, now having to renege on the date I'd engineered for her and Perry. My mother? She'd voiced optimism about Perry as boyfriend potential the minute she'd heard that a male resident of The Margate was helping me hang paintings. I could call her, but phrase it how? *I'm seriously considering a sexual alliance with that neighbor you met, the art handler who brought the ice wine. But don't say anything to Jackleen.* No.

I decided I'd be my own counsel. But then again, many of my law school classes had been conducted in the Socratic method, with give-and-take, asking and answering questions to stimulate critical thinking. Who was nearby and smart and good at drawing out some presuppositions about my situation?

Mandy, a fellow woman and an elevator-ride away. We'd discuss the pros and cons. After two years of medical school and two more of dental school, wouldn't she have had a thorough exposure to male thought processes, behaviors, and hormones? So far, over several glasses of wine and cups of coffee, her reactions to my mistakes, personal and criminal, had been supportive, albeit in her characteristically clinical fashion. We'd discussed the potential man in her life (tricky, a patient, no action taken), plus she and I had shared eyerolls over Jackleen's theatrics, from her late arrival to her two attention-getting layer cakes.

I texted her: free for dinner tonight?

Sure. My turn. Come up to 8-B.

A welcome change of scene! Love to. Text me when you get home.

In contrast to her sartorial efforts (splashy sundresses, tie-dyed T-shirts, and asymmetric skirts), her apartment was depressingly old-school. The furniture was mid-century-old-lady and slipcovered, the living room crammed with too much of everything. Mandy volunteered, "I bought it, as is, from the dead owner's estate. Not one of her kids wanted a single thing, except *of course* the priceless art."

I nodded. The couch was nubby gold. The side chairs were striped in satiny champagne and beige. Between them, brown end tables holding candy dishes and ashtrays. I silently chastised myself for being critical. I couldn't help asking if she was planning to redecorate.

"Maybe when it wears out. It's all serviceable," she said, "and obviously high quality."

"True," I said.

We decided on BBQ and went overboard on the order: ribs, chicken, cole slaw, chili beans, black-eyed peas, corn bread. Her treat, she insisted. I told her I had two things to discuss of a personal nature, a very personal nature.

I knew I could be blunt. Mandy had never exhibited any queasiness over anything I'd confessed over the course of our short friendship, not about my crime or my FitzRoy loathing. It wasn't that she was cool and casual; it was quite the opposite, an odd kind of cheerleading. And there was something I found amusing in her unfiltered takes on almost everything. I jumped right in with "Perry has suggested that we give friends-with-benefits a go."

She let the drumstick she was holding drop in a dramatic fashion. "And you said . . . ?"

"Not . . . no."

"So? How was it?"

"Hasn't happened yet."

Now she was shaking the retrieved drumstick in a thoughtful, analytic fashion. "You know, it makes perfect sense."

"It does?"

"The two of you, both confined. Lots in common. Lots to commiserate over. It's as if you're in a zoo, and there's only two of your species, and he's the male and you're the female, so they put you in the same cage to procreate. You don't have to fall in love. You just do it."

I said, "Not to romanticize it or anything . . ."

"Was I being too me just now?" she asked.

I said it was okay. She was a scientist. I'd grown accustomed to her less-than-sentimental reactions to my . . . various testimonies.

She asked if I wanted to share another beer. I did. We took seconds of everything, buttered more corn bread, unwound more paper towels for our greasy fingers. "What about your sister?" she asked.

How smart of her to guess that Jackleen was the other agenda item that needed discussing. I said, "We have . . . a conflict of interest."

"Such as his interest in you and not her?"

"Very insightful . . . yes. Unfortunately, I arranged for her to attend one of the dinners I cook for him. I'd have a drink, then disappear. This

Friday, in fact. Oh, and there's the added complication of me having told Perry that she liked him."

"Yet . . . yet . . . I'm not hearing that he asked *her* to have sex with him. He's not interested! Case closed! Call her. Tell her Friday's off. Things have changed."

I said, "I know her so well. Even if she doesn't say it, she'll think, 'You had no interest in Perry until I did.'"

"Am I missing something? Do you two not get along?"

I took a swig of beer. "We do. But right now there's a power imbalance. She's helping me out financially."

"Weren't you a partner in a New York City law firm? You must have decent savings and/or investments. Will the well go dry? You're young. You'll fill it up when you're back in the saddle."

I said, "I was supposed to be writing a complexion-happy food blog for her website, but we both knew it was charity, and an answer to 'How's your sister/what's she doing?' Now at least she can say, 'She's a private chef with a TikTok platform.' It hasn't been easy for her. I've embarrassed a lot of people."

"Too bad! This is about *you*. *Your* sex life. Every night my mother says, 'Mandy! What's your goal in life? Visualize it! When you visualize, you materialize.'"

I said, "Not really my thing. . . ."

"Get it over with! Call your sister now. You'll say, 'Perry guessed you're interested in him, but the timing is bad. He and I are planning to have sex.'"

Blunt enough? Quite the diplomat. I said, "Before I tell her anything like that, I should wait and see how it goes."

"With him? The sex? As if he's going to say, 'Sorry this isn't working. Next sister!'"

I looked at my phone. It was 7:05, unlikely that Jackleen would be reachable.

Mandy said, "I'm finding some vicarious satisfaction in this. The way she threw herself at him. I felt like I was back in high school, watching the popular girls in action . . . not that he was buying."

"Welcome to my whole life," I said. I hit the first name under "favorites" and Jackleen picked up. "I'm in a taxi," she announced. "The driver's having a fight on his phone with his wife or girlfriend. In Arabic, I think. Can this wait?"

"I'll be quick."

"Sir!" she was yelling. "I can't hear with you shouting. Can you whisper or call her back?" Then to me, "What's up?"

I said, "Friday dinner's off with Perry."

"Oh . . . no problem. Send me some alternate dates."

"I mean *off*-off. There's been a development." I checked with Mandy, who was nodding vigorously. I continued, "I'm going to be completely honest with you: He asked me out." I checked with Mandy: *Close enough?*

Jackleen asked, "He asked *you* out? Did you accept?"

"I intend to."

"Sudden," she said. "Quite."

"Believe me, if I thought you had genuine feelings—"

"Don't be ridiculous. It was nothing. As a matter of fact, I'm headed to meet an orthopedic surgeon now for a drink, then a radiologist at eight for tapas."

"Good for you," I said.

"I have a ton of matches on Tinder," then to the driver, "South side, far corner."

"Okay," I said. "Have fun."

"You, too," she said unconvincingly. "Talk soon."

"How'd she take it?" Mandy asked.

"She sounded surprised, but she recovered. She's on her way to serial dates." I stood, picked up my plate, and reached for hers.

"We're not done. Sit. Now you're going to call Perry."

"There's no hurry. I'll call him when I'm back in my apartment."

"I don't trust you. It's already Tuesday night. You're feeding him tomorrow, right? Tell him your answer is, 'Yes, thank you, I'll be your fuck buddy.'"

I said, "I'll text him."

"Now."

I typed, erased, typed, and finally sent Hi, it's me. Your invitation re us? My answer is yes for tomorrow night. I think we should eat first. I'll bring a light meal.

He sent back a thumbs-up emoji, not exactly a fulfilling response, given the magnitude of what I'd just agreed to.

"Ask if he has condoms," said Mandy. "He might assume you're taking care of it."

I wrote back, Condoms?

Another thumbs-up.

What to emoji back? Not a blown kiss, even though I sent that to all and sundry, almost automatically. Should I just match his thumbs-up? Or maybe a glass of wine? A salad?

Mandy asked what I was overthinking.

"The right emoji."

"How about a heart?"

I said, "I hope you're kidding."

"I wasn't. But how about a bed? It's like saying, 'I know what I agreed to, and I'm looking forward to jumping into it with you.'"

"That wouldn't be too . . . literal?"

"Visualize your success, then take action, remember? Plus, he might find it charming."

I was overdue on charm. It was only a piece of furniture, wasn't it? I typed "bed," which brought forth a head-boarded emoji. I added a bolt of lightning, erased it, substituted a simple black checkmark. And without further cogitation, sent them.

Chapter 24

As Ready as I'll Ever Be

I made Salade Niçoise with canned tuna already on hand. Potatoes, anchovies, and olives also in stock, along with eggs I hard-boiled. Would Perry notice if green beans were missing? I guessed not and substituted a jar of artichoke hearts. I whisked together a vinaigrette, which waited in its travel jar while I did the main prep work: on me. Hair to be washed and much work with an abandoned pink disposable razor. *Was I trying too hard?* I asked myself as I painted all twenty nails Romancing the Red.

I found myself thinking that there was something escort-y in what lay ahead, one stranger hooking up with another. But it wasn't an altogether unappealing fantasy. And not exactly a stranger. Wasn't I luckier than the average pro on a date, who didn't know what kinky monster could be answering the door of his hotel room? In my case, I knew whom and what to expect: Perry Salisbury, a not-unattractive man in his early forties; clean, smart, polite. Dress code? I chose a peasanty yellow dress, easy-on, easy-off.

As I was applying eyeliner and considering mascara, I wondered what extra ablutions Perry, as a guy, was up to. Probably just a shave, a shower, a clean shirt, and probably a change of sheets. I stopped mid–mascara application. Had I made it clear in my texts that this was the night we'd be doing it? Yes, I had. Wednesday spoken aloud and confirmed in writing. And if he'd gotten the night wrong, no big deal. I'd suggest we carry on anyway, me as ready and well-groomed as I'd ever be.

* * *

"Well, well, well," said Perry upon answering my knock. "I wasn't expecting . . . *this*."

I didn't have to worry that he meant *Wait? Is tonight the night?*, because he was wearing, to my astonishment, a tux, with a blossom I recognized from the roof plantings in its lapel. I said, "And I wasn't expecting *this*. You look so . . ."

"Handsome?"

Like prom dates unsure of the customs, we traded a hasty peck on the lips, my picnic basket between us. "Please come in," he said.

As usual, I headed straight for the kitchen table, to find it not set.

"We're eating in the dining room tonight," he said. "Champagne?"

As I was starting to unpack the salad components, Perry said, "Leave it. Come with me."

There were white roses in a vase and unlit candles. "Don't look so surprised," he said. "I wasn't raised in a barn." He handed me a glass and led me to the sofa.

Once seated, closer than usual, I said, "You didn't have to fuss. The tux? Very grand. Did you mean it to be ironic?"

"Ironic how?"

"You know—maybe you stood in front of your closet and said to yourself, 'Wouldn't it be funny if I opened the door wearing a tux?'"

He said, "I just thought it was a nice gesture. And I'm noticing that you're not exactly dressed for the gym. Did *you* pick out your dress ironically?"

I deserved that. I said, "Sorry! I was making nervous chatter." I smoothed the fabric of my skirt. "I thought to myself, 'This is pretty. . . . I'd like to look pretty tonight. I've only worn it once. It's about time I got some use out of it.'"

"Same here. I bought this a month before I was canned, for my parents' fiftieth. We all know how that went."

"You look . . . very nice," I said.

"Who doesn't look nice in a tux?" he asked.

"I meant *especially* nice."

"Thank you. Likewise." We clinked glasses. What to toast? *To us? To recognizing what's been . . . never mind.* I settled on a noncommittal "Cheers!"

"I almost texted to give you an out," he said.

"But you didn't. . . ."

"Right. Because I didn't want to hear 'Thank God. I was just trying to be a good sport, but I have zero interest in changing the game.'"

Regretting how lukewarm I might be sounding, like a mouse misrepresenting the real me, I said with conviction, "Our plan makes sense." And then, editing Mandy's zoo analogy: "Two people, two normal people, a man and a woman, under one roof, confined, on friendly-enough terms."

"Both lonely."

Neither one of us had used that word before, and it struck me as a rather huge confession. I said, "But here we are, stumbling on companionship, one Wednesday at a time."

"And possibly expanded to other nights?"

"Don't you think we should wait and see how it goes?" I pointed in the direction of what I knew from my own floor plan to be the bedrooms.

He said, "I'm not worried about that. Even if the first time isn't great . . . I mean, haven't you had that experience: getting to know what the other person likes?"

Did that portend . . . ? Had I just heard the kind of question a thoughtful lover asks? "For sure," I said.

"What about Friday?"

I said again, "We'll take it one day at a time."

"Not that. I meant is your sister still joining us for dinner?"

"It's off. I told her . . . well, not about this. I gave her the PG version: I said that you'd asked me out."

He smiled. "And when does the R-rated version commence?"

"After dinner? Or now?"

"If you're game." And then, to make me laugh, he called out, "Alexa! Play something Jane will find seductive," rendering a robotic "Sorry, I don't know that one."

I said, "Let me put the salad in the fridge."

He stood up. "We'll cut through the kitchen on our way. . . ." He was walking backward, smiling, gesturing, *Come on, this way, follow me.*

I did, salad forsaken. His room was painted a dark gray with white trim. Two bureaus, a highboy and a lowboy, one displaying a framed photo of a bunch of smiling guys in caps and gowns, and on the other surface just a hairbrush and a saucer holding pocket change. The bed was expertly made in blacks and whites, but he'd turned the corner of the bedclothes down at an angle. The blinds were drawn.

I said, "Close your eyes."

"Why?"

"I'm going to take my dress off."

"Good. I'll help. Turn around."

I said, "No need. No zipper." And then with unnecessary particularizing I explained that the bodice was elasticized so it just pulled off, over my head. *Comme ça.*

I didn't have much on—just the dress and carefully chosen lace panties. If only my ankle monitor could be prettier. In seconds I was under the covers. "A little chilly in here," I explained but said no more, spellbound by his meticulous disrobing. It wasn't hurried or slapdash. First, his shoes and socks. Then vest, cuff links, studs, bow tie. Then boxers, the jersey kind, navy blue. *Is this a deliberate striptease*, I wondered, *or just the tasks required by so many tuxedo accessories?* I watched, extra attentive when the long shirt and its obscuring shirttails dropped, revealing a penis ready to participate.

Funny how I'd had low expectations about our first go. But then a warm body slipped in beside me. And as my college roommate liked to say, *boom!*

Chapter 25

Are You Sitting Down?

Disinclined to recap dinner-plus-benefits for my sister, I hadn't spoken to Jackleen in several days. Luckily, I knew how to distract and, if necessary, dissemble: go directly to her newly expanded social life.

How were those guys u met last Tues nite? I texted.

No chemistry.

W/ neither?

One was 60+ w/ a daughter my age. The other got mad when I didn't want to go up to his hotel room. Then, off-topic, Did u have yr big date w Perry yet?

Dinner as usual, I wrote.

That's it?

That's it, I lied.

My phone rang. I heard, "Then why disinvite me to dinner because he—quote-unquote—asked you out?"

I said, "'Out' in our case means *in* since, as you know, we can't go anywhere. I cooked. I packed it up and brought it. I stayed and ate with him, which is why it was different from the usual meal transport."

What was I afraid of—that I as the sidelined sister had more going on than the unshackled one? She never would've held back if the situations were reversed, if she'd just left someone's bed and I'd been returning from two dud dates. It was a habit, a bad one: me leaning into my role as the beta twin. To dramatically change the subject, I said, "How about this? Are you sitting down?"

"Not bad news, I hope."

"More like crazy news: Would you believe that before Frances Fitz-Roy died, she told the police that if anything happened to her, they should focus their investigation on me?"

"Whaaaat? Who told you this?"

"She left a note! I saw it!"

"As if you're free to commit murder! How, when, where, sudden heart attack?"

Having been sworn to secrecy by Sergeant Terrence, I didn't mention poison. "To be determined," I told her.

"No autopsy?"

"Autopsy for sure, but only next of kin can see the results."

"What gall! What did you ever do to her?"

"Nothing! It had to be her own guilt. Purely projection! Having wrecked my career, she assumed I had a motive."

Jackleen asked who else knew about this libelous letter.

"The cops of course. They're the ones who came knocking on my door."

"Just what you need—more cops showing up at The Margate, asking for you."

She meant witnessed by the doormen, the staff, the fellow residents, and the dog-walkers who happened to be in the lobby when New York

City's finest came around asking for Jane Morgan. I said, "Au contraire. I think it makes their day."

She asked what I was doing to exonerate myself. Had I spoken to a criminal lawyer? And the whole idea, the accusation, the slur—ridiculous on the face of it, given my constricted life.

"That's exactly what I told the cops—I'm stuck here! I'd set off some alarm in ankle-monitor central."

"Can you appeal to the brother and sister?"

"For what?"

"Cause of death. You can't be blamed for a heart attack or an aneurism! Or have your lawyer call their lawyer. Wouldn't it be . . . what's it called?"

"Discovery? Not yet. Besides, I don't have a lawyer."

"You're a lawyer. Call them yourself!"

"I did."

"And?"

"I told Dani that I lived across the street and had some history with Frances. We had a very civilized conversation."

"When?"

"When she came over for a drink."

"Just like that—'Come over for a drink?' How'd that happen?"

"I told her I was a lawyer, so if she and her brother had any questions—about probate, wills, trusts, co-op board, et cetera, maybe I could answer them. As it turned out, there *are* problems with their visas. So she and I had drinks on my roof."

"You're friends with these two now? Mom and Dad thought they were obnoxious."

"I think, over drinks and Polish appetizers, I can get them to tell me how she died."

"They're coming over?"

"Maybe. The invitation's been issued."

"For when?"

"Soon."

"Don't be coy," she said.

"Tomorrow."

"May I point out," Jackleen said, "that two siblings plus two siblings would make the sides even. I can be very useful."

It was true. I might be the lawyer, but Jackleen could be a charming cross-examiner and diagnostician. And an extra set of eyes and ears would come in handy when I was in the kitchen, plating the food.

"Is she fair, light, medium, or dark?" Jackleen asked. "And how old is she?"

I knew exactly what she was asking: *What samples should I bring?*

"Thirty-three-ish."

"Alpha-hydroxy then. And a vitamin C serum."

*   *   *

I called her back when Dani confirmed, six-ish on Thursday for cocktails. "Be on time. I don't want a grand entrance."

"No grand entrance! I'll get there early and I'll have done my homework."

"On . . . ?"

"Poland . . . and Polish! A useful phrase or two."

Before I could tell her that both Grabowskis spoke English, I heard "Give me a sec. I'm on Google Translate. . . . Okay, how's this: 'Ow-top-see-ah nyahn-ee.'"

"Which is?"

"Your nanny's autopsy," she said.

Chapter 26

Good Cop/Bad Cop

Whole Foods sold potato and cheese pierogis, so that was a promise easily fulfilled. I arranged them on a platter with coins of pan-seared kielbasa, alongside a shot glass of toothpicks and a jar of Kosciusko mustard.

As promised, Jackleen arrived early. The Grabowskis came separately, first Dani, a mere fifteen minutes late, in a dress that looked like a black satin slip; her brother, in Lycra bicycle shorts and a jersey, a half hour after that. I introduced myself and Jackleen, who said in ambassadorial fashion as she shook each hand, "Welcome to our city."

Krzysztof was, as described by his sister, "hot," his hair streaked blond and his very blue eyes fringed by unexpectedly dark lashes. I could almost see Jackleen calculating the difference between his age and hers. *Please don't flirt*, I thought to myself. Then immediately, *Why the hell not?* She could be the good cop and I could be the immigration expert.

It was clear to me that he'd been pressed to come, barely disguising his impatience. He never let his phone out of his hand, unless it was perched on his thigh while he ate and drank. Dani would periodically bark things to him in Polish. Upon hearing "veeza," and surely the enticement that got him here, Krzysztof looked up from his phone, waiting for my counsel.

I asked if their current visas had expired. Yes, they had. Last month.

"Is that big deal?" asked Krzysztof.

I knew, without experience beyond general knowledge and a law school elective, that it was a *very* big deal. The most charitable question I could ask was "Did you lose track of the expiration date?"

"It's summer. We were busy," said Dani.

"In Hamptons," said Krzysztof.

Instantly engaged, Jackleen asked, "Which one?"

"Many," he said. "We sleep at many nice houses. We like it there. We take Jitney."

Jackleen asked me, "Are they safe if they stay under the radar? I mean, do visitors walk around carrying their visas so anyone can check them?"

I said, "If they're not caught, they're . . . not caught. But let's say you two traveled—"

"Where?" Krzysztof asked.

"On a plane—"

"Out of country?"

"For sure, but let's say . . . okay, take Florida—"

"Miami, South Beach," Dani translated for her brother.

"Presumably you'd be flying. You have Polish passports?"

"So?"

"TSA would ask to see your visa. And if it's expired, that would be that."

"Jail?" asked Krzysztof.

"You'd be deported, and you wouldn't be able to return to the United States for ten years," I said, quoting what I'd looked up an hour before.

"What if we flew on private plane?" asked Krzysztof.

I had no idea. "That airline would probably know."

Jackleen said, "I have a patient who has a pilot's license. I could ask him."

Her good-cop routine was starting to annoy me. "Didn't someone explain all of this when you got your visa—presumably at an American embassy?" I asked them.

"We'll be fine," said Dani.

"Why do you think that?" I asked.

"We won't fly anywhere."

"What if you apply for a job? Any respectable employer is going to ask about your status."

"We don't apply for jobs," Krzysztof said. "We audition."

"We know people who could change the date," said Dani. "Make us not late."

"Here? At Citizenship and Immigration?" I asked.

She pantomimed: pen in hand, writing, forging.

"Don't even think about that," I said.

"What about the reason we had to stay, for funeral?" said Krzysztof.

Though she knew every detail, Jackleen said, "I'm sorry. Whose funeral?"

Dani looked to her brother for permission.

"Tell them. I don't care," he said.

"Our au pair's," Dani said. Pointing at me, most likely having forgotten my name, said, "She knows all about her."

"But *I* don't," said Jackleen brightly.

"Our nanny for years and years, for much longer than children need one," said Dani.

"*How* long?" Jackleen asked.

"Into our teens."

"Because she was fucking our father many years," said Krzysztof.

Would *shocked* look phony, since Dani knew I'd been versed in the family's dysfunction? I tsk-tsked anyway.

Jackleen asked me, wide-eyed, "Wouldn't that constitute workplace sexual harassment?"

"It was an arrangement," said Dani. "She was brought to Poland to speak English with us. To immerse us. But also to help my parents with something they wanted but couldn't get on their own."

"Such as . . . ?" asked Jackleen.

"A baby to carry on the family name."

"OMG," said Jackleen. "*Did* she?"

"A son, first try," said Dani.

"Would that be you?" Jackleen asked Krzysztof.

"She gave birth to me, yes. That did not make her my mother!"

"Was she a gestational surrogate?" Jackleen asked.

"Maybe you should restate that," I said.

"Was it IVF, using your mother's egg and your father's sperm?"

"No more eggs. They did it in bed," said Krzysztof.

"It was an arrangement," Dani repeated. "A contract. She was checked out by a British doctor before she came to live with us."

"Did your parents' marriage survive this?" Jackleen asked.

"You don't get divorced where we come from. Not in our station," Dani said. "You have your liaisons, and you carry on."

"And the former au pair is definitely the decedent, whom I've heard so much about?" Jackleen asked.

"Definitely," I said.

"Except no one's told me *how* she died?" said Jackleen, her eyes signaling to me, *Just like that! It's our lucky day.*

"She was allergic," said Dani.

"Allergic to . . . ?" Jackleen asked, quicky adding, "I'm a physician. This is professional curiosity."

"Nuts," said Krzysztof.

"Tree nuts," Dani amplified, "which are nuts that grow on trees."

"She went into anaphylactic shock?" asked Jackleen.

"And hit her head," said Krzysztof.

"On?" Jackleen asked.

He checked with his sister. "Plantaseena?"

"A planter," she said "Big, heavy . . . a wooden box. It had metal corners."

"Sharp," said Krzysztof.

"Made of lead," said his sister.

I asked which of those tragic events—eating nuts or hitting her head—was the actual cause of death.

"Both," said Dani. "Plus a little drunk."

"I assume there was an autopsy," I prompted.

Krzysztof said, "That's how they know she ate nuts," adding, "Autopsies are very careful."

"There was dirt in her mouth," said Dani. "The whole planter fell on top of her. Dirt everywhere."

"And there could've been lead in the dirt," Jackleen speculated. "Her bloodwork must've been a holy hodgepodge." She asked if they had a copy of the autopsy report, because, as a physician, perhaps she could answer any questions they had.

Krzysztof, phone at the ready, scrolled, clicked, then handed his phone to Jackleen.

Scrolling, she murmured, "Looking for . . . here it is . . . stomach contents. Ahh, there's the culprit."

"Poison?" I asked.

"Pesto," she said. "Obviously, the pine nuts caused the anaphylaxis. But . . ." More scrolling, more reading. "It was the traumatic brain injury that killed her . . . plus, here we go: alcohol, a lot. The olives could mean she was drinking martinis . . . dirt in the lungs with some nasty elements . . . nitrates." She looked up. "Undoubtedly when her face hit the dirt, she was struggling to breathe."

"What a way to go," I said.

"She was in love with fertilizer," said Dani. "I mean, too much, like every week."

Jackleen consulted the report again. "There was mozzarella, tomatoes, bread, herbaceous matter. So that makes perfect sense."

"What does?" I asked.

Jackleen looked up, surprised. "That her last meal was a caprese sandwich, with pesto."

I asked the Grabowskis, "Does that sound like something she'd eat?"

Dani said, "Why would it be in her stomach if she didn't eat it?"

"I meant why would she eat something she knew she was allergic to?"

"We don't know why she did anything," said Dani.

"Was she a drinker?" I asked.

"Did she have martinis every day at five o'clock? Yes. A few," said Dani.

Jackleen said to Krzysztof, "It must've been very painful."

He shrugged. "Maybe if drunk, it didn't hurt so much."

"I meant for you, losing someone who'd taken care of you your whole life."

"His whole life he thought Ma was his mother," Dani said.

"Until the 23andMe results came back?" I asked.

Krzysztof said, "My big-mouth sister told you about DNA tests?"

Jackleen said, in her best bedside manner, "It's quite the thing. I've read so many articles about people who found siblings who'd been conceived with the help of sperm banks—"

"I had *kuzni* in England with her name. Dani didn't! Who was I now?"

"I assume you went to Frances with these DNA findings," Jackleen said.

Dani jumped to her feet, striking a pose that was remarkably Frances-like, witness-stand straight and severe. Her expression turned superior, that of someone about to shock her audience with a bottled-up secret. "'Stupid boy,'" Dani mimicked in a British accent frostier than her own. "'Did you never realize who gave birth to you? Who was brought to your country to give your father the son he couldn't get from his wife?'"

"Wow," I said.

Dani took a slight bow.

"She really said 'stupid boy'?" I asked.

"Yes!" Krzysztof said. "Imagine finding out that woman is your mother!"

"I can't imagine keeping such a thing from your own flesh and blood!" said childless Jackleen.

"She said she couldn't tell me," said Krzysztof. "She signed something—a do-not-tell document."

"Was she at *least* a good nanny?" I asked.

"We didn't know about good or bad. We didn't know that a nanny could be nice," said Dani.

"Until we got VCR," said Krzysztof.

Jackleen asked, "Did you ever say to your parents, 'Can't you fire her? Can't you hire someone who has'—what was missing? Warmth? Affection?"

"She stayed because was still fucking our father," Krzysztof said.

"And your mother knew they were carrying on still? Even after Frances produced a son?"

He squinted at his phone and said something that sounded like "pool knots."

"Midnight. It's midnight there," Dani translated.

"You're calling your mother now?" I asked. "In *Poland*?"

"She never sleeps," he said. "Is okay. I call this time often."

With one tap, and presumably one ring, Krzysztof was speaking Polish, his voice sweet, affectionate, boyish.

"He's her favorite," Dani explained. "It's why his English isn't as good as mine."

After listening for another minute, I whispered, "Is he asking her about Frances?"

"Only about how long the affair went on. Ma doesn't know that he found out from 23andMe that Fitzi was his biological mother. And why would he drop that bomb? She thinks it's her big secret. She worships him."

I heard Krzysztof pronounce "Danusha," which I assumed was a lead-in to *Danusha says hello*, because it produced a thumbs-up. He put the phone down, smiling. "She laughed when I asked about Ta-toosh and Franciszka."

Jackleen asked, "How is that possible?"

"She had men," he said. "And also she pretends their sex was nothing, just what happens when there are extra women who work in the house."

"She has serious boundary issues," said Dani. "She tells Krzysztof things that most parents wouldn't tell their sons."

"He doesn't seem to mind," I said, watching Krzysztof happily stabbing and chewing kielbasa coins.

He answered for himself. "Do I want to make her sad? Burst her bubble? I play with it."

"He means he plays along, pretending my *matka* is his *matka*, too," said his sister. "It's easy because he thought that his whole life."

Jackleen asked, "How old were you when Frances left?"

"Too old," said Dani. "Teenagers don't need nannies. She didn't want to leave."

"Poland?" I asked. "Or Krzysztof?"

"Her home, her lifestyle. Our father. The house has a movie theater, a staff, a cook. She never had to make a bed."

"There must've been some ginormous golden parachute if she could buy a penthouse apartment in Manhattan," said Jackleen.

Dani yelped, "She didn't buy it! My grandparents bought it when they thought they might be sent to Communist prisons. Fitzy would live there until one of us wanted it."

"Sitting house," Krzysztof confirmed.

"Then she suddenly died," said Jackleen, "after ingesting something she knew she was allergic to. Did she *not* have an EpiPen with her at all times?"

"How would we know that?" asked Krzysztof.

I stood up. We had all the information I needed. "We've been keeping you way too long," I said.

"Can you do anything about our visas?" Dani asked.

No; no one could. My inexpert pro bono parting advice was "Keep doing what you're doing, lying low."

"Good luck, you two!" said Jackleen.

❊ ❊ ❊

When the half-siblings were out the door and the elevator had descended, I pretended to call after them, "If you're caught, expect to be deported on the next boat."

"And my sister didn't kill your nanny-slut!" Jackleen added.

She and I returned to the couch, poured ourselves a glass of the red wine Jackleen had brought.

"Want to report them?" Jackleen asked.

I said nah. They're annoying, but no threat to me or national security. And if I turned them in, wouldn't I be fulfilling the warning in Frances's posthumous letter: *Watch out for Jane Morgan?*

Jackleen was shaking her head. "Amazing," she said.

"I know! And creepy—his phone call to his mother, asking her how long his father slept with the nanny. Creepy but . . . almost funny. I actually enjoyed the whole dysfunctional exchange."

"Not that. I meant you. Your being entertained by those two."

"Weren't you?"

"It's something else. I think you're not telling me everything."

"Such as . . . ?"

"I think you've made some kind of peace with your situation. You're practically cheerful."

As my British detectives often said about uncooperative witnesses, I remained *shtum*.

Chapter 27

Count Me In

On Wednesdays, faithfully, Perry would cock his head in the direction of his bedroom and I'd pretty much jump to my feet. We'd return for dessert, a course I added so that our get-together seemed less transactional. Sometimes we got right to it upon my arrival, and I'd reheat dinner in the microwave. Cold food was showing up more and more on the menu.

There was the matter of invoices, too. I told him that I felt odd leaving the biweekly bill on the counter the way I did before we were having sex.

"Ridiculous," he said. Of course he'd continue reimbursing me. This wasn't Meals on Wheels. This was haute cuisine; okay, haute-retro cuisine, but that was fine. Very fine.

Our conversations remained pleasantly neutral. We didn't discuss feelings. We were always mindful of how our six-month sentences were ticking down. Topics discussed at the table: weather vis-à-vis waning days of roof visits; renovations to the building that were increasing our identical monthly maintenance fees, New York City politics, absentee ballots, places we'd go to and eat at, shows and museum exhibitions we hoped would still be running when we were free.

I was careful not to imply that we'd be doing such things together. After one such wish-list recitation I asked as casually as I could, "What about your dance card?"

"Meaning?"

"Going out on dates when you're free . . . with new people?"

He just shook his head, and looking disconcerted, took a spoonful of my first-ever vichyssoise.

I was immediately sorry I'd asked a question that had a relationship ring to it. For the first time since I'd been a prisoner of The Margate, a wholly new thought invaded my brain—*Is it so bad being stuck here?*

"What about you?" he asked finally. "New people?"

I shrugged. "It's a long way off."

He put his spoon down, wiped his mouth with his napkin, said carefully, "You seem to enjoy what we do. Quite a lot. Am I wrong?"

I knew what he was referring to: the certain heights I regularly reached. "For which you deserve all the credit," I said.

"For which you're very welcome."

We returned to our soup. I couldn't be tongue-tied, could I? I was a litigator. My job was to think on my feet, yet I was holding back in case an unreciprocated declaration slipped out. Perry asked what was in the soup. I looked down at it, its uninterrupted whiteness in his plain white soup bowls. "Potatoes, leeks, cream. It's Anthony Bourdain's recipe, may he rest in peace. But I forgot the chives. Don't move."

As I was chopping at the counter he surprised me with the question "Does your sister know what's going on?"

I returned to the table and garnished our bowls. "If she does, you can bet it's along the lines of lonely man plus lonely woman, confined to the same building, end up attending to each other's needs."

"Like you're the only woman in the building?" Perry groused. "Is that what she thinks? Like that movie where we're the only two people left on earth after a nuclear holocaust?"

I said, "No, no. I'm only projecting what Jackleen would deduce, because she rarely gives me credit for anything."

He tapped the back of my hand. "I'm fishing for a compliment here. Maybe something like, 'I'm not having sex with you, Perry, just because you're the other person in the building with an ankle monitor.'"

"Clearly," I said.

"Or maybe, 'I try to act cool and nonchalant, but I'm really glad I agreed to our . . . arrangement.'"

"Very true. Extremely true."

He walked our bowls to the sink, barefooted, shirt never buttoned back up, and asked from there, "In that case, how would you feel about adding Sunday night to the lineup?"

"On top of Monday-Wednesday-Friday?"

"I don't mean the cooking. We'll order in, my treat. Or it could be just a late-afternoon . . . social call, your place or mine."

"I accept," I said.

❋   ❋   ❋

Wasn't it obvious to an outside observer such as my sister what had developed between Perry and me? I thought so, until Jackleen asked me in a late-night phone call, "Does Perry have any single male friends he could introduce you to?"

"Introduce *me* to? For what?"

"For dates, at least until you can meet someone IRL."

Hello, habitual sister-diminishment. "You realize what a passive-aggressive question that is?"

I heard an indignant "What? Why?"

How much to give away? I settled on "It would be a slap in the face for him to fix me up with another guy because . . . we're extremely and regularly satisfied with each other's company—" Emphasis on "satisfied."

With a cynical laugh she asked, "Right. And when do men play matchmaker? Never." She switched to another unfriendly question: "Does he think he's going to find a job when his six months are up?"

"We don't discuss that."

"I'm not surprised."

"Because you think I just drop the food off and return to my cell?"

"No. Because discussing what, if anything, is ahead professionally probably reminds him of the idiotic thing he did that got him arrested."

I said, "I'm sorry I told you about that. And, by the way, I view his crime as slightly more altruistic than idiotic."

"It says so much about his character. I'd be very careful if I were you."

I said, biting off each word, "I'm doing just the opposite of being careful, thank you."

"You know what I think he should do?" she continued, unfazed. "Throw himself on the mercy of his old boss at Gladstone's. Hat in hand, say, 'I paid for my crime. I served my time. I made a mistake. I take responsibility. Let me prove myself. I'll take half my salary.'"

"Where is this coming from? Suddenly you're strategizing about

Perry's reentry into the workforce? Is it transference—what you're really worrying about is *my* reentry?"

"I'm not worried about you. *You* can set up a private practice. What kind of private practice can Perry set up? Does 'felon' get swiped from his record after he's done the time?"

I said, "Jack—are you still interested in him? Is that what these tortured questions are all about?"

"Don't be ridiculous. I'm hanging up."

Before I could say, *Fine, good night*, I heard, "Weeks ago, you said he asked you out. Anything since then?"

What was I waiting for? "There's been movement," I said.

"To the bedroom?" she snapped.

"Regularly."

I expected follow-up questions, but there were none. "Surprised?" I asked.

"Why would I be? When I call you on your catering nights—even at eight, nine o'clock, you don't pick up."

"So? I call you back."

"Gloating!"

I said, "That's ridiculous. And untrue."

"Maybe 'gloating' is too strong. I meant . . . self-involved. You don't ask what's going on with me, or the practice, or maybe if I have news from Mom or Dad."

I asked, surely unconvincingly and lamely, "Anything new?"

"As a matter of fact, I'm going to an AAD conference in Chicago, and I have theater tickets for Saturday."

"For?"

"*Hamilton*, finally. A fortune."

"Tickets, plural? Are you taking someone?"

I heard a weary sigh. "We're almost forty, Jane. I don't need to be running out on dates. Do I want to get involved with just anyone? Right now, for me, at least, 'just anyone' would be worse than having no one."

It was a reprimand wrapped in a sermon. I said, "Point taken," and hung up.

Chapter 28

And the Goal
Here Is What?

W e'd changed venues, cutting out the commute to Perry's apartment, now that we were regularly having dinner à deux. A dozen episodes into my TikTok debut, I reached over to my night table, where Margaret's cookbooks were still my bedtime reading, and announced to Perry that I had something I'd like to run by him.

He propped himself up on one elbow. "Fine. I'm listening."

I left the bed and stood next to it. "Okay. It's . . . me on TikTok. I start with personal stuff, such as the good and the bad parts of twindom, or being under home confinement, or various miscarriages of justice I've suffered. Then I narrate and record as I cook."

He pointed at me. "Presumably not naked?"

"Fully dressed, so ignore that. Ready?"

"Ready."

I read from the script in one hand and the cookbook in the other. "Today we have the deceptively titled Fried Chicken, and I say 'deceptively' because—dramatic pause . . . it's not what you get when you think, *fried chicken*! Okay, now I read word for word from the recipe: 'Blah blah. Place in a frying pan with a tablespoon of butter or lard . . . et cetera.' Then I might editorialize along the lines of good luck having lard on hand. 'Use more butter or Crisco or bacon fat.'"

I checked with Perry. Was his one-eyed squint mystification? I carried on, reading faster and faster. "'Season with salt and pepper. Cover tightly until the water has boiled away. Uncover, add more butter if the chicken sticks to the pan. Fry to a golden brown, turning the pieces frequently. This may be made a rich fricassee by adding a gravy made of one and one-half cups of milk, and one scant tablespoon of flour to the browned chicken, just before removing from the fire.'" I smiled a professional smile and closed with 'Another bad recipe and another glimpse into my hard-luck life.' What do you think?"

"And you're reading this to me why?"

"Because I may not have mentioned the TikTok posts before."

"You haven't. This is what you do on TikTok—read recipes?"

"With some autobiography thrown in."

He reached for his phone. "I have TikTok. How do I find you?"

"I go by—and this isn't set in stone—'hashtag unfortunate food.'"

Not keen on hearing my own voice, I threw on a seersucker robe and said I'd get the gazpacho out of the freezer, where I'd put it for a quick chill, and prep the salad.

After the table was set and the watermelon and feta tossed, I returned to the bedroom and slipped in next to him, his phone on his chest, from which the recorded me was reciting a recipe for something called Dainty Indian Pudding. He hit pause and said, "In terms of the real-life parts, did you mean to be this blunt? Because there's no holding back."

"It's very stream of consciousness. It's like I'm talking to myself, or maybe to the jury I would've had if I hadn't opted for a bench trial."

After some throat-clearing he asked, "Have you mentioned me in any of them?"

"No. You don't have to worry—"

"I wouldn't mind," he said.

"But, here's the thing: I talk about what's wrong: my failures, my mistakes, my enemies. It's all cynical, all grudge-y. If I talked about you, it would be way off, tonally."

"Because?"

I poked him. "You know. . . ."

He touched his screen, listened to another unappealing recipe I'd chosen because it called for mutton broth. "And the goal here is what?" he asked.

"In the beginning, no goal. It was Jackleen's make-work project for me. She read about kids who made it big cooking on TikTok."

"And she talked you into it?"

"Into one episode. I just went with 'Hi, I'm Jane, cooking under house arrest for public indecency'—like I was mocking the whole idea. To my astonishment, when Jackleen saw it, she said, 'More.'"

"And you do everything Jackleen tells you to do?"

It was a question I hated because these days it was true. I said, "It's only polite. She underwrites a lot, pretending that certain posts could grow her practice, 'hashtag MorganDerm.'"

Perry said, "You sign off each time with 'my hard-luck life'? *Still*?"

I knew what he was asking with the *still?*. Even now that we were enjoying our semiweeklies? I kissed him, something we didn't do very often, given the pragmatic origins of our arrangement.

He returned the kiss, several times. And then, to my surprise, asked if my parents knew where things stood now.

"Do you mean . . . ?" I lifted the sheet: one naked man and one naked woman, whose uncinched robe had fallen away.

"Exactly."

"No. Do yours?"

"Totally different situation. I met your parents. Remember?"

Of course I remembered—the dinner that was supposed to demonstrate that I had friends in the building. I asked if *his* parents ever visited, and did they know he wasn't merely downsized, and what were their names?

"DeAndra and Calvin. Now they do. Everyone with a phone knows what I did. And no, they haven't visited since I hit the skids."

"The skids?" I laughed. "If we were in your bed instead of mine, I'd point to the Warhol silkscreen and the—I'm guessing—thousand-thread-count sheets. You haven't hit any skids, my friend."

"'My friend'?" he repeated. He inched closer until our hips were touching. "Is this what friends do before supper?" And for emphasis, he gave my closest breast a tweak.

I said, "I stand corrected."

* * *

He was quieter than usual over dinner, stirring his gazpacho in a distracted fashion between spoonfuls. "Something wrong?" I asked.

"No. It's great. I even like the frozen bits."

"Is there something else you wanted to say about the TikToks but think I'll be offended?"

"Only what you've heard already—they're kind of blunt."

"I know. My mother agrees. She hates the narratives, which she thinks are too honest. Home confinement! Losing my license! Why advertise all of that? What if any future employers are watching?"

"I disagree . . . well, not about the posts but about the job part. Tell her you'll be up and running on January 1, briefcase in hand. I, on the other hand, am a lifer."

"No, you're not!"

"What's my way up and out, then? Who the hell would hire me? The Art Students League to model for Figure Drawing 101?"

I said automatically, "Someone will!"

"No one will. And it's what keeps me up at night."

Was it possible that our prior conversations were only about what we did or didn't do that day, what we'd watched or read or ordered online, never slipping into more significant topics such as our futures?

I said, "There must be plenty of other auction houses, not to mention galleries and—"

"I worked at Gladstone's! I don't want to settle. I don't want to spend the rest of my career at some low-rent auction house, crating and shipping. Which"—finally a small smile—"I happen to be very good at."

What else to say that could help, could elevate his mood? I knew nothing about the auction world, let alone its job opportunities. Of course, that same auction-house ignorance hadn't stopped Jackleen from prescribing a course of action. *Do I quote her or pretend it's my own advice?* I said, "Not that it's any of her business, but Jackleen was wondering if you could get your old job back by throwing yourself on the mercy of a higher-up at Gladstone's."

"Out of the question. Zero tolerance. No second chance. A felon handling millions of dollars of artwork? No way. I wouldn't get past the greeter in the lobby."

I tried again. "What about previous jobs? Anything? Any old boss who'd welcome you back?"

"No! My previous job was at an auction house run by a crook."

I didn't want to look too animated by that, but I loved hearing about crooks. "In what way?" I asked, refilling his wineglass.

"A cash-flow dodge."

I took a deep, hopeful breath and whispered, "Embezzlement?"

"Not quite. The way it's supposed to work is that the buyer has thirty days to pay, and the auction house has to turn the money over to the seller within thirty-five days. The buyer usually pays up right away, but this guy would wait till the last minute to pay the sellers, and make them beg for the payment. In the meantime, he'd put the money into the stock market."

"And this was common knowledge among the staff?"

"Regular customers kept complaining, so it *became* common knowledge."

"And you quit in protest?"

"I was fired."

"Because you blew the whistle?"

"Three of us did. And all of us were canned. He denied it all, went crazy, and that was on top of him being a lunatic to begin with, always screaming at us, always firing people. We learned to show up the next day anyway. But not this time."

My worried expression must've telegraphed, *Does this guy get fired from every job?*, because Perry said, "That particular gap in my résumé isn't what'll hurt me. Everyone knew—dealers, other auction houses, galleries—that he was a lunatic and a crook, so it was a badge of honor."

I felt it was only polite to say, "I lose sleep, too, over what *I'm* going to do next."

"Law," he said. "You're going to be a lawyer again. You're only suspended, right?"

"True."

Perry said, "If I were a law firm, and you came in and you owned what you did—public indecency? That's it? Are you kidding me?—I'd hire you in a minute."

I said, "That's very nice of you, but the last thing clients want is an ex-con representing them, period, end of story."

"I disagree," said Perry. "It says, 'She knows her way around the system. That's why she's here.' Especially valuable if I were a criminal myself." He smiled a rueful smile. "Oh, that's right. I *am*."

For the first time in a long time I had a lawyerly ambitious thought: What could I do for him when and if I were back in the saddle? Anything? Request a meeting with the brass at Gladstone's? Be the one who threw herself at their mercy? Hadn't I observed, after six binged seasons of *Line of Duty*, that a bent copper who showed up for an interview always has a solicitor at his side? And didn't the parties always walk away with an immunity deal?

A good idea; brilliant, actually. I'd work on it, starting tomorrow.

Chapter 29

The Mission Is What?

Upstairs in 8-B, I took in Mandy's decor, once again, unhappily. No changes in the four-plus months since I'd first seen this clutter. She pointed down the hall. "Come. I'm all set up."

What she was set up for was trimming my hair in the bathroom. I'd chosen her for the job, guessing she wouldn't just chop off the four months' growth willy-nilly but would be root-canal-careful. I sat atop a two-step kitchen ladder, a bath towel over my shoulders, newspapers spread on the floor, as she measured and cut, measured and cut. I said, "I knew you were the right person to ask."

It was taking a long time but that was fine, except that the conversation inevitably turned dental. Did my six-month confinement allow a timely appointment for my next cleaning? "Yes," I lied, "the week I'm freed." I changed the subject by asking how the would-be romance with the patient was going.

"It's not. There never was a romance."

I said, "I knew you were being careful because you wouldn't cross the sacred doctor-patient line."

"I was being *too* careful. I dropped the ball." She explained what had given her the impression that the man was interested: He'd asked her receptionist if Dr. Zussman was married.

"Which she reported to you the second he walked out the door, I bet."

"Correct."

"Was there an adjective in the request, like 'the attractive Dr. Zussman'?"

"I doubt it."

"Then what?"

She shrugged. "I checked his schedule. He didn't have another appointment."

I forced myself to ask calmly, "Could you have invented a reason to call and suggest a follow-up?"

"It wasn't indicated," she said. "And he didn't have dental insurance."

"So that was it? End of story?"

"I blew it. It would've been appropriate to give him a call and ask if he'd had any swelling after the implant. Worse: It's not like I'm his regular dentist. I can't say, 'See you in six months.'"

Worse than what? Her lonely heart? I said, "Don't worry," followed by the universal well-wish, "You'll meet someone. You'll make an effort. I'll help."

She met my gaze in the mirror. "Do you know anyone who'd want to sleep with me?"

Yikes; just like that. I checked her expression in the mirror to see if she'd been joking. No. She was looking not only serious but also single-minded. I said, "Then you should go online. I guarantee there'd be no shortage of guys who'd want to sleep with you, especially if you hinted that was a goal."

She returned to her painstaking snipping while I continued to stare at her reflection, hating myself for having makeover thoughts. Mandy was pretty in a severe, unadorned way. Of course, she wouldn't be wearing makeup or plucking her eyebrows to cut a friend's hair or hide under a face shield at work. "Do you always wear your hair in a bun?" I asked.

"Too schoolmarmish, right? But I can't have my hair fall into patients' faces. Even a ponytail can flop over at the wrong time."

I reached for my phone on the edge of the sink and googled "attractive ways to wear your hair up." Clicking on "Messy Buns," a YouTube demonstration promising three different ways to make long hair prom-pretty, I invited Mandy to watch it with me.

After the third styling, Mandy said without much conviction, "I'll try it sometime. Do men really care if your hair is up when they're lying down?" And then with a loud sigh: "I don't have to tell you that peak fertility started declining at thirty. At thirty-five I'd already be a geriatric primigravida."

Thirty-nine-year-old me didn't love being reminded of that. "So the mission is what? A husband? A baby daddy?"

"Both. I missed some chances," she said.

I asked with whom and when.

"When I was in dental school." She shrugged. "I had no shortage of grateful sex partners. But I wasn't in love with any of them and I thought I had a lot of time." Snip, snip. Then "I've heard you can check a box on OkCupid that says you're fine with casual sex. And I can vamp up my photos." With that she leaned forward, pushed her breasts upward to mimic the work of an aggressive bra.

By now I was staring at her reflection in the mirror. "Where have you been hiding this Mandy?" I asked.

She didn't answer that. She said, "They all want sex. Which I don't think is incompatible with wanting to be a husband and a father, do you?"

How best to end this conversation? I didn't agree or disagree. Stuck at home, I was in no position to play matchmaker. I said something that would ultimately prove prophetic. "You'll get there. Whatever it takes."

Chapter 30

Holding Me Harmless

Weeks later, my new nonfriend Dani/Danuta texted me, Need to talk. Can u come over?

I can't. What's up?

With no prologue and no more gravity than if she were asking me to recommend a nearby dry cleaner, Dani typed: Do u know a U.S. citizen who could marry Krzysztof? Like now?

Coming from her, on behalf of him, I was hardly surprised. I wrote, Forget it. Citizenship and Immigration smells a fake marriage a mile away.

Apparently, her fluent English didn't cover that particular idiom, because she wrote back, Someone here, in NYC, I meant. Not long-distance.

I assume this is to get him a green card?

I to get Form I-130.

With that grammar and syntax, I knew the wannabee groom was also on the thread.

Trust me! USCIS knows when it's a fake marriage!

Im actor, he wrote back. Did u no that?

I *didn't* know that, but I knew what he meant: He'd pretend to be in love. I texted back, You can't do that, to counteract anything incriminating in writing.

Then, against my better judgment, and after a Google search, I called Dani. She answered her phone with "You know someone?"

I said, "Why would any woman enter into such an arrangement? If caught, she'd face criminal penalties. And you shouldn't be asking for my help."

"It was off the record," she said. "It was only a text."

"*Why* would the wimmins do this?" I heard her brother repeat, presumably to his sister. "So she can be married to *Krzysztof*!"

A long, noisy pause followed while the two yelled in Polish. Then it was Krzysztof saying, "Why would I be breaking laws if I fell in love and proposed to marry her?"

I said, "Krzysztof, trust me; it would be painfully obvious to the authorities that you were marrying to stay here." Now on speaker, I heard Dani ask, "What about your sister?"

I expelled a loud, dismissive laugh. "Trust me, my sister would never agree to a green card marriage!"

Dani said, "Lots of women want to get married. Let's say Krzysztof knocks on a woman's door and she opens it and he says, 'Hello, lovely lady. Will you marry me?' Don't you think she'd be very pleased?"

"Maybe in another century," I said.

"What if they have a nice time, a glass of wine, some nuts, and then come back here, maybe have a martini on the terrace? He would intrigue the person. She'd think, 'How does someone so young have an apartment where the elevator opens directly into it?'"

Having met and attempted to make conversation with Krzysztof, I said, "I haven't experienced the intriguing side of your brother."

I'd forgotten I was on speaker. He said, "I didn't do that with you, because we were getting advice. I wasn't having a date."

Dani said, "Baby steps. A glass of wine. Maybe you know someone who'd say yes to meeting a handsome man for a drink. We pay."

I said, "The last thing you want to do is to pay someone to marry him!"

"I meant pay for the drinks. Maybe dinner, too. Like a blind date."

Put that way, I didn't think I'd be perverting the cause of justice. I said, "I'll check with my sister. She has a staff, mostly young women. But, let me repeat, framed as a date, period. Not buying a wife."

"When?" Dani asked.

I said, "I promise nothing."

* * *

Jackleen huffed, "You've got to be kidding. You're helping them? Mom and Dad thought they were the brattiest mourners they'd ever seen, and, in my own experience, utterly charmless."

I said, "I'm not endorsing this. Maybe one of your nurses or physician's assistants or your receptionist might like to meet a handsome Pole who just inherited a penthouse on Billionaires' Row."

That stopped her. "How old again?" she asked.

"You met him. Thirty-one? Thirty-two?"

I heard a disappointed "Oh."

"Maybe someone there would like a very short engagement."

"Are we talking green card?" asked Jackleen.

"Exactly."

"I know a joke when I hear one," she said.

* * *

A few nights later, Mandy was in my kitchen, this time as cinematographer on a new TikTok recording. I'd been studying the competition and noting how they achieved close-ups that weren't selfies. I didn't ask Perry for help. Though I knew he'd oblige, I hadn't forgotten the semi-pained expression on his face as I narrated.

For this shoot, I chose a recipe that was retro but edible, a Cream Cheese Salad that made good theater: me trying to fashion lumps of cream cheese, moistened with milk, into miniature footballs, tapered and tossed with walnuts, green peas, and French dressing ("cooking oil," vinegar, sugar, tomato, paprika).

We did it in one take. "I'm serving this," I told Mandy, "just like Julia Child, who would sit down and eat what she'd just cooked on *The French Chef*. But don't worry. I made a chicken salad. The cream cheese is at your discretion."

We toasted, we chatted, we ate, agreeing that the dressing and embellishments did nothing to transform the cream cheese into anything but its uninteresting self. She told me she was taking my advice, was working on a dating profile and the questions needed before she went online. Did I have any tips? She wanted to sound like fun. Should she say she was a dentist? Plus or minus? So many people have dental phobias. And where it asked about favorite activities and favorite places, what if she said *between the sheets*? Would that be too cute? Would that be censored?

I said I was not a good person to consult. I lied and said I'd never signed up for a dating site. She'd do fine. Then, merely to change the subject, not to enlist but to entertain her, I told her that someone had asked me, a lawyer, to help engineer a green card marriage. The nerve!

"For a man?" she asked.

"Yes. A man who's overstayed his visa."

"A green card marriage as in . . . the two people would actually, legally marry?"

"Yes. Like immediately. That's the whole point."

"What's he like?"

"Immaterial! It's against the law. Several laws."

"Have you asked anyone else?"

"I told my sister about it, but just for fun."

"What kind of fun? She's single, too, right?"

"I was kidding. I couldn't resist. I asked if someone on her staff would like a date with a handsome Pole—just a date, not a marriage, holding me harmless."

"What about me?" Mandy asked.

"If you mean *your* staff, you can ask if anyone wants a blind date, period. Not to marry the guy the next day."

"Both of my hygienists had their own green card marriages— successfully." Followed by "What about children?"

Were we having parallel conversations? "What *about* children?" I asked.

"Would this man who's looking for a wife want to have children with her?"

Finally I understood that Dr. Amanda Zussman was asking on her own behalf. She was also reaching for her phone, asking how to spell his name. Halfway to speechless, I picked up my phone, sensing it was easier to google "Krzysztof Grabowski" than to spell it. When I hit "Images," up came a whole gallery of Krzysztofs, each handsomer than the next. His blond hair was tousled, a stray lock always in the same place on his forehead, his frown both intense and come-hither. He looked like the last guy on earth who'd be eager to father a child.

After a long pause, and more swiping, Mandy said, "I don't have a good photo of myself. Will I need one?"

"No, because you're not doing this! You're not marrying a total stranger. You're not entering into an illegal marriage, because believe me—"

Shaking her head, she countered, "You know how people who are living together but are anti-marriage say, 'It's just a piece of paper'? If you can help someone get American citizenship, save them from being deported, then why can't I say, 'It's just a piece of paper'?"

"Because you'd be facing criminal penalties."

"Only if the marriage is a fake. Some people meet and they just know."

"Yes, but—"

"A date. That's all. You said so yourself." She handed back my phone. "Call him. I'm free tomorrow night."

I stared at my phone, did nothing. There was the illegal part of it, and there was the potential hurtful-rejection part of it. Was Mandy a woman that Krzysztof would want to bed and marry? I said, "Sorry, no. I can't be your broker here."

"Then *I'll* text him."

I said, "But it'll be on my phone, which puts me in the frame, so—"

She hit my messages icon. Visible was the last text from Dani, asking if I knew a U.S. citizen who'd marry her brother.

Mandy typed, Yes. A friend. A dentist with her own practice.

It earned an instant Send photo!!!!

Unfazed, Mandy wrote, Better to meet in person.

Is it you?!!!! Dani wrote back.

No. A friend.

Attractive?

Mandy wrote, of course. *Free tomorrow for a drink at Carney's, 7 p.m. and if that goes well . . .* ❤

"If it goes well, what?" I asked. "And won't you miss your mother's nightly call?"

"I'll call her earlier. Then I'll be free to extend the evening." She smiled and added, "Having seen his photos."

I knew that smile; it had intercourse written all over it. "You'd jump in with both feet if you liked him?"

"I like him already. And, really, is it so different from an OkCupid hookup?"

I said, "It's totally different! It's not a one-off. It's—"

"I know: potentially till death do we part. I'd consider it an adventure. You hear about people who meet for a drink at a hotel bar, total strangers, maybe at a conference, and after a cocktail or two, one of them asks, 'Want to go upstairs?'"

"That's how you see it? Not as a potential felony but a hookup?"

"So? I've never understood people who save themselves for marriage. What if he turned out to have lousy technique, no chemistry, a penis you wouldn't look at twice? And that's who you spend your life with? One guy, one body? Shouldn't you get a test run?"

I was both dumbfounded and riveted as she continued. "He shows up and says, 'Will you play my wife? I need to get married.' It would be a challenge, but for me at this point, a very welcome one."

What to say? I didn't have to respond, because she was explaining that *Sarah, Plain and Tall* was her favorite middle-grade book. Did I know it?

I said yes, no, maybe, didn't remember.

She summarized reverently, "Sarah travels west from New England to marry a widowed father who advertises for a wife and mother. She comes, sight unseen!"

"And you're identifying with Sarah?"

"That worked out. It won a Newbery Medal."

I was now thinking, *Something's very wrong with her.* How had I missed that? I said carefully, "You're a smart woman. You like his picture. I get that. What about his IQ . . . his character . . . his personality?"

She sent me a pitying look. "Call me shallow, but don't you think a hot actor is a good place to start?"

Was Mandy playing me? I laughed just in case. I was about to say, *You had me there!*, except that she was explaining that she'd picked the closest bar, so if all went well, she could invite him upstairs.

"If by 'all goes well' you mean attraction, chemistry, et cetera . . . but you know it's not always mutual."

"In which case I'd remind him that this was not about choosing a girlfriend. It's about staying in the country, right? Believe me, men don't play hard to get if someone's offering them sex. I'll dress for the occasion and I'll do that thing you showed me on YouTube, with my bun. With tendrils."

I said, "In my wildest dreams I wouldn't have thought that this idea would appeal to you. You're the woman who didn't call a patient back who'd expressed interest, because it would be crossing a line."

"That woman learned her lesson: Strike while the iron's hot. It's common knowledge that arranged marriages have lower divorce rates than love matches. The more I think about it, the more I'm liking this. What games need to be played? None. 'Hello, yes, I'm applying for the job. I'm attracted to you. It's not about love. That can grow.'"

I had ignored the ping that Dani's text had generated. It said, He's in for a drink tomorrow. Both of us are.

At Mandy's insistence, I typed, Why are you going if it's just a date?

He'll need me 2 translate, Dani wrote.

It's not about words, Philosopher Mandy dictated.

The screen went silent for several minutes. Mandy took back the phone and typed, Her name is Mandy. She'll take good care of him.

After a long silence: K.

Chapter 31

The Morning After

Two days later I woke up to a text from Mandy: IT'S A GO!!!!

It could mean only one thing: Krzysztof liked Mandy enough to green-light a bogus, doomed marriage. I didn't want to commit words to the Cloud that would identify me as anything but an ardent dissuader of illegal actions, so after some mental editing, I wrote back, So u had a good time?

❤❤❤!!!!! Didn't sleep a wink!

Were these enthusiasms for show, for my benefit, should I be called to testify on the legitimacy of their union? I wrote, Can we talk? In person.

Now?

Come down.

Be there ASAP . . . followed by a showerhead emoji.

It was 8:15. With her dental patients waiting, how much time would I have to shake her out of her connubial stupor, if it was even genuine?

What I didn't expect was that she would arrive with a wet-haired

Krzysztof, wearing an unbuttoned shirt, the trouser-half of scrubs, and a look I read as *Play along with this.*

"You remember Kris," Mandy said.

I didn't even manage a *good morning* or *come in*, just pointed to the living room couch. "Sit. Debrief."

They obeyed, Mandy looking exultant, Krzysztof more like an embarrassed teen in the company of a girl whose crush was unrequited. Having spent the last ten minutes on uscis.gov/green-card, I started with "If a marriage is proved to be fake, it's punishable by up to $250,000 and an instant deportation."

"Except," said Mandy . . . and she turned to Krzysztof. "Tell her."

"I like her," he said. "I could like her very much. For real."

I was not expecting a declaration. And what about his odd conditional tense? "Now what?" I asked.

"We go to city hall," said Krzysztof.

"For the license," said Mandy.

"But his visa! It's a dead giveaway."

Krzysztof said, "A passport is enough for ID."

"And yours is current?"

"It's very current!"

Mandy said, "I adore his accent."

"How will you explain applying for a marriage license like five minutes after your first date?" I asked.

"They don't know that, and they don't ask how long you've been dating when you apply for a license," said Mandy. "I looked it up, even before I got to Carney's."

"I meant in an interview down the road, where it counts."

Mandy said, "If anyone asks, 'Why so quick?' we'll say, 'Quick?

Not quick at all. We met at the memorial service for—I think you know this—his nanny who turned out to be his biological mother.' And we'll say we just *knew*. Like in *The Godfather* when Michael Corleone falls madly in love at first sight with the beautiful Sicilian girl, and marries her, ASAP."

"Which didn't end particularly well," I pointed out.

"People get married fast in Vegas, don't they?" said Krzysztof.

"It's not as if we met at a casino, drank too much, and went to a drive-through wedding chapel. It *really*, truly feels as if I've known him for months," Mandy added.

"So, Krzysztof," I said. "I'm going to be frank. If interviewed, it can't look one-sided. Will you be able to say under oath that it only took one awesome date for you to propose?"

Mandy said, "Tell her about last night."

With minimal eye contact, Krzysztof said, "We drink, and then another. It was nice. She told me about being dentist. We went to her flat." He shrugged. "What can I say? She has a hot body."

Mandy laughed. "Who knew, right?"

"Before that? At the bar? You talked for hours?"

Krzysztof said, "I told her about my life, how I grew up thinking my mother was my mother, then I found out—found out at fucking thirty years of age!—that the au pair was my birthday mother. Amandy was warmed by this—"

"Touched," Mandy explained. "Who wouldn't be?"

"We talked. We had some crisps. She says, 'Come to my apartment.' We go to bed there," he said. "She is very nice, very enjoyable, which is what I want in a *żona*."

"Wife," said Mandy. "I love how it sounds in Polish."

I said, "If I were interviewing you, the first thing I'd ask is 'You had a hookup like millions of people do every night, then never see each other again, yet you two ran to city hall the next day? Why?'"

Mandy whispered, "Tell her."

He straightened up from his slouch. "Here's what I say: 'I made a promise to myself that before I turned thirty-one, I would marry. First I had to meet a nice and pretty wimmin, especially if she was warm and enjoyable and felt the same way exactly. I'd marry her right away.'"

Mandy added, "Because in his country, they still arrange marriages." She snapped her fingers. "Like *that*. You meet one day, the priest comes the next. It's better to take matters into your own hands."

I said, "Not in the least convincing. And highly questionable about arranged marriages in Poland. Who told you that?"

With a wink, Mandy said, "I forget, but it was on good authority."

"These agents have heard it all. They're not gonna fall for speeches about love at first sight."

Mandy said, "Oh ye of little faith. We'd do a very good job. We'd study—what are our mothers' maiden names, our parents' home addresses, what color are our toothbrushes?"

Was she the best actress in the world or had I misread her wink? I must have, because now her eyes were filling. She said, her voice shaky, "My story, my true story, is 'I met Krzysztof. It was just a casual date, a drink, a fix-up. But then . . . something happened. Something huge. We combusted.'"

I was afraid she was heading down a sexual road, especially because Krzysztof was looking newly alert, bordering on cocky. I said, "Wait. You can get specific in an interview at USCIS but I'd rather not hear it."

"Can I use synonyms? Euphemisms?"

I said, "Please don't—"

"On a scale of one to ten, it was a twenty. With fireworks, and I think you know what that means."

I said, "Mandy? Is this a script? Is this what you two brainstormed?"

She said, "We did brainstorm, but that doesn't mean we have to spin anything. The feelings are real."

Krzysztof said, "And she looks like girl in Warsaw the first to have sex with."

"Which is fine with me," said Mandy.

"Not a girlfriend," he said. "Just someone in our house."

"In what capacity?" I asked.

"What job? A maid. We didn't go out. I made invitations to my room."

"He showed me her picture," Mandy reported. "Really the only resemblance is her dark hair—"

"You carry around a photo of an old girlfriend?" I asked him.

"She's not girlfriend, and she is only in it because someone had to hold the new puppy so my father could make the picture."

"We both love dogs," said Mandy.

I said to Krzysztof, "I hope you had consent."

Mandy said, "She means she hopes you had permission; didn't force yourself on her."

I was glad to see that he looked offended. "She liked me, too. I knew that. I did not need to push. It was time for me and she had the experience. I asked if she'd like to meet me in my room, and she said a very happy 'Okay.'"

Mandy said, "It was the first thing he told me when he sat down at Carney's, that I reminded him of someone very attractive at home. I took it as a good sign."

"Are you still in touch with this woman?" I asked.

Mandy answered for him. "It couldn't go anywhere—he's the son of a count and Magdalena's a maid. It wasn't a bad thing. I'm sure you know from history that kings took up with pretty maids and ladies-in-waiting every day of the week."

Could a smart woman be brainwashed overnight? I said, "Fine. Now back to the United States and the twenty-first century, where I'm worried that you're serious."

Krzysztof smiled. "She was not faking last night. You can believe me. I can tell."

Now I was the one failing to make eye contact. "Are you auditioning more women for the job?" I asked him.

Mandy translated, "Are you going on more dates?"

"No," said Krzysztof. "This is good."

Mandy said, "Jane! We're going to city hall today!"

All I could manage was "Don't you have patients this morning?"

"No implants. This is when you're glad your hygienists are dentists in their home country."

"I like her being dentist," said Krzysztof. "I'm going to see her place of business today."

"And I'm going to see his apartment."

"We'll live there," said Krzysztof.

"With your sister?" I asked.

Mandy said, "That won't be for long. Her visa's expired, and she can't stay under the radar forever."

I said, "Between now and the actual wedding, will you be living together?"

Mandy said, "Not sure. There's a lot to do before Tuesday, and I'm a little superstitious—the groom not seeing the bride, day of."

"You're getting married next *Tuesday*?"

Mandy took Krzysztof's hand and caressed it as she spoke. "I picked it because my parents got married on a Tuesday and the rabbi told them that the Talmud or maybe just the Bible said it was a good day."

I asked Krzysztof if he knew Mandy was Jewish.

"She told me. I'm fine with Jewish. We can't marry in church, but . . . ," he said, ending with an insouciant shrug. "Here, they don't care. We go to city hall. No priest. No problem."

Mandy was mouthing something, which, after several retries, turned out to be *circumcised*.

I was out of questions and out of words. I couldn't even tell what was truth-telling and what was acting. I asked Mandy if I could talk to her in private. When we'd gotten only as far as the foyer, she said, "I'm in. I'm committed. I mean, who wouldn't be?"

Who wouldn't be? Someone thinking straight. Someone who didn't break laws. I said, "There's no question that he's a very handsome man-child, but you're a doctor, a scientist. Where's the logic to this?"

"The logic is that I don't want to lose him. How else to keep this going? He could be on the next plane to Warsaw."

"Is it because of your age? Are you feeling this is your last chance, because it's not—"

"I want to help him. It's personal, but it's also political."

I asked, one last try: "Is this what your mother's been telling you to visualize? Do you think he's going to set up housekeeping with you? Live a married life, be a real couple? What if he abandons ship after getting his green card—if he ever pulls that off, which is highly doubtful?" And while I was at it: "Do you think life-changing sex lasts forever?"

She said, "Don't ruin it for me. I'm willing to take a chance. I'm writing our vows, and going beyond 'for richer, for poorer, in sickness and in health . . . .' I'll bring in Emma Lazarus, and . . . and . . . Kościuszko. And I'll mean every word of it."

I said, "I'm pretty sure that civil marriages are cut-and-dried."

"I don't care. The city clerk or whoever can give us two minutes."

What to say? I couldn't endorse their recklessness on the record, in a text or email, or on paper, but I could say here in the privacy of my apartment, sidestepping a hug, "Good luck. I hope I'm wrong."

Chapter 32

Sidelong Glances

They went through with it on Tuesday, confirmed on Instagram: Mandy in a white lace dress borrowed from a married hygienist, and Krzysztof in a black shirt, black jeans, and a skinny silver tie.

For better or for worse, they wanted to celebrate, or at least put on a show of celebration. Not at a restaurant, not at the groom's penthouse, not at her parents' house in New Jersey, but at The Margate! Why? Because they owed it all to their fairy godmother–matchmaker, who could party only within the confines of her building: me.

The newlyweds presented their plan at my front door, Mandy smiling as if she was bursting with news that was so adorable I'd jump for joy: Would I do them the honor of hosting their reception?

"Wait. Where?"

"Here! Your apartment. You'll be the guest of honor! Saturday!"

They must've interpreted my frown correctly—*The work, the expense, the cleanup before and after . . . how does that make me the guest of honor?*—because Mandy quickly added, "You wouldn't have to lift a finger. Dani's taking care of everything: the caterer, the florist, the booze, the bartender, and a cake you wouldn't believe!"

A party? I liked parties. No work, no expense? And not to be discounted: I'd get to wear a dress and the five-strand faux pearl necklace I'd recently bought on Etsy, so far unworn. I asked how many guests.

"A dozen. Maybe twenty."

"Short notice, we know," said the groom. "So maybe small-scale."

Steamrolled and semi-inclined, I said okay.

* * *

I reported back to my sister that the potential marriage I'd offered her staff, completely and totally in jest, on behalf of Frances FitzRoy's Polish émigré love child . . . well, my dentist friend Amanda *bit*, thanks to the excellent job he'd done fucking her brains out.

"I met her," Jackleen mused. "She seemed the embodiment of . . . sensible. Why would she do this?"

"It might be an act, some excitement and lawbreaking she craved. Or it's political: Give an immigrant a green card. Or as a shortcut to the husband and sex and babies she's been yearning for."

"How old is she?"

"Thirty-five. I think that milestone did something to her brain."

"She should try forty," Jackleen murmured.

* * *

The doorman called to say a Miss Grabowski was here to see me, his voice protectively dubious. I said, "It's okay. Send her up."

Was she here to discuss visas again, or the commoner-dentist-Jew who was suddenly her sister-in-law? A prenup? A dowry? No; she wanted to remind herself what the venue looked like.

"The bar," she said after her tour. "Will it have to be"—pointing unhappily into the kitchen—"here?"

"It's a Manhattan apartment. Your friends won't be expecting an event space."

"They'll know we had no choice," she granted. "It was either here or Amanda's apartment, which is like old ladies died there."

I said, gesturing toward the couch, "Sit. No one's thought this through. He can still get deported. And, worse, not allowed back for a good ten years."

Propped conditionally, impatiently, on the edge of the sofa, she said, "It's done. If he's deported, Amanda will go back with him. She said that in her vows."

"Are you in on the act as well?"

"What act?"

"The instant marriage! The true love!"

"It was a real wedding. I signed something. I cried."

I didn't ask *Happy tears?*, because I was determined to display nothing but pessimism and disapproval about this union. One positive takeaway: Since the marriage charade had come my way, I'd felt like a lawyer again—advising, dissuading, warning of the dire consequences of thinking you could fool the United States of America.

"Can't stay," said Dani. "I have an appointment with a personal shopper at Bloomies. . . . Is that a good choice for me? For a jumpsuit? In silk crêpe?"

I said, "You'll know soon enough. You're only one stop away on the Q."

She looked baffled.

"Subway," I said.

* * *

I confessed to Perry over dinner, "I never should've opened my big mouth," and was relieved to hear him ask, "Why so guilty? It was a runaway train."

"Because I brought it up in the first place. Because I'm a lawyer. Because I let it go forward. I could've threatened to turn him in. I could've lied to Mandy when I saw her eyes light up. I could've said, 'No, no, you wouldn't give him a second thought. He barely speaks English. He doesn't have a job. He's a burden on society. . . .'"

"Instead of . . . ?"

I winced. "Pretty boy–actor–minor Polish royalty."

"C'mon. They're adults. It's not your fault. Also . . . I'm not that surprised that she jumped at the marriage proposal."

"To a total stranger? Talk about impulsive."

When he didn't answer, and only winced, I asked, "What?"

He allowed an apologetic half-smile. "Once . . . ," he began. Then: "It was nothing."

"Mandy?"

"At that dinner party with your parents, remember how she excused herself when I did and said she was going to call it a night, too?"

I didn't. I said that was a fraught night—my parents' first visit, which I'd been putting off for weeks. Why? What did I miss?

"Trust me, nothing. It was only a few seconds. But waiting for the elevator, she said it was really nice to meet me and kissed me."

"On the lips?"

"Sort of. Straight out of left field. I dodged it."

I said, "Stranger and stranger. Was that all?"

"The elevator came. When she got on, I didn't. She said, 'Call me.' I think she knew right away from the look on my face that it wasn't going to happen."

"Anything since? I mean, since she's known about you and me?"

"Nothing since. She'd have to have a chip missing to try something again."

I said, "Chips are missing, believe me."

* * *

We'd brought our supper to the roof, two trips required from my kitchen, given the food, the wine, the dishes and side dishes, the glasses, the pie, plus the hibachi and its accessories. As soon as I lit the briquettes and headed back to our table, I noticed undue attention being paid to us by two couples at a nearby table. Was I violating any NYC ordinances? Were they worried about liberal use of lighter fluid and the resulting flames? Or, as I guessed from their judgmental stares, had they recognized the Margate Two?

When Perry and I sat down to eat, the whispers and sidelong glances escalated, all subtlety abandoned, as if these two couples couldn't believe their gossipy good fortune.

I tried to ignore them. I launched into a discussion of tonight's Cold Slaw versus Hot Slaw. Did he think that "cole slaw" might be a corruption of the Gay Nineties "*cold* slaw"? Had I made an etymological discovery? Faithful to the Hot Slaw recipe, I'd boiled slices of cabbage for a half hour, tossed them with butter, a well-beaten egg, and vinegar. I quoted the last line of the recipe, "'Very nice with meats of any kind,'" pointing to our festival of sausages, charred and burst.

Obligingly, Perry stabbed a few shards with his fork, chewed unhappily, and said, "Not good. And weird . . . So yes, definitely on-brand."

The nearby diners were still looking at us spellbound. I whispered, "You can bet they're saying, 'birds of a feather. . . .'"

"Should we let them know we don't appreciate their gawking?" Perry asked.

I told him how I'd once handled a similar situation: It was at Union Square Café, when some guys at the next table were whispering and pointing—maybe they were opposing attorneys, or maybe tourists who'd never seen a woman eating alone, or just plain assholes. So I'd taken out a pen and written, "Take a picture, why dontcha?" on a cocktail napkin and given it to the waiter to deliver. They sent over a drink.

"No waiter here. . . . Shall we?"

Why not? We scraped our chairs back and walked with faux-friendly faces to our neighbors' table. They looked up with a range of expressions, from surprised to forced pleasantry to guilty-as-charged. I said, "I guess we don't need to introduce ourselves, but you are . . . ?"

The first to answer, after a survey of his tablemates, was the oldest, sixty-five-ish, napkin tucked into the neck of his linen shirt: Dr. Aaron Fields.

"And I'm Susan Fields," said the woman opposite him, her blond hair in a stiff bubble, her tone worried.

The other man said more cordially, "I'm Bruce Wiseman and this is my partner, Rebecca."

"Rubel," she finished. Both younger, maybe fifty, in matching horn-rimmed glasses.

"I'm Bonnie and he's Clyde," I said.

Was that a joke or a scold? their expressions asked. Either way, total silence.

Perry helped by asking almost cordially, "Do all of you live in the building?"

Yes, they did. Tenth floor, east side, corridor-mates.

I said, "You're lucky. It's not easy to meet people here."

"You're on the sixth floor, correct?" Susan asked. "No one welcomed you with a bottle of champagne or a box of chocolates? Not even the Sloanes or the Freedmans? I'm surprised. They're usually so friendly."

I knew a sarcastic question when I heard one. I said, "That's correct. No one, even when I first moved in as a law-abiding lawyer." I took a step back. "We'll let you finish your"—I checked and raised my eyebrows—"takeout."

But Perry didn't retreat. He said, "This space, this amenity, it's for everyone. And you made us uncomfortable."

Never having heard him say anything confrontational, I was inspired to add, "Very high school cafeteria behavior."

Rebecca the partner surprised me by saying, "You're right. Some of us were being rude. I apologize."

The other three murmured syllables that sounded vaguely contrite.

Perry and I said our good-byes, and to drive our point home, moved everything to another table, out of the busybodies' line of vision. Once seated, glasses refilled, I said, "I'm not used to your being cheeky. I found it delightful."

"Where do you think I'm getting *cheeky* from?"

"Would that be me?"

"Entirely," he said.

"I'm over them," I announced. "I'm enjoying the sunset and"—raising my glass—"my excellent support system . . . speaking of which, can you come to the fête I'm hosting for Mandy?"

"*You're* hosting? Like a bridal shower?"

"No, a party. It's Saturday night. I'm inviting you."

"I'll come if I'm free"—a favorite ironic answer we often used. I laughed and said, "My fingers are crossed."

"I'm serious. My parents are coming in."

"From?"

"Home. Cincinnati."

There were two tracks I could follow: either *By all means bring them*, or the untraveled, personal route, best summarized as *Wouldn't you want them to meet me?* I chose a synthesis of the two: "Bring them. They'll see you've met people in the building."

"But a wedding reception for two strangers?"

"What else are you going to do with them?" I asked. "Order in? Watch a movie?"

"They could go out. Dinner and theater."

"They'd visit their housebound son, then abandon him?"

"Would I rather we sit around and discuss my future, such as it is? No, thank you."

"What if you told them your very good friend Jane was hosting the party. Believe me, that piques a mother's interest."

"About the green card marriage? I wouldn't call that an enticement. Just the opposite."

The marriage of Krzysztof and Mandy was not the card I was playing. I gave his knee a squeeze. "You could tell them that the party's host is . . . your *special* friend."

When he greeted that with silence, I said, "Never mind. I get it. You're a guy. Guys don't tell their mother whom they have a horizontal relationship with."

"You don't know my mother. Do I want to hear afterward how the forks were plastic and the bartender didn't know how to make a Sidecar? And what was that black thing Velcroed around your special friend's ankle?"

I said, "Thanks for reminding me. I'd forgotten for half a second about that. I'll leave it at this: You and your parents can drop by for a drink and some high-end hors d'oeuvres. Maybe you'll introduce us; maybe not, then you send them off to see *The Lion King*, never mentioning that we have sex on a regular basis."

He smiled. "Speaking of . . . ?"

I dropped the parental line of questioning. It was Wednesday. Not only had I not forgotten, but I'd misted the sheets with lavender water. I said, "Let me give the briquettes a douse. They're still red-hot." I poured some melted ice into a wineglass, headed for the hibachi, watered the briquettes, and got a satisfying hiss.

One of my guilty new friends called out, "Smart!"

I said, "Thank you. I have to be careful." Unspoken: *Because if the building burned down, I'd be the first person they'd come looking for.*

Chapter 33

You Must Be Mrs. Salisbury

Had someone estimated twenty guests? My living room was packed with friends acquired over holidays and summers in the city, unless half of them were patients of Mandy's or—not out of the question in New York City—nonunion extras.

The waitstaff managed to circulate, trays aloft, offering the latest in canapés if you didn't count the obligatory herring and kielbasa skewers, with backups on shelves I'd cleared in my refrigerator. Should there be leftovers, I hinted to the chef, this host would put them to very good use.

Mandy had risen to the occasion, appearance- and beautification-wise. Eyes, eyebrows, lipstick, cheekbones—highlighted or shadowed or outlined, surely by a professional. I'd never seen her hair in anything but a bun, but tonight it was down, shiny, straight, and asymmetric. When had there been time for such a transformation? And surely the halter jumpsuit in a silky bridal ivory had been chosen by her influencer sister-in-law.

I circulated without making conversation. An hour into the festivities, I texted Perry, Coming or not?

On our way. ASAP.

I didn't wait by the door; didn't want to appear overly hospitable to those arriving whenever they damn well felt like it. Let them find me in the kitchen, where I was watching the chef pipe rosettes into deviled eggs.

"Jane?" I heard.

All three Salisburys had arrived. His tall, blue-blazered, white-trousered mother offered her hand, charm bracelet jangling, and said, "So you're Jane," before taking a step back and adding, "Well, Coco would approve."

Meaning? Her husband, gray-haired with the thin mustache of a 1950s bank president, translated, "Coco Chanel. Her beau ideal."

I said, flicking my faux pearls, "Not quite."

"Little black dress? Bold necklace? Did you know she invented costume jewelry?"

I didn't, but I was pretty sure I'd been complimented. To underscore her mislaid manners, I said, "You must be Mrs. Salisbury."

"DeAndra," she corrected, looking around. "Did we miss the ceremony?"

"The wedding was Tuesday. This is the after-party. I'll introduce you to the bride and groom."

"But first I'll say hello to the handsome bartender."

"Of course," I said.

Then, extending my hand to her husband, I said, "I'm Jane Morgan. Glad you could make it."

Without even the suggestion of a smile, he said, "Cal Salisbury. I don't like parties, but I was outvoted."

"Same here," I said. I joined his wife in line behind a couple speaking presumably Polish, who kept repeating what sounded like "brood-nay martini." Translating their pantomiming and pointing, I jumped in. "I think they want dirty martinis," I told the bartender.

More waiting; lots of clinking and stirring. Should I fill the time with girlfriendy chatter? I said, "The bride's parents didn't come. They don't approve of the marriage."

"I heard it's a green card ploy. Perry filled me in."

Hardly the polite or politic thing to say aloud, but I wasn't going to shush her. I called to the bartender, who was fashioning one drink at a time, "Can't you fill the flutes and put them on the bar so people can just grab them?"

"Flutes are being circulated," he said.

More time to kill. Where was Perry? I tried, "The groom's sister is the real host. She lives across the street . . . at The Gloucester. I'm just supplying the venue."

"You're a very good friend, then . . . considering."

Finally, the bartender asked, "What'll it be?"

"Can you make a French 75?" Mrs. Salisbury asked.

"I make a great one. Just not here. How about a vodka martini? A vodka tonic? A cosmo?"

"Vodka on the rocks, then. And my husband—where did those men of mine disappear to?—would like a scotch. Surely you have scotch?"

He didn't. But my liquor cabinet was only steps away. I left her side and came back with my own bottle of Johnnie Walker Black. "Will this do?" I asked, proud to accommodate.

"It'll have to. Neat, a double," she instructed the bartender.

Perry had returned with two flutes. I took one, which was at least my third drink of the night, took a sip, and over the rim shot him an SOS.

"It's a madhouse out there," he said. "Shall we?"

"Shall we what?" I asked, wishing he could say, *Hide in your bedroom*.

"Mingle. Congratulate the newlyweds."

What else was there to do but that? "Follow me," I said. At the living room threshold we were met by the sound of a knife clinking against glass. Krzysztof, wearing a T-shirt silkscreened to look like a tux, took the floor.

Uh-oh: his English, his vocabulary, his lack of affect; but then, not quite as badly as I'd expected, he delivered the generic groom-appreciation toast. "To this beautiful bride. Not every vimmin would say yes to be short engaged, but here we are legally married, happily." And then, from the script they'd fashioned when the deal was struck, "Didn't I always tell my *kolega* I'd be married before I turned thirty-one? And here I am." He raised his glass. *"Na zdrowie!"*

Half of the crowd echoed the toast, followed by a shouted "L'Chaim!" Just as I was thinking, *Whew, that's over*, Dani called my name in the interrogatory manner that was an unmistakable *Next!*

What choice did I have? I tried a silent protest without success, a flapping of my free hand that was supposed to mean, *No, can't, too shy*. But Mandy was looking so fond and hopeful that I had to raise my glass. "Who knew," I improvised, "that from the first moment these two crazy kids met, things would . . . combust! We've all heard about *love* at first sight? Well, this was even bigger. This was . . . happily-ever-after at first sight. Cupid was on the job and he got two bull's-eyes. Their first date went on for hours—the talking turned into flirting. The flirting went all the way to . . . last call. Did they even remember to order food? Before the night was over, they were choosing a wedding date. Everything clicked." I smiled and raised my eyebrows. "Boy, did it *ever*," I said, netting a few lusty hoots.

Was that enough? I hadn't mentioned Krzysztof, who looked to be taking proud ownership of the sexual marathon I'd alluded to. I continued, "And Krzysztof . . . what a lucky guy, rising to the occasion. Hats off to you for recognizing a good thing when you saw it: Mandy, the total package. Brains and . . . so many skills. May love conquer all."

Someone called out, "Hear, hear," which prompted as much clapping as people can execute while holding drinks and plates.

But it wasn't over. Mandy was making her way to my side. After kissing me on both cheeks, and slipping her arm around my waist, she asked for everyone's attention. "Krzysztof and I owe it all to this woman, Jane Morgan—for her friendship, for this beautiful party, but most of all for being that Cupid she spoke of. Mythological? I think so. Was it the Fates who prompted her to ask her nerdy dentist neighbor if she'd like to meet the most eligible man in midtown? Did she know something I didn't know? She'll testify that I didn't have to ponder for very long. I said yes, *tak*, *sí*, *oui*—I *do* want to meet Krzysztof Grabowski! He's looking for a wife? Well, count me in! So . . . to Jane!"

I was finding every word excruciating. Had she used *testify* on purpose, a wink? *Please let the toasts be over. Please let there be no government plant here. Please don't let my parole officer choose this night for a random visit.*

Mingling resumed. I received a few "very nice"s, though not one compliment about my apartment, my artwork, my parquet floors, my moldings, my recessed lighting. Now Mrs. Salisbury was coming my way, looking relatively animated. Perhaps a conspiratorial thought we'd share about my coded speechmaking? But she said, "The bride's a dentist! Does she have her own practice?"

"She does. She's a specialist, an endodontist."

"And I found out another fascinating thing, thanks to photos on the mantel—that our hostess is a twin!"

Our hostess? Could it be any more impersonal? I said yes, true, everyone's favorite fact about me.

"Perry says your sister is very successful . . . a skin doctor. Is she also unmarried?"

I said, "Yes, an unmarried dermatologist."

"Cosmetic? Because I didn't see a wrinkle."

"She does do some cosmetic procedures, but mostly she cures cancer."

Perry and his dad were back with plates of chic canapés—dumplings, shrimp wrapped in green vegetal strands, and ceramic spoons holding tartare. Perry had the most crowded plate, topped with two plump sliders. Was one a spare? And if so, for me or his mother? I didn't have to wonder long, as he gave me one of the black cocktail napkins, and said, "It's wagyu. I asked."

His mother looked at him and then at me. She said, "Some people think only children are spoiled and selfish, but Perry has always been thoughtful, even as a little boy."

I'd heard about his lonely-little-boy life, in the nursery with the nanny, eating pureed food after he should've moved on to mac and cheese. I said, "I'd have to agree."

"I haven't formally met the bride or the groom," she said. "Their circumstances intrigue me."

"You won't mention the intriguing circumstances, will you? They're kind of illegal," I felt the need to advise.

She didn't. While patting and evaluating Mandy's left hand, she delivered proper receiving-line sentiments. "We wish you a lifetime of happiness . . . and may I say, you're aglow. No wonder: The way you met was storybook. The groom, something like a hereditary count, I understand. That fix-up that your Cupid friend engineered—kismet!"

That Cupid friend would be me, Jane Doe. Mandy gushed her thanks, then further gushed, "I want the same for these two."

Oh, God. I said, "Mandy's just . . . it's like she's throwing her bouquet to all the single women in the room, right?"

Mandy caught on and said, "Jane's right. I've turned into such a romantic that I see every couple . . . well, not even *coupled* couples, through rose-colored glasses."

Perry jumped in to introduce his father, who shook Mandy's hand and offered a mispronounced "Mazel tove."

"And your handsome husband?" asked Mrs. Salisbury. "Is he still with us?"

Mandy said, "Taking a break."

"DeAndra," Mr. Salisbury commanded, tapping his wristwatch. "Remember our reservation."

Was that true? Either way, I said to Mandy, "I'll be back. Just showing them out."

At the door I said, "Very nice to have met you both," in case this was the end of my social intercourse with the Salisburys this weekend, or ever.

"Thank you for inviting us," said his mother.

Perry was already heading for the elevator, but stopped, returned to my side, and kissed me.

"Now you're in for it," I said.

* * *

When I woke up, there was a text asking, Brunch today?

I wrote back, Are they still there?

Yes. Flight's at 5.

Did you fill them in?

Nothing for a few minutes, then: She noticed the ankle monitor. Drilled me about yr legal status.

Bad?

Public indecency—not a big hit.

Did he have to give her the exact mortifying infraction? I asked, You couldn't make up something less trashy?

Didn't come from me. She googled you.

Whose idea was brunch?

Doesn't matter. Any of those nice Hor-deurves (sp?) left?

Tons. Should I bring?

👍 👍 Noon?

That way you can claim I'm just your caterer.

TOO LATE, he wrote back.

* * *

What to wear? I didn't want to care, but nonetheless I spent some time deciding what was suitable, knowing how his mother judged and pigeonholed. Should I or shouldn't I? Only I would know its provenance . . . so yes—I put on the cotton sundress I'd been arrested in. It had, ironically, an innocent and sweet look to it. Would Coco have approved of tiny bouquets of flowers in pale blue? Probably not. Added a cardigan and left my ankle bare, a challenge.

I made it to 9-C, balancing two large platters, double-sealed in plastic wrap, the canapés arranged on my best earthenware. With neither hand free to knock or ring, I called out a melodic "Hello!" Perry answered in seconds, greeting me with a whispered "She's promised to be civil. Dad's fine. He's reading the newspaper in the living room."

Mrs. Salisbury didn't turn around when we entered, devoting herself to stirring a pitcher of what turned out to be Bloody Marys.

"Mom? Jane's here. She's brought a ton of food."

Mrs. Salisbury turned around, feigning surprise at my arrival. "These look marvelous," she said, peeling off the plastic wrap, helping herself to a caper atop a smoked salmon tart. "Do you think the caterer makes her own gravlax?"

Not the icebreaker I was expecting. I said, "Without a doubt."

Perry said, "Jane is a fabulous cook herself."

"Which is how I met Perry . . . through cooking."

His mother smiled, having been handed a diminishment opportunity. "You know what they say? The way to a man's heart is through his stomach. . . . Clever of you."

Clever of me? That's what you call civility?

Perry kept trying. "When Jane found out that I never cooked and I got takeout seven nights a week, we worked out an arrangement—"

"My sister did, actually. She was over for dinner, along with Perry—I forget why now—"

"Eczema," said Perry with a wink.

"She's the one who lobbied for the catering. And one thing led to another. . . ."

"So I understand," said Mrs. Salisbury.

"It took some fine-tuning," Perry said.

"I was reluctant to commit to producing meals three nights a week. I'm a lawyer, not a caterer."

Perry said, "It was all business. She'd bring the food, leave the Tupperware—"

"In and out," I said. "Just one course."

Mrs. Salisbury asked, "At what point did you start dining à deux?"

"Dee!" I heard from the living room. "Don't be like that."

Could that have been Perry's grouchy father, who just told his wife to behave?

"Like what?" she called back, adding a phony *ha-ha*.

Perry said, "Some mothers might be happy that in the worst, most humiliating time in my life, I'd have . . ." He paused.

He'd have what? I sent him a look that was part question, part dare.

" . . . found someone."

Mrs. Salisbury said rather cheerfully, "Well, then, thank goodness it's allowed."

Perry asked, "Allowed?" but I knew what was coming.

"I mean legally. Isn't there some condition in your respective paroles about not associating with . . . others in the same situation?"

I wanted to slap her, leave, and take my food with me. Having run this very thing by my parole officer, I said, feeling white-hot, "I can answer that. If Perry and I had been collaborators, fellow gang members, or cellmates up the river, planning our next bank robbery or kidnapping or murder or embezzlement, we'd be off-limits. But we're not a threat to anyone."

Smiling, Perry said, "Except my mother."

She matched his smile with an even brighter one. "Maybe we should put these goodies on smaller platters so we can pass them around?"— the implication being *on anything but these oversize, peasanty platters.*

Provoked, I said, "I know this kitchen inside and out. He doesn't own any platters. But I can put everything onto three or four of "— with all the class disparity I could muster—"his Limoges dinner plates? Clever?"

"Very," she said.

"Highball or water glasses for the Bloody Marys?" Perry asked.

"Either."

Now Mr. Salisbury had joined us in the kitchen. "Everyone getting acquainted?" he asked.

Perry said, "If you want to call it that."

"Is Mother playing judge and jury?" he asked.

"Anyone in my shoes would," she said.

"Which shoes are those?" asked Perry.

"A mother's shoes. And any mother of a son would want to know, under these unusual circumstances, 'Who is she?'"

I said, "I get it. He's your baby. You need to know who I am and where I went wrong."

His dad said impatiently, "The nonsense about—what's the legal term for naked on the roof?"

"Indecency," his wife supplied.

". . . mountain out of a molehill," he grumbled. "Why would it even be a misdemeanor? Are we such a nation of puritans?"

Perry said, "Exactly! The judge was making an example of Jane because she's a lawyer. No ordinary person would've been sentenced so harshly."

"Does committing a crime keep you permanently barred from the practice of law?" his continually horrible mother asked me.

"May I point out," said his father, "that not all felons are undesirables—starting with your precious son, who was also arrested and sentenced—"

"Unfairly!" I cried.

"See?" said Perry, putting an arm around my shoulders.

"What does your father do?" Mr. Salisbury, the new master of ceremonies, asked.

"Professor emeritus, art history."

"Very good," he said. "And with your sister a doctor, he must be proud of his girls."

"He is. So is my mother."

Not to be out-niced, Mrs. Salisbury took back the floor. "I apologize if anything I said might have offended you. . . ."

I stifled a *Thanks for that textbook example of a nonapology apology*, and said instead, "Let's move on to *kanapki*."

That yielded three puzzled faces. "Polish for 'canapés,'" I said.

Chapter 34

States of Mind

Whats wrong with her!" I asked, slumped on Perry's couch after his parents left. "Is she always like this? Was it me? I mean, I've gone through life not worrying about the kind of impression I'm making, because . . . I don't *have* to worry! I do fine. But with your mother, I couldn't say or do anything right."

Rhetorical questions all, no answers needed, because I knew what motivated her: She was a son worshipper. No one would ever be good enough for her one and only; certainly not me, whose moral turpitude could be googled by any Cincinnatian in possession of a smartphone.

Perry kept repeating, "I'm sorry."

"Sorry you introduced us?"

"If you're this upset . . . maybe I shouldn't have."

"Maybe you shouldn't have told her about us"—I motioned back and forth between us—"and just said I was an acquaintance in the building throwing a party for another acquaintance in the building."

He plopped down next to me and said, "What a crock. We'd be having an entirely different argument if I didn't tell them about"—both hands energetically mimicking my back-and-forthing.

That was true, but I still had some ranting left in me. "We're not arguing. I'm stating the obvious, that she's made up her mind, and I'm a bad choice for . . . whatever she thinks we are. I can't be the first woman you ever brought home, so to speak."

Perry said, "You want to know about her choices? They'd picked out a wife for me, a daughter of some mixed-doubles-friends of theirs. Not that it was ever framed as 'your future wife'; not that I ever saw her except for one Sunday dinner at the club, parents looking on. That was their plan: I'd come to Cincinnati. We'd run into her and her parents at the country club. Then this, the disgrace. End of nonstory."

"Did they *not* know about your Gladstone girlfriend?"

"When my mother asked over the years if I was dating anyone I'd say, 'Yes, someone I met at work,' 'Someone I met through a friend,' 'Someone I met on a plane.' She was fine keeping it at arm's length."

"Ice-cold arm's length! Why bother being nice to Perry's comfort woman? Surely he just selected Best Available?"

"What would you like me to do?" he pleaded. "Both my father and I told her she was being rude. In her own fashion, she got it. She's never going to change. They live in Cincinnati. I don't care what she thinks."

I was losing steam, as he was sounding so reasonable. "You could write her a letter. . . ."

He got up, crossed to the table, sat down, pushed up his sleeves, and pantomimed putting pen to paper. "Dear Mother," he intoned. "Good work: Jane hates you. Don't expect any more invitations from me. Sincerely, your son, who makes up his own mind. PS Any normal mother would be happy for me, if you don't count the pitiful state of everything else in my life. PPS Don't disinherit me."

I said, "I hate hearing that you think your life is pitiful."

"Isn't it? Where am I going? To work every day? And how would I ever have gotten that work? 'Sorry, sir, I can't come for an interview. Can we do it on Zoom or Teams or FaceTime or WhatsApp because I'm on home confinement for a few more months'?"

I said, "You're going to land on your feet. We'll be a job-hunting team. And may I point out how you've enriched yourself? All the books you've read? How many online courses have you taken? Art history, Russian history, ancient history . . . how many Ken Burns documentaries have you watched? Not to mention . . . our one-on-ones."

But even as that teased a smile, even as I was cheerleading, I knew this: Perry saw his crime as stupid, unethical, regrettable, embarrassing. I saw mine as minor, forgettable, and my punishment the whim of a priggish judge. We had identical sentences but very different degrees of shame.

* * *

There were several voicemails from Jackleen, which, regrettably, I didn't play back until Sunday night. The first was "I have huge news. Call me!," followed by increasingly impatient orders to do the same with a final, sarcastic "Busy much? Call me, for crissakes!"

I reached her, explaining that between the party I'd been obliged to throw and—a guaranteed interest-piquer—meeting Perry's parents—

"Jane! Okay! Later! Duncan and I are back together."

Not sure from her tone, I asked, "That's good, isn't it?"

"It's very good. It's great."

"When? How? Who initiated what?"

"Friday night. We had dinner at Vice Versa, which used to be 'our place'—so when he asked me to meet him there, I kind of knew. Then he ordered an appetizer to share, our old favorite. You don't share an appetizer with someone you're estranged from."

"Everything's good, then? Settled?"

"He came prepared. We talked about the issues that led to the breakup. Yes to a baby: just one. If I don't get pregnant in six months, we'll consult a fertility specialist. And as far as me helping you, he realizes that wasn't his concern."

That was blunter than previous breakup diagnoses had been. I couldn't help grumbling, "For putting food on my table? *That* issue?"

"He regrets that! And it's not like you're treating yourself to filet mignon and caviar."

What to say? *Thanks for my chicken thighs and ground chuck?* Instead, I asked, "Has he told his charming daughters?"

"They were on alert. He texted them—a photo of my hand with the ring on it."

"Ring!" I squealed. "Right at the restaurant? You said yes? Is it beautiful? Did it fit?"

"Yes, over dessert. It's *so* beautiful."

"How did the girls take it?"

"They're all in because he'd been moping. They kept saying, 'You're in love with Jackleen. We've never seen you like this. What are you waiting for?'"

If the difficult daughters had given their blessing, who was I to withhold mine? I said, "Duncan really stepped up. I'm impressed. The right restaurant, the right appetizer, the ring in his pocket. Talk about a vice versa!"

"I'm texting you the photo . . . right . . . *now*."

I squealed again. "It's gorgeous. And may I say—huge!"

"Two carats and flawless."

"He knows your taste, that's for sure."

"We'd window-shopped when we were still together, so he had a good idea."

"So much for the famous twin ESP. If I'd known why you were calling, I'd have picked up before it rang! I thought you were just checking in." I repeated my alibis: party on Saturday that I didn't volunteer for, and brunch today with Perry's parents, whom I was meeting for the first time.

"You met them as in . . . 'this is Jane, my in-house . . . friend'?"

I couldn't let that pass. "'House friend.' Is that like *hausfrau*?"

"Don't be so touchy. I only meant, how did he introduce you?"

"It went from 'We're invited to a party downstairs, and the host is a good friend' to 'She's a very special friend, so read between those lines.'"

"Were they happy about that?"

I said, "You'd think. That'll be another conversation."

"Now is fine. They'd better appreciate how lucky their son was to find a catch like you in the same building."

I said, "Not so much. Not after googling me."

"Did you point out that people who live in glass houses shouldn't throw stones?" Jackleen said.

"Perry did, more or less."

"But still, meeting parents is a big deal. I'd say it's been a red-letter weekend for the Morgan girls."

"No comparison: ring on your finger, a green light for having a baby, and a thumbs-up from future stepdaughters!"

She asked if I was okay with all of that. And oh, by the way, another thing that was negotiated: If I needed a letter of reference when the time came for me to petition the New York Bar Association for readmission, Duncan would write one. He promised.

Except Duncan hadn't ever passed the bar. I said, "Thank you. I hope that wasn't one of your contingencies."

"I had all the cards," she said. "I was in an excellent bargaining position. You'll call Duncan? Tell him you're happy for us?"

"Of course. Were Mom and Dad thrilled?"

"They knew before I did! Duncan called to ask Dad for my hand."

Interesting. My parents had not been fans of inhospitable Duncan. I said, "Dad must've been caught off-guard, thinking, *Last I heard they'd broken up.*"

"He was. But you know Dad, always diplomatic. He gave a provisional blessing, based on my saying yes. We called them as soon as we left Vice Versa to say it was official."

"I'll call them as soon as I get off with you."

"Good idea. Mom was worried how you might take it."

"I'll tell her how I took it—like a champ!" And to sound even more sisterly and involved, having ignored two days of messages, I added, "I'm picturing a beautiful wedding in Harrow, maybe at the college chapel, and hopefully I can be your maid of honor—in person!"

Wasn't it easy enough to say reflexively, "Maid of honor, no question." But what I heard was "It's too soon to know what kind of wedding it will be, or where, or if we'd want attendants."

I refrained from a readout of my thought bubble: *Really? Maybe Duncan has a twin sister who needs a boost, who needs to get dressed up after being confined for half a year. Or maybe one of your nurses or PAs or your receptionist could stand up for you, wearing whatever backless fuchsia dress you chose.*

"Janie? You still there?" And again: "You're happy for me, right, despite everything?"

By "everything" she didn't mean Duncan-redux. She meant was I okay with her perfect life, while I was making due with best-available. How to answer? Nicely, because this was not the conversation to end with sarcasm. Unrelated to her big news, yet sounding magnanimous, out popped "I couldn't be happier."

Chapter 35

Christmas Miracle

Who'd have predicted which of my #foodtoks would go over well, let alone big, let alone viral? Certainly not me. Numbers? Followers? I avoided looking, expecting no gains. My sister's nurse's boyfriend, who knew about such things, explained that a video can have a life of its own after making it onto TikTok's "For You" page, aka FYP, and from there can be pushed out—wherever that means. Apparently, that very thing happened to "Aunt Jane's Bread Pudding" in *Hood's Practical Cook's Book*, page 224.

I'd chosen the recipe for its eponymous title, its degree of difficulty (simple), its holiday properties (rum), and its quaintness. ("Butter three thick slices of stale bread, and put in a greased pudding dish with one pint of milk. Set this on the back of the stove or on a stove shelf if there is one and allow it to soak one hour.") But apparently what did the trick was my waxing nostalgic about a meaningful bread pudding episode in my life. I took up the whole three minutes, unable to stop once I started reminiscing about my contribution to a bygone office party. Always competitive, I had guessed that its lumpy, cinnamon-y presence in its Pyrex casserole would announce "homemade," as opposed to the aluminum trays of cold cuts from the deli downstairs.

One of our associates at that gathering was an observant Muslim. When he got to my bread pudding—me presiding, cake knife at the ready, no doubt a hard-sell and possibly intimidating because I was a partner and he was a second-year associate—I described what it was and what was in it. He held out his empty plate and I put a few square inches on it. He tasted it, smiled, finished the sample. I took that as a green light and cut him a generous square. Before the night was over, half the pudding was gone and the remainder sent home with him.

It became a minor legend around the office. *We laughed when Jane brought a humble bread pudding, but Nadeem put it on the map.* No one thought his multiple servings piggish, just endearing. Besides, he'd graduated from Harvard Law School, a rare, welcome bird at Sullivan Schwartz.

Inevitably my retelling on TikTok turned bittersweet. I couldn't help segueing into how quickly I'd been banished from that disloyal, thin-skinned group. As ever, I spoke my mind, assuming no one was listening. I ended with "Nadeem, if you're out there, hello. And please know that the glug of Jamaican rum I added in today's demo was not in the pudding you devoured." I started to blow a kiss, thought better of it, turned it into a worried wave.

The next morning I scanned the unusually high number of comments, fearing accusations of cultural appropriation or religious insensitivity or any other offense committed or taken. But every one was supportive, and most damned the "assholes," "pricks," and "shitbags" who'd abandoned me.

Did this mean people were listening? The nurse's boyfriend-mentor said to keep it up, keep posting, assuming incorrectly that I had TikTok ambitions. Semi-obediently, I recorded on Monday-Wednesday-Fridays, when Perry was coming for dinner, should that day's posting be appealing enough for our dinner. The bad recipes were plentiful. I'd bought another cookbook, a collection of recipes first published as *The Compleat Housewife, or Accomplish'd Gentlewoman's Companion* in Williamsburg, Virginia, in 1742. Though my copy was the thirteenth edition, published in 1966, they'd retained the original lettering to be cute, so that most of the *s*'s were *f*'s, rendering titles such as "To Dreſs Parſnips" and "Veniſon Paſtey," "A Fricaſy of Lamb" and "Deep Diſh Apple Pie." For fun, I added subtitles so anyone watching could see the written directions and figure out the "ſtrew with nutmeg before covering with Pie-cruſt . . . bake forty Minutes or until brown and Apples are thoroughly ſoft."

My mother sent suggestions for more cheerful posts. What about a chowder, and then I could talk about our vacations on the Cape? Or "What about fudge? The word *penuche* is always fun to say." What about her meatloaf or mine or one of my handsome entrée salads?

But I stuck to my brand, #unfortunatefood layered with cynicism. Cold Water Cake fit the bill, the ultimate halfhearted dessert, instructing the baker listlessly to "flavor to taste and frost if you like." Having many times described my professional limbo, I starting adding a countdown worthy of a CNN crawl: how many days left in my house sentence. I didn't come right out and ask if anyone out there in a firm, a company, or a federal, state or local government agency was in need of an excellent lawyer. When the time was right, when I could foresee daylight outside The Margate, I'd add a discreet #resumeuponrequest.

* * *

Two days after I'd delivered my bread pudding chronicles, my seldom-answered landline rang. As ever, I let it go to voicemail. The first four words I heard were "This is Nadeem Malik." Frozen, hand on the receiver, I listened for the threat of an imminent lawsuit. But the friendly, unlitigious tone of "My daughter starting following you on TikTok and to her great delight—" was all it took for me to pick up and shout, "Nadeem! It's Jane! Wow, you saw the video. . . . I didn't embarrass you, did I?"

"On the contrary. I found myself tickled. We've watched it many times!"

"I don't edit myself! I started with the recipe, and suddenly, while buttering the exact same casserole dish I'd used for the office party—"

"And I've never forgotten the source of my bread pudding addiction! Whenever I see it on a menu, I order it. Sometimes even for breakfast."

I asked if he'd listened to the whole long ramble.

"Of course I did. I was mesmerized."

"Even when I moved into dissing the firm?"

"Jane . . . please know I felt very bad when you were terminated. My reaching out to you is overdue. I apologize."

I was so happy to hear anyone apologize for anything firm-related that I immediately forgave him the months it took to call. I said, "I've asked myself almost daily, what would *I* do if another partner—or anyone!—was kicked out for the reason I was? Wouldn't I find a way to show my support, even if there was a gag order? I always come up with the same answer: Yes, I would . . . but I don't mean to guilt-trip you."

He apologized again, then switched paths to "Are you keeping yourself busy? Are you putting this fallow time to good use?"

I said, "I'm reading. I'm cooking, obviously. I've made friends in the building. Not practicing law. I can't yet."

"Remind me: disbarred or suspended?"

"Suspended."

"Will you be automatically *un*suspended?"

"No. I need to petition the New York Bar . . . prove I've stayed out of trouble and won't be a danger to society. Considering what I was arrested for . . ." I stopped there, not knowing whether the crime of indecent exposure would offend.

He said, "I didn't approve of the partners' choice to protect Noah, considering other infidelities that went unpunished in those ranks."

"I know! The judge made an example of me and so did the firm! My sin was the failure to disclose the relationship, but I'd have needed ESP to know I was going to run into Noah at the market and that . . . nature would take its course."

"I'll never understood how Jane Morgan—a great lawyer, in my opinion—became persona non grata, given your . . . well, *popularity* is not too trivial a word to apply here."

I found myself expressing aloud what I chronically brooded over: "Why couldn't the firm stand behind me? I could've been put to some kind of use—a paralegal, a researcher. First-years are hired right out of law school, before passing the bar, and they work their asses off, don't they?"

Nadeem said, "I assure you, some of us asked that same question. Litigators can keep their heads down, work and write as ever without going to court. As you know, I was too junior to have a vote."

Perhaps it was time for me to tread more lightly, lest he regret making this call. What to ask or say that didn't sound crazy? I tried a calm "Anything new at the office?"

"I wouldn't know. I left the firm right after you did."

For a few seconds I entertained a fantasy that he'd walked out in protest and solidarity. But no; surely I'd have heard. So all I asked was "To go where?"

"On our own, my wife and I: Malik and Khan, LLP. My secretary jumped ship, too. Do you remember Bridget? She came with us."

"Here? New York? Specializing in what?"

"We're above Tip Top Shoes on West Seventy-Second. Meera does trusts and estates. I'm still doing tax law."

"Exciting," I said.

He had the good grace to laugh. "We like it. As Malik and Khan, we seem to have caught the eye of a good number of South Asian clients."

I said, "Good for you. No small matter to go out on your own."

"I'll never forget your kindness," he said. "You're the only partner who ever invited the lowly associates to her home."

He'd remembered incorrectly. The holiday buffet had been at the office, but I didn't correct him. I said, "You're giving me too much credit."

"Our fifteen-year-old tells us you are quote-unquote dope. She's the cook in the family. Her grandmother started her off, but TikTok has become her recipe bible." He laughed. "Not always the meal you want to come home to. A lot of peculiar mélanges and glorified nachos."

I told him that I did that as a teen. My working mother left instructions, and I made dinner after school, between soap operas and homework.

"She's just worked up the courage to post one video in which she is decorating her unconventional cupcakes. We find sprinkles every-where."

I asked if it would be okay if I did a follow-up video, in which I'd talk about how the last one brought us back in touch.

"Of course. Could you mention my daughter as the agent who brought it to my attention?"

"Will do! What's her name?"

"Laela. Laela Malik. *L-a-e-l-a*. I won't tell her. I'll let her be surprised."

I said, "Before you called, if I'd asked myself why I was cooking on TikTok, I wouldn't have had a good answer. But now, if it's brought us back in touch . . . it gives the whole stupid thing meaning."

"I appreciate that very much. It's been meaningful to me, too, and also propitious. Meera and I would like to pay you a visit. Is that allowed?"

"It is! When? I'd love that."

"Soon," he said. "She and I have some talking to do first."

I thought that meant *We'll talk; she'll ask why the hell I'd suggested a pity visit to a total stranger, and I'll never hear from them again.*

But then I heard a lilting voice in the background ask, "Would Thursday or Friday of this week work?"

"Thursday. The sooner the better."

"We'll bring the sweets," he said.

Chapter 36

Case Closed

After not hearing from any Grabowski, not even a thank-you for hosting their wedding reception, I sent Mandy a text asking, How's everything?

Her As expected arrived a lackadaisical thirty-six hours later.

Call when you can, I wrote back, livening the message with Jackleen is back with Duncan, followed by a diamond ring emoji and several exclamation points.

I expected a response worthy of that startling announcement but got nothing. Sensing something was off, I called her at work.

A man answered, a man with a Polish accent, whose pronunciation of "Dr. Grabowski" was too authentic to be anything but his own surname. "Krzysztof?" I asked.

"Who is this calling?"

"Jane!"

"May I help you?" he asked, clearly reading from a front-desk script.

I repeated my name, adding "Morgan" and "Mandy's friend from The Margate. You're working at the office?"

"Dr. Grabowski is with patient," he recited.

"Will you tell her Jane called?"

"I write everything. Please spell it the last name."

I did, then asked, "How are you two doing?"

He said, "The other line is ringing. People make appointments by landline still. Good-bye."

* * *

Mandy called me that night, late, waking me up. "His parents are furious," she said. "He never gave them a heads-up about the marriage. They want an annulment."

"Mandy? What time is it?"

"Late. I don't know. Yes, Mandy . . . *Grabowski*, in fact, despite their objections."

I said, "If this is a legal question, parents can't annul a marriage. And what are they so furious about?"

"They're furious because it's me. They were holding out hope that he'd come back to Warsaw and marry some young, fertile countess."

"Do they know it was all about getting him a spousal visa?"

"You mean do they know I'm his ticket to citizenship, and they should be grateful? Ha!"

Her use of "ticket" was the first unromantic note Mandy had sounded since the whole charade began. She must've sensed her own shift in tone, because she corrected it with "We're going to make this work. We're going to prove we're legit. How's honeymoon cystitis for proof? I'll hang on to the prescription for nitrofurantoin and say, 'You think this was a fake marriage? Well, fake marriages don't give you bladder infections.'"

Did this woman have no other confidante? She added, "He's a machine. It would be flattering, if I didn't remind him of the palace scullery maid."

Uh-oh. "It's a little late to ask, but did you sign a prenup?"

"Not exactly," she said.

Before I could ask what that meant, she said, "I've never had even two minutes on FaceTime or Skype or WhatsApp with his parents. They don't want to meet a Jewish commoner. Or maybe they were saying 'communist.' Krzysztof's useless as a translator."

"What about Dani? She must be on your side after setting this whole thing up."

"Who knows? It's like she didn't expect me to be moving in. But I *do* know one thing: She wants to be next."

"For what?"

"A spousal visa. She's going to put something on Craigslist?"

"To find a husband?"

"She's not going to say, 'Need green card marriage pronto.' More like *I'm a European fashion model who'd love to find an American husband.* She'll post a gorgeous, hot photo. She thinks there must be lots of guys who'll come forward for the price she'll pay—"

I yelled, "I don't want to know this! 'Putting the word out' is crazy; it's beyond stupid, let alone paying someone to marry her."

"She's not the brightest bulb," said Mandy, "which is masked by the fact that she speaks English with a British accent."

It didn't take anything more than the mention of a British accent to remind me of their late governess. I couldn't help but ask, "Do either of them ever mention their old nanny's death?"

"A *lot*, and believe me, nobody's grief-stricken." She'd already been whispering, but now I could barely catch "It's why I waited until they were both asleep to call you. And this is *totally* in confidence; totally off-the-record, maybe just a hunch."

Once again I said, "I don't want to know anything."

"I *have* to tell you. And when you hear it, you'll know why. You might need a lawyer."

That woke me up fully. I turned on the bedside lamp, reached for the pen and memo pad I kept on my nightstand, and said, "What? Tell me."

"Okay, Frances . . . Fitzy . . . left a handwritten note warning that if she died, the police should track you down—"

Oh, that. "I know. Two cops came looking for me and showed me the note."

"But here's the thing: They seemed to be laughing over that piece of paper as if it was funny, as if they got away with something."

"'Something'? As in murder?"

"I don't know. I asked what they were laughing about—not in a suspicious way. I tried to sound as if I were asking so I could join in the fun."

"And . . . ?"

"They clammed up."

I asked, "Do you know if those two were ever interviewed by the police?"

"I don't. It would've been before I met them."

"Are you telling me this because you're scared? Or want me to follow up?"

"Someone's in the hallway," she whispered. "Gotta go."

* * *

She was at my door just after eight the next morning, recanting. "I wanted to clear some things up—an impression I might've given you last night."

"Which was what?"

"That Krzysztof and Dani found something funny in his mother's note . . ."

I asked her to come in. Coffee? Or I could scramble some eggs. She said, "Neither. I just wanted to let you know that I'm not worried. Or scared. No need for you to give it another thought."

"What happened to 'I heard something that made me suspicious and made me wait till everyone else was asleep to call you'?"

She'd already taken a few steps toward the elevator but returned to my open door. "Here's the thing . . . in terms of the timing? You might as well know: I'm ovulating. That means I have, basically, tonight and tomorrow to get pregnant. So please don't do anything."

"Such as?"

"I don't know. What lawyers do."

I said, "This has to be obvious, but the father of your future child could end up in prison for matricide."

"But she wasn't *murdered* murdered. She wasn't stabbed or shot or pushed out the window. She ate pesto then fell onto a planter, face-down."

"Does Krzysztof know you're trying to get pregnant?"

"He's . . . um . . . not exactly. He thinks it's just what you do before you go to sleep and when you wake up in the morning. Did you know the Polish word for sex is *seks*? *S-e-k-s*. Or *seksa*. I've had enough recreational *seksa* to last a lifetime." She said she had to go; her first patient was at eight-thirty. Dani and Krzysztof had been laughing, but it was over a joke. She knows that now. They kid around all the time.

* * *

I let her twenty-four-to-thirty-six fertile hours pass before wondering aloud to my detective pal, Sergeant O'Malley, if he was satisfied with Frances FitzRoy's autopsy result. I left a purposely off-topic message, not using the word *murder*. Had that inculpatory letter been destroyed? Could he give me a ring?

He called me back with the usual absent greeting, just "O'Malley. We don't destroy evidence. Why are you asking?"

"Because I'm worried that there are duplicates out there. Why leave just one or two copies? She could've sent it to newspapers and, who knows, my law school alumni office and the New York Bar Association, to which I'm applying for readmittance."

"Couldn't tell ya."

Should I squeal—tell him about Krzysztof and Dani's inappropriate and disrespectful behavior? As a halfway measure I asked, "Can I tell you something off-the-record?"

He said, "Nothing's off-the-record."

I said, "Okay, bear with me . . . my friend Amanda is married to Krzysztof Grabowski, the son and love child of the deceased. Amanda heard him and his sister, Danuta Grabowski, aka Dani, holding that letter and laughing over it."

"That's it? They were laughing?"

"That's not nothing. It was as if they were saying 'Ha. We sure got away with that one.'"

"Did your friend hear them say that?"

"No. But my friend is a good reader of people. She's a dentist. You should talk to her."

I could tell it was the last thing he wanted to do. About to be hung up on, I asked, "Am I the only one whose suspicions were raised by the contents of her stomach?"

Sigh. "Remind me."

"Even though she was allergic to nuts, there was pesto on her sandwich, still undigested. To me that raises the question: Who made the sandwich? Certainly not her."

"Maybe she didn't know there was pesto on it, or didn't know pesto had nuts in it."

I said, "Believe me, if you're allergic to nuts—"

"This was determined to be an accidental death. She ate something she was allergic to on top of martinis and she went into shock, causing her to fall, right? Hit her head. Died from that. You wanna know how many autopsies I've been to where the guy was drunk, fell, and died?"

I said, "In England the pathologist or the DI solves the crime because of something just like this—a light bulb goes off and the detective says, 'Pine nuts! Of course.'"

Another unhappy pause. "The marriage? Trouble in paradise?"

"You mean, is my friend unhappy and trying to get him in trouble? I know for a fact she's trying very hard to get pregnant with that husband."

I could tell from the clacking on a keyboard that he was distracted. I said, "Okay, never mind. Case closed, even if my name is forever linked to her death because God knows how many of those paranoid and defamatory letters of hers are in your active file."

He asked wearily, "Let's get this straight: Do you think there's something there?"

"Could you follow up . . . and maybe *not* say that we talked?"

"I find her where?"

"She's at her dental practice," I said, and gave him the address. "Her husband works there, too. Two birds with one stone," but without a word about him being undocumented, working without a green card, or that his visa had expired. Why would I? Apples and oranges. Detectives on the immigrant-friendly New York Police force wouldn't ask about visas or green cards, would they?

"Would you like me to review motive, opportunity, and means?" I asked him.

"Please don't," he said.

* * *

I waited to hear anything from anybody. Nothing. On Friday I texted Mandy, How's everything?

She wrote, Disaster!!!! My cell rang, Mandy, angry. "Krzysztof and Dani were arrested by your bosom buddy detective!"

"For what?"

"For disturbing the peace!"

"Disturbing what peace? That can't be right."

"I was there! In the office. It was awful."

"Awful how? Was someone hurt?"

"No. Not like that. It's a mess! They're in jail!"

I said, "I'm going to make a call"—probably sounding as if I'd be hustling to find them legal representation. But that wasn't the case. I called Sergeant O'Malley, who, to my surprise, answered. "What happened?" I asked, expecting to hear, *Sorry, can't discuss an open case*, but the opposite happened. He told me everything.

* * *

He'd gone to Mandy's office. Krzysztof was manning the front desk, his English seemingly limited to his receptionist script. O'Malley asked who could translate, and heard "My sister. Around corner."

It took Dani only minutes to get there. "Then it hit the fan," O'Malley said. "Even before I said a word, she asked both me and my partner if we were single and American citizens. Sort of flirty. Ignored that. Then, before we could say why we were there, and after an exchange in Polish with her brother, no translations offered, she tells us she's Emily and he's Emil.

"Knowing that was bull, we asked to see IDs. The sister immediately started yelling, 'How dare you? Do you know who I am? Why would I have an ID with me—I ran out of the house without my purse when my brother called and said the *poleetzia* were there. I know the Polish ambassador to the United States and the American ambassador to Poland!'"

"You weren't cowed by that, were you?" I asked.

O'Malley said, "I don't get cowed by bullshit. There were several patients in the waiting room while all this was going on; him, too, yelling in Polish about who knows what. The dentist comes out from the back and asks if we can conduct this interview outside. I said no. I mean—interviewing people on West Fifty-Seventh Street? I asked if there was a place where we could talk. But the sister's already on her way outside, screaming about harassment of naturalized American citizens. Obviously she thought we were ICE, so I told her, 'Okay, I know you don't have an ID with you. Calm down. . . . Listen, on another matter, miss, where were you the day Frances FitzRoy died?' More yelling, more abuse, like nutcases. Half the people passing by were crossing the street to avoid us. The other half were recording on their phones, some yelling at us, the usual abuse. My partner and I looked at each other. Is this for social media? We knew it was going to be a cheap pinch, but we did it anyway: We arrested them, both bagged for disorderly conduct."

"Wow. Where are they now?"

"At the precinct. Locked up."

Was this gratification I was feeling? What did I have against the Grabowskis other than their brattiness, entitlement, green card marriages, visa-flouting, and possible murder? I told him, "Excellent, excellent summary. Much appreciated, but I have to admit, I'm surprised you're being this forthcoming."

"Once arrested, it's public record. You're a contact. I keep those channels open."

My first and second thoughts were *If he's making me a contact, he must not consider me a pain in the ass, let alone a misdemeanant. Maybe he could write a letter of reference on police letterhead in support of my reinstatement to the bar.* I said, "I appreciate your trusting me—"

I heard a cynical laugh.

"No?"

"You wouldn't want to meet most of my contacts in a dark alley. You keep them, you talk to them, good or bad."

Okay, so not exactly a character reference. I said, "Thanks, I think."

* * *

Then what happened? Where was my follow-up? I pestered O'Malley, leaving messages for two days until he finally picked up. "Are they still in jail?" I asked.

"They're gone."

"Gone? Released? Dead?"

"One, two, three," he said.

I asked what that meant.

"As soon as I got back to the precinct and booked them, I ran their names through NCIC. That's what you do."

"And?"

"Got hits. Found detainers from ICE for visa violations."

"ICE took them away?"

"Not before their arraignment."

"It didn't help that's he's married to an American citizen?"

"You're forgetting they'd been arrested. The DA made this deal: He'd throw out the disorderly conduct charges if they left."

"As in go back to Poland? They agreed to that?"

"They did. On effectively the next plane, home to Mommy and Daddy."

"Were you in court for all this?"

"I was. Quite the show she put on. 'Stupid *poleetzia*, stupid judge, stupid laws, stupid country.'"

"What about Mandy. Amanda, the dentist-wife?"

"I wasn't taking attendance. If she was there, she behaved herself."

"But what about the nanny's death? Did you get a chance to dive deeper into that?"

He said, "No offense, Ms. Morgan, but even if you're trying to kill someone, you can't count on an allergic reaction on top of alcohol guaranteeing she'll fall, hit her head on a sharp object, inhale fertilizer, and die. Even if they wanted her dead, which we can't prove, they just got lucky."

"Maybe a good point," I allowed.

"Let it go," he said.

* * *

What to say to Mandy? Before I figured it out, she called, her voice as cold as I'd ever heard it. "I suppose you know that they're gone, both of them. I need a lawyer who can practice in Europe. Can you at least help me with that?"

"If it's an immigration lawyer, I don't—"

"Too late for that. I need someone who can sue for breach of contract."

"Are you talking about a prenup?"

"No, not a prenup, a contract. He promised to pay me a hundred thousand euros for marrying him and also granting me sole custody of our future issue in case of divorce or deportation."

I gasped. "In writing? Documenting that your marriage was a fake? Who drew this up? No ethical lawyer would've."

"*I* did. Krzysztof signed it in front of a witness."

"Let me guess: Danuta Grabowski."

"What difference does it make? I haven't seen a cent. Plus, I got my period, so thanks for nothing, Mr. Sex Maniac."

"But, but . . . why would someone as smart as you put it in writing?"

"Only a dummy wouldn't get it in writing! What was I supposed to do—trust him to make good on the offer?"

"You married him! You took his name. You moved in with him and tried to have a baby with him. How's that for trust? And what do you need a hundred thousand euros for?"

"My apartment needs everything, from the ground up. A new kitchen alone could eat up all of that. By the way, I'm back at The Margate. The penthouse is going on the market ASAP. And you know how much I'll be getting from that sale? Zero. Not one zloty! His name wasn't even on the deed, just his father's, the anti-Semite."

I had to say, "You must've known putting this on paper was a terrible move, or you'd have told me about it."

Which is when I heard with pronounced sarcasm "Of course you'd never have approved. But I'm the expert now. I *lived* this, which seems to be more than your law school immigration course covered."

I didn't deserve that. She hung up before I could answer, but what was I going to say? I'd only been trying to save her from herself. Now I knew whose side I was on in this whole Mandy-Krzysztof-Danuta mess: nobody's.

Chapter 37

A Reunion for Sure

Was it pandering to make bread pudding for the Malek-Khan visit? But how could I not? I ordered brioche two days in advance, leaving it unwrapped on the counter for the right degree of staleness. I baked it and wrapped the finished product in aluminum foil, tied with ribbon. Swag.

I'd dressed up to what I thought was an appropriate degree for professional hosting, quite sure they'd be coming from work. They arrived with a box of assorted homemade cookies, exactly on the dot.

Did they drink wine? They did not. Having predicted that, I'd ordered clementine-flavored Italian soda that seemed more festive than supermarket bubbly.

I realized I'd met Meera, or at least had spotted her waiting for Nadeem in the firm's reception area—tall, elegant, beautiful. After welcoming them and thanking them for reaching out, I said, "Trusts and estates, I hear."

"And you?" she asked.

I said, "Last job: litigator. Mostly all civil cases. Shall we sit?"

I'd made a mental list of topics, should the conversation stall, starting with their daughter, my fan. It was an excellent opener, producing broad grins. Meera said, "She bakes and bakes. I've had to buy pans of various shapes that produce things I'd never eaten—"

"Popovers," said Nadeem. "And mini cupcakes." He patted the slight paunch at his midsection.

"We had to make a rule about homework before baking," Meera said.

"For her fifteenth birthday, she asked for a stand mixer. Who does that?"

"We obliged," said Nadeem.

"We do worry," said Meera. "At her age she should be socializing."

Her husband, smiling, said, "Homework first. She can socialize on weekends. She's a very good girl and an excellent student."

"Soccer starts up in March," said her mother. "So there's that."

"She's a midfielder," said Nadeem. And with a slight shift in his chair toward me, "But perhaps we've exhausted the topic of our child."

I said, "As promised, I'm going to record another video when I tell the story of this reunion and I'll give Laela a shout-out."

"A reunion for sure," said Nadeem, "but we have another reason for visiting you."

"A professional one," said his wife. "First, a question about your legal status. When your six months are up—of course Nadeem explained to me about your unwarranted and, I suspect, misogynistic sentence—will the offense be erased from your record?"

I said, "That's my goal."

"Is your lawyer working on that already?"

I said, "Stupidly, I represented myself, but I fully intend to hire someone to get my record cleared."

Did I detect some mental message being passed between husband and wife? Yes, because Meera said, "We aren't experts in getting offenses expunged, but we do practice law in the state of New York."

"Criminal law, phffff," said Nadeem. "How hard can that be?" with a sly smile that reassured me he knew exactly the opposite.

I said, "That would be . . . beyond wonderful. I've just started working on this."

"We rise to the challenge," said Nadeem.

"Let's get to the point," said Meera. "Nadeem?"

He said, "We have more work than we can handle."

I said, "If you're saying what I think you're saying . . . I don't do tax or estate law or trusts."

"We want to round out the practice," said Nadeem. "We have loyal clients. When someone comes along and says, 'Thank you for my estate plan. Can you now represent me in the purchase of a condo?,' we'd like to be able to say, 'We are one-stop shopping here.'"

"Like a concierge medical practice," said Meera.

I wanted to throw my arms around both of them, but I thought I should at least offer a composed "I wouldn't want you to be doing me any favors that you'd end up regretting."

"A favor? Why a favor? I know your work. We need someone who could do what needs to be done in court. We sometimes think juries could have biases."

"To hell with those juries," I said. "If you think there's overflow work or new work or litigation you'd rather not handle, count me in. I'd bat cleanup . . . if that expression means anything to you."

"I played softball at Penn," said Meera.

Nadeem said, "The only bat I ever picked up was a cricket bat, but how is this for an aphorism: I'm keeping my eye on the ball."

"Which ball?" I asked.

"The excellent lawyer who, to our great good fortune, is currently unemployed," he said.

Chapter 38

Double Date

Suddenly I had prospects and champions. With Nadeem and Meera's encouragement, I filed my application for reinstatement to the New York Bar. But what about Perry, both of us fearing that "larceny by trick" would be hard for any upstanding employer to overlook. Who could rescue *him*?

I'd suppressed the fact that my sister's fiancé was a real estate agent who found ways of succeeding outside the box, which is a polite way of saying that he didn't let ethics stand in the way of a big sale or a compelling pitch.

The two men met for the first time at a double-date dinner I hosted to celebrate his and Jackleen's engagement. Despite my offer to invite friends of theirs or Duncan's daughters, Jackleen turned me down. She said she'd like to keep it at four so the guys could get acquainted.

And so they did. Duncan, as soon as he'd handed me his coat and said yes to a margarita, was peppering Perry with questions. They didn't seem to me as much conversation as a self-styled Myers-Briggs personality test: Introvert/extrovert? Thinking vs. feeling? Judgment or perception? Seemingly pleased with Perry and his answers, Duncan asked for a tour of his apartment.

"Sure," Perry said. "Any reason?"

"Now?" I asked, my enchilada pie needing only another fifteen minutes in the oven.

Duncan said, "Busman's holiday! I've never seen a two-bedroom on the west side of The Margate."

That made sense, sort of, but still, as we took the elevator up to 9-C, Perry and I exchanged puzzled glances.

"Nice," Duncan said in each room. "*Very* nice." He complimented Perry on the dark gray walls of the master bedroom, the tufted headboard, the many uncluttered surfaces. Onward to the study, admiring the alternating books and photos and signed baseballs on his shelves.

"Did you have help?" Duncan asked.

"With . . . ?"

"I meant were you your own decorator? Did you choose this color palette yourself? That print in the master bedroom—Warhol, obviously. I like how you knew that was enough."

Last stop: the living room. Duncan praised the white paint above the chair rail and the midnight-blue below, which he said had a grounding effect. He nodded with approval at the bronze gladiator on the mantel. He asked where Perry had bought the couch. Really liked the ebonized dining table. Persian rug. Everything worked. Light fixtures great!

I was growing increasingly nervous with each compliment. Was this a scheme I wasn't in on? Was Perry moving away when his six months were up? "Are you putting your apartment on the market?" I finally hissed.

"No! I think this is just . . . what he does."

Back downstairs, over dinner, Duncan asked Perry more questions about his employment history. He recited obligingly, Gladstone's most recently, before that a smaller auction house, and before that an auction house in Hudson, New York, and right after college—

"Anything lined up?" Duncan asked.

"Not yet. It's going to take a climb back, given what I stupidly did. I assume Jackleen filled you in."

"So why are you smiling?" I asked Jackleen.

"Tell him," she instructed Duncan.

"It's about your eye," he told Perry. "That isn't something you lose, no matter what your CV says. You know I own my agency, right? I hire anyone I want to. Totally up to me."

"Real estate?" Perry said. "I don't have a license, and I'm not inclined to get one. Besides, I'd be terrible at it. I'm not—"

Duncan said happily, "An aggressive asshole? That's where I come in."

"Then what?" I asked.

"One word," Duncan said. "Staging."

Though I knew what that meant in a real estate context, I waited for Perry to react.

"Staging? Like an interior decorator?" he asked.

Duncan said, "Let's say I'm going after an exclusive on a property— which is, like, every day of my life. With you on board, I could tell a potential client, 'What do I have that other agencies don't? A specialist to do your staging, included! My guy"—he pointed to Perry—"worked for the most prestigious auction house in the world. He'll step in. You won't have to fluff a pillow yourself.' What I won't say is 'Presto: tackiness gone.' In walk potential buyers who don't have to see past all the crap to envision it as their own."

"And even things like repositioning and rehanging their artwork can make a huge difference," said Jackleen, who'd obviously retained the Perry-Dad art-hanging collaboration.

Duncan continued, "Is this not a selling point: 'My stager was an art consultant for Gladstone's.' Name another real estate company in the city who can match that."

Perry said, "Art *handler*. Big difference."

Duncan batted away that minor distinction. "How are you at feng shui?"

Perry smiled. "How hard can feng shui be?"

Chapter 39

MEMORANDUM AND ORDER

JUDICIAL DEPARTMENT, ON MOTION

Any attorney seeking reinstatement from suspension must establish, by clear and convincing evidence, (1) that he or she has complied with the order of suspension and the Rules of this Court, (2) that he or she has the requisite character and fitness for the practice of law, and (3) that it would be in the public's interest to reinstate the attorney to practice in New York (see Matter of Attorneys in Violation of Judiciary Law § 468–a [Smith], 152 AD3d 960, 960 [2017]; Matter of Attorneys in Violation of Judiciary Law § 468–a [Ostroskey], 151 AD3d 1377, 1378 [2017]; Rules for Attorney Disciplinary Matters [22 NY-CRR] § 1240.16[a]). A reinstatement applicant must also provide, as a threshold matter, certain required documentation in support of his or her application (see Rules for Attorney Disciplinary Matters [22 NY-CRR] § 1240.16[b]; part 1240, appendix C).

In light of the length of her suspension, respondent appropriately completed the form affidavit contained in appendix D to the Rules for Attorney Disciplinary Matters (22 NYCRR) part 1240 (see Rules for

Ms. Demeanor

Attorney Disciplinary Matters [22 NYCRR] § 1240.16[b]) and such
affidavit is properly sworn to (compare Matter of Attorneys in Violation of Judiciary Law § 468–a [Hughes–Hardaway], 152 AD3d 951,
952 [2017]).

As to her character and fitness, respondent attests to having no criminal
record or other disciplinary history during the time of her suspension
(see Rules for Attorney Disciplinary Matters [22 NYCRR] part 1240,
appendix C, ¶¶ 14, 30).   Considering the foregoing along with respondent's responses provided in her form affidavit, we conclude that she has
established, by clear and convincing evidence, her character and fitness
to practice law in New York (see Matter of Attorneys in Violation of Judiciary Law § 468–a [Squires], 153 AD3d 1511, 1513 [2017]; Rules for
Attorney Disciplinary Matters [22 NYCRR] § 1240.16[b]).

We further conclude that respondent's reinstatement will be in the public interest (see Rules for Attorney Disciplinary Matters [22 NYCRR]
§ 1240.16[a]; compare Matter of Leibowitz, 153 AD3d 1484, 1484
[2017]).   Respondent's misconduct had no impact on a client, and she
has expressed contrition for the deliberate public exposure of her body
parts in a manner contrary to local standards of appropriate behavior.

ORDERED that the motion for reinstatement by respondent is
granted; and it is further

ORDERED that respondent is reinstated as an attorney and counselor-
at-law in the State of New York, effective immediately.

Chapter 40

Window Table

Freed two weeks ahead of me, Perry went straight for a long, cold, overdue jog in Central Park, then over to the Frick, then had two lunches—oysters at the Oyster Bar in Grand Central and a cheeseburger at the Burger Joint—then disappeared into Argosy Book Store, and from there to nearby Bloomingdale's for new underwear and socks, then to Just Bulbs on East Fifty-Eighth, then to a wine store, a barbershop, and finally on a stroll through the Village, returning with a fresh mozzarella from Murray's Cheese for me.

I didn't want to tempt the Fates by wishing upon a map of New York or tempt the gods of liberation by plotting in advance where I'd go when sprung. All I let myself visualize was a haircut and a long soak in a hot bath as soon as my ankle monitor was removed.

A few days before *my* six months were up, Perry asked, "Favorite restaurant?" The question didn't sound like a pie-in-the-sky, best-case-scenario destination, but a real invitation. I named a five-star Indian restaurant on West Fifty-Sixth, where I'd eaten before home confinement ruled my life.

"Maybe someplace more atmospheric?" he suggested.

Without hesitation, I said, "Robert, on the top floor of the Museum of Arts and Design."

"Easy. We'll celebrate your return to the law, to the bar, to defending the Constitution."

I said, "Should we ask Nadeem and Meera to join us? I wouldn't be returning to the law straight out of the gate without them."

"Not this time," he said.

*　*　*

We were shown to a table—remarkably, by a wall of windows, the Upper West Side glittering over Perry's shoulder "Don't you have to reserve this weeks in advance?" I asked.

"Maybe. I must've won the special-occasion contest." He smiled and pointed at the menu. "They have a drink called Rosé Colored Glasses. You should get that."

"Because . . . ?"

"It sounds like you."

I said, "You're in a fanciful mood."

He didn't confirm or deny that. He said, "I should get the Mad Manhattan . . . for courage."

Oh, no: *courage*. That word collapsed my smile. Our six months were up, and everyone knows that this is how a civilized man breaks up with a geographically convenient partner, in public, at an elegant restaurant to discourage the making of a scene. Before I could ask him to get it over with, a waiter was at our table. Did we have any questions about the cocktail menu? Of course the bartender could make anything—

Perry said, "A Rosé Colored Glasses for the lady and a Mad Manhattan for me."

"Champagne?" the waiter whispered.

Perry said, "Later. I'll keep you posted," and when we were alone again, "I told them we were celebrating your new job."

"You were lucky; not everybody likes lawyers. Did you throw in that I was starting as an equity partner?"

He murmured, "I must've."

When the drinks came, Perry uncharacteristically took a gulp, ahead of any toast, and without eye contact. He cleared his throat, once, twice, while I sank lower into dread. He began, "Jane . . . okay. Here goes . . . I think you know I'm not the kind of guy who gets down on one knee, especially in public . . . but on the other hand, I didn't want to do this in your kitchen. Or mine." He stopped, as if waiting for ratification.

Down. On. Knee. I whispered, "Go on."

He started over. "Jane. You know I'm not the guy who'd propose at Madison Square Garden, on the Jumbotron."

"Propose," I whispered. "Is that what you needed courage for?"

"Did that not come across?" He glanced around, presumably checking for gawkers, then asked, "What I mean is: Would you want to get married? To me."

All I managed was a strangled yes and the noisy intake of a sob.

Looking stricken, he asked, "Are you all right? Did I fuck this up?"

I reached across the table for his hand, too choked up to answer.

"We're good? You're happy? We're engaged?" he asked.

I nodded vigorously. He leaned back and slumped a few inches in his chair. "Phew." Then he sat up again, leaned forward, and kissed me—

confessing that a kiss was the signal the bartender was waiting for to send over the champagne.

Love? Had he declared that? I didn't need him to. Now *his* eyes were red, and he was blowing his nose on a tissue I supplied.

"You weren't worried that I'd turn you down, were you?" I asked.

"I didn't know! You could've said, 'It's been fun, *but* . . .' or 'I'm a modern woman. Why get married? Why spoil a good thing?'"

"A *great* thing," I barely managed to say.

Not only did the preordered flutes of champagne arrive with a flourish, delivered by the grinning manager himself, but the heretofore unobtrusive cellist struck up the opening notes of Mendelssohn's "Wedding March."

"We knew it happened," said the manager. "You both looked so happy," which made me laugh, given our sniffling and red eyes.

Perry of few words, Perry who hadn't wanted to make a scene, stood up, raised his glass, and announced to the room at large, "You might have gleaned that someone just proposed marriage. That was me. And this amazing woman accepted."

Cheers, applause, raised glasses. Some joker called out, "Let's see the ring!"

What nerve! What bourgeois values! I answered, with a lawyerly forced smile, "I'd rather that money go to charity."

Perry sat down and said quietly, eyes on the menu, "Charity! Ha, good one." He tapped the ring finger of my left hand. "We'll shop tomorrow."

At actual brick and mortar stores, out in fresh air and real life. I sniffled again and said, secretly hoping for tomorrow, "No hurry."

"Except I'm too old for a long engagement. I'm thinking a small wedding somewhere warm, a good excuse to get the hell away from here."

"It's called a destination wedding." I smiled, eyebrows raised. "Not Cincinnati? Maybe something discreet at the country club . . . small, quiet, a little tragic, considering your choice of brides . . ."

"Whoa. You're way off the mark. My parents are waiting to hear. My mother wanted to overnight some family ring."

I said, "Um . . . darling husband-to-be . . . did you tell her *not* to?"

"I told her you'd want to pick your own."

"Did she ignore that and send a picture anyway?"

She had indeed, several, front and side views, in its satin-lined box, another above the knuckle of someone's index finger, another lying on a Hermès scarf. The diamond was square, art deco–ish, big without being ostentatious, and breathtakingly beautiful. I said, "Tell her yes. Tell her I fainted."

He texted, It's official. She loves it. Send.

A minute or so later: Will have it sized by our jeweler. Get her finger measured.

Her finger? Did she mean Jane's finger? Is that how a mother responds when her only son gets engaged at forty-one? Where were the best wishes? I'd heard her muster more vigorous congratulations to scofflaws Mandy and Krzysztof. Clichés and platitudes welcome!

I fished out my phone and texted the newly ringed Jackleen, What's your ring size?

If yr asking what I think you're asking, OMG. We're a 6!!!!

"Six," I told Perry. And back to Jackleen, Call u later.

6, Perry texted his mother, but we'll size it here.

Mrs. Salisbury wrote, I think it IS A 6!!!! It was my Gran Edwina's.

"The robber baron's widow," Perry told me.

Why not start with a clean slate? Why not take the high road? I asked for his phone and texted, It's Jane. I love your son!!!

Gray bubbles were churning. What appeared was We love him, too! It's rose gold. Is that OK?

Perry answered for me: It's SO OK that she's speechless. Talk soon. Haven't ordered dinner yet . . . followed by food emoji.

I waited a polite interval, feigning menu absorption, before asking if his parents had pushed back when he told them he was going to propose.

"They're fine. My dad's a fan. Besides, I led with your new, highly respectable job and the expunging of your bogus crime. Gone! Like it never happened."

My phone pinged. Was it from DeAndra, belatedly expressing her delight, having been chastised by Cal? No, it was a text from my mother that said, Call me!

Jackleen, obviously, hadn't wasted a minute. I wrote, At dinner. Talk later.

"Or now?" asked Perry. "Want to tell them?"

I said, "I'd rather talk to them when I won't sound like I'm still in shock."

"I think they knew from Day One." He grinned. "Same as I did."

He knew from Day One? I wanted to react in an appropriately swoony fashion, but we were new at romantic proclamations, and I was prone to cross-examination. I asked, "But I'm remembering the first time we met, when I came around with brownies. You weren't particularly friendly. Did you mean *that* Day One?"

"No. You caught me off guard. I was in a constant state of humiliation. I hated what I'd done, so I wasn't thinking, 'Oh good, here's someone in the same boat' because I was so friggin' ashamed of that boat."

I reached under the table and gave one of his thighs a squeeze. "Maybe Day One happened on *Night* One."

"That, too. But it was at your apartment, the night I met your sister for the first time. She was lobbying for you to be my personal chef, and you were having none of it. When she asked what you were serving us, you said, 'Dead chicken.' I didn't laugh, but I wanted to." He shrugged. "That did it."

Love at first wisecrack certainly was nice, but I was processing an even better takeaway: Jackleen's subsequent aggressive flirting didn't trump my "dead chicken." Faced with a set of identical twins, only one of us had registered: me. I said, "You'll never know. . . . ," tears welling again.

He asked, "What about you? I mean, was there some point . . . ?"

I checked around us before whispering, "When you made a case for us having sex? And then we followed through? For weeks, I told myself we were just you-know-what buddies."

"But . . . ?"

"The 'buddy' part was a lie. It wasn't 'love the one you're with,' because I actually *did* love the one I was with."

Perry said, "So did I."

✳   ✳   ✳

We shared everything: the tuna tartare appetizer, the lamb shank, the salmon, the complimentary goat cheese mousse topped with a sparkler. I raised my glass, barely one sip left, and said slowly, composing between phrases, "To us. To you, for courage . . . and to observant doormen, and to The Margate, without which . . ."

Instead of clinking glasses he said, "The Margate? I've had it with that penitentiary."

"Meaning you want to leave? I mean now, when I'm starting a new job? With a wedding to plan."

"I have to, Janie," he said. "And not to sound Kafkaesque, but the walls closed in on me a long time ago."

I looked out the window. It had started to snow. Wasn't that supposed to symbolize something—like innocence and purity? Or maybe, in a context that applied more closely to Perry and me, a fresh start?

I said, "I go where you go."

Chapter 41

I Suppose It Wouldn't Kill Me to Take a Look

Duncan pointed out that if we sold both our respective two-bedrooms, we could buy a bigger place. Did we know there was a three-bedroom on the market right now, in our own building? I surprised myself with the vehemence of my no. "Not here! We've had enough Margate to last a lifetime. I want to live in a place where the doormen haven't called upstairs to announce that coppers are here to interrogate me."

"Me, too," said Perry. "Jane and I could be just the respectable newlywed law-abiding couple who don't play loud music or own a yappy dog, who'd sail through an admissions committee interview."

Eagerly, Duncan rattled off, "New? Old? Prewar? Landmarked? How much?"

"Something in the price range of two people who sell their apartments and pool the proceeds," said Perry.

It took exactly one week for Duncan to call back. He knew of a place that wasn't even on the market yet. A complicated situation, but he was really good at navigating complicated situations, and he could get us in to see it. He had an exclusive.

We asked where it was. "Here. Your neighborhood. You wouldn't have to change dry cleaners or gyms."

I asked what the complicated situation was.

"The tenants were deported. The owner is in Europe and doesn't need it anymore. Wants to dump it. No plans to come back, and his kids can't. How's this afternoon?"

Very funny. Shouldn't he have known he was sending us a kryptonite listing: the penthouse in The Gloucester, previously occupied by my late mortal enemy Frances FitzRoy and the deported Grabowskis? I said, "Is this a joke? This listing just happened to fall into your lap?"

"Not exactly. Your sister clued me into the circumstances—a death, a deportation or two. But this guy doesn't wait for things to fall into his lap. I made a call. Six-hour time difference factored in."

I said, "Is my sister nuts? Did she think I'd ever want to live in that place?"

"Have you seen it?" he asked. "Because Jackleen has now."

"No! And I don't want to."

At which point Perry asked, "You're not even a little curious? C'mon."

"Have fun," I said. "And don't send me pictures."

I'd known Duncan through two iterations of his relationship with Jackleen, so it was in a brotherly fashion that he said, "Don't be stupid.

The Poles don't want to drag it out, and best of all, they don't know shit about Manhattan real estate prices."

I said, "As if that co-op board is going to approve us."

"Why wouldn't they?" Duncan asked.

"Duncan! Until two minutes ago we were under house arrest!"

"Who's telling them that? Not me; not any of the glowing personal recommendations you'll be submitting. And never in my entire career, representing all kinds of sketchy buyers, has an admissions committee asked, 'Either of you a felon?'"

I said, "I know for a fact that admissions committees google prospective buyers."

"Then here's what you two charming people say: *Morgan is a common name. That wasn't me.* Besides, you don't swear to tell the truth, the whole truth, and nothing but the truth at a co-op interview."

"We'll pay cash," said Perry, whose money I'd never counted, whose trust fund I'd only joked about after the single mention of a robber baron great-grandfather.

"If it's such a great deal, there's going to be a line out the door and down Seventh Avenue for the open house."

"What open house?" asked Duncan.

I said, "There must be some regulation that says you can't just show it to one potential buyer."

"There isn't. It's a broker's dream."

"What about other people in the building who will want to move up from a lower floor to a penthouse? That always happens."

"What are you, their lawyer? President of their co-op board? I show it to you, you make an offer, the Grabowskis grab it. End of story."

* * *

Perry went alone and was across the street for much longer than it should have taken an uninterested party to walk through an apartment his fiancée would hate. When he returned, I pretended to have forgotten where he'd been. He helped himself to the Arts section of the *New York Times*, and after feigning absorption and humming for effect, he said, "Aren't you going to ask me how I liked the apartment?"

I knew what the answer would be. I picked up the Food section and from behind it asked, "Okay. How was it?"

"Let me put it this way," said Perry, newspaper abandoned. "The kitchen. They left the copper pots. They're hanging above the stove. . . . Oh, and Duncan says it's an AGA."

An AGA. The stove often found in the homes of British landed gentry. "What else?" I asked.

"There's a faucet over the stove that's called a pot-filler. And for some reason, two dishwashers."

I didn't respond, but I was listening. He continued, "Lots of closets. Built-in bookshelves everywhere. With a sliding ladder so you can reach the highest shelves. Views."

I said, "But the terrace . . . very bad juju."

"I didn't check it out—snow out there. Which is very cleansing, I'm told."

"The kitchen . . . what are the counters?"

"I knew you'd ask." He took out his phone. I saw stainless steel countertops, gleaming, begging for food prep, graduating into double sinks. I said, "I suppose it wouldn't kill me to take a look."

Mandy had told me the apartment was beautiful, but I'd seen first-hand what her taste had rendered up in 8-B. "In what way beautiful?" I'd asked her.

"The views. Nice furniture. Pretty wallpaper," she'd said.

I'd seen Mandy's furniture. And wouldn't her idea of pretty wallpaper be cuckoo clocks and flocked fleurs-de-lis?

Perry said, "Duncan said he could take us back tomorrow."

He did. And Mandy for once had been right. The bedrooms had William Morris wallpaper, classic Arts and Crafts, one with dark green leaves and four different flowers; the other a pale blue with lemons, so beautiful that I wanted to copy these choices in whatever other, future apartment we bought or rented. And Perry's kitchen counter photo had missed a marble insert for kneading bread.

"I'm thinking, for what I'd get you for both apartments, you'll make a very decent offer," said Duncan.

Perry said to the stunned and reluctantly entranced me, "Obviously, I'm not going to talk you into anything. We'll keep looking."

Duncan said, "No, you won't. You're going to put in an offer today. It's gorgeous. You'll repaint. You'll steam off the wallpaper and paint every wall whatever color you agree on. You won't even know who lived here before you. You'll make it your own."

"But that's the problem," I said.

Duncan raised his eyebrows, a silent question for Perry. "Here's her dilemma," he explained. "She loves everything, but the owner who made those choices is haunting the place."

Duncan asked me, "Do you know who lived in your apartment at The Margate? Would you know if they were a rapist or a racist? My point is, they could've been terrible people. Who cares?"

"We'll talk," I said.

Two hours later, at the bar at Red Rooster in Harlem, one of the destinations on my restaurant bucket list, Perry said, "I don't think we could do any better. And last night, I even dreamed about it."

I couldn't resist asking what the dream was about. His smile told me it was fiction: "Babies . . . rescue dogs . . . a big turkey roasting in the AGA. You and me weeding the heirloom tomatoes and two kinds of basil growing on the terrace . . ."

I said, "Talking about rosé-colored glasses . . ."

"Just saying, you'd have the last laugh."

"When did I ever laugh about Frances FitzRoy? Even when I learned that she died from ingesting fertilizer, I didn't crack a smile."

"Are we doing it?" he asked.

I said, "We'd need a contingency in the purchase and sale that says we have to sell both our places."

"Pretty standard, I'm sure."

"And I want everything of hers out of there. Well, maybe not the copper pots and the umbrella stand by the front door."

"Easy. What else?"

I said, "We'll make a list."

He waited, pretending to be studying the menu.

I said, "I'm having the shrimp and grits. . . . Okay. Let's give it a try."

"Is that 'I give up, so let's do it'? Or 'Let's do it. I want to live there as much as you do.'"

I said, "If we can get Penthouse-Two for the price Duncan thinks we can, I'm in."

"What if we had to meet the asking price?"

I said, "Let's not get ahead of ourselves. Let's make an offer—"

"When?"

"Tomorrow?"

"Be prepared to have it accepted," Perry said.

The bartender was a woman, which I thought might account for her noticing my conspicuously beautiful ring. Two glasses of prosecco appeared. She said, "If that's what I think it is, congratulations."

I said, "I'd forgotten what nice things can happen out in the world."

*　　*　　*

We made the offer. Warsaw countered. Perry's parents, of all people, when consulted, said, "Do it. How much do you need?"

I protested to him privately on the principle of us not being kids, not paying off student loans or scraping together a living. We could do it on our own. Plus the unstated: Who'd want to feel indebted to parents who hadn't been civil upon meeting their son's nearly intended?

Perry said, "You can bet they talked to their estate lawyer about what made the most sense, inheritance and probate-wise. And I think you remember: I'm their only child." And knowing I liked hearing about what much better parents they could and should have been, he said, "I think it's their way of making up for having very little interest in the child who later sacrificed his career to their golden anniversary."

I said, "That's something to consider: their guilt."

When I told Jackleen of the Salisburys' offer, she told me to stop being proud-stupid and accept their down payment graciously. Wasn't grace something those Cincinnatians would relate to? And wasn't it an early wedding present?

I said, "What if they start making frequent trips to New York, feeling like they have a stake in the guestroom."

"Yes, they will," she said firmly. "That's what in-laws do."

In Warsaw, Count Grabowski apparently failed to read about desperate buyers in a sellers' market, and he'd been told by Duncan that New York real estate regulations mandated that sellers accept offers that meet the asking price.

I said, "That can't be true."

Duncan said, "I can be creative when I have to. Congratulations."

*　*　*

He scheduled open houses for our Margate apartments on two successive Sundays, and to no one's astonishment, both got offers above the asking price after bidding wars. Perry's got more for, among other things, the higher floor and its finished, polished, uncluttered good taste. It meant that together we could afford the bargain of a penthouse without parental help. I made the call myself, happy that Calvin answered. I said we deeply appreciated their offer, their generosity, but we could swing it. We'd been so lucky—our future brother-in-law was not cutting himself a commission for either 9-C or 6-J, quite unheard-of. Wedding presents, he insisted. With Perry listening, twirling his index finger, prompting me, reminding me of the invitation we'd rehearsed, I said, "We hope you can make the wedding."

*　*　*

I had to break the news to Mandy, who had thought, as Krzysztof's wife, she'd get Penthouse-2 in a settlement—a pipe dream rooted in a notion that their marriage would be deemed kosher.

I was delinquent in catching her up; hadn't told her that Perry had proposed and I'd accepted. There was a time when she'd have been aware of the passage of time as it related to my six months' confinement, but that deadline came and went. Inevitably, just the way I'd first seen her, our morning departures for work were the same. The elevator doors would open, and there would be Mandy, staring straight ahead, not acknowledging her fellow passenger. The third time that happened, I said, "Good morning," and got a clipped "Morning" in return.

Because we didn't have the elevator to ourselves, it wasn't fitting to mediate our falling-out, but when we'd reached the lobby, I kept up with her race-walk, crossing the street in the opposite direction of my own route to work, and said, "Mandy! Do you want to talk sometime? Maybe a drink? I can go out to a restaurant now."

She stopped. She said, "I was an idiot. I thought if I married Krzysztof he'd get a green card and I'd get pregnant, and the children would be adorable."

"I know."

"Did you know I have a huge fine I have to pay for going through with it?"

"I knew it was a possibility." I refrained from saying, *But there was no stopping you.*

She picked up my left hand. "I heard. You're lucky."

I was *lucky*? No credit due to me or to love, just to timing, geography, crime and punishment? All desire to have a drink—let alone pick up the friendship—drained out of my better instincts.

Chapter 42

Woman to Woman

How my mother summed the two couples up: Jackleen and Duncan? No surprise. He'd left and come back before, hadn't he? That previous time—something about resistance from his daughters? Or not seeing eye-to-eye on a few matters very important to Jackleen, now negotiated and fixed. She and Dad had sensed they'd end up together eventually.

"But what about me?" I teased. "Sensed anything?"

Mom, the eternal optimist, wondered aloud if . . . was it possible that down at the bureau, the office, the department, the court, wherever decisions are made about sentences . . . that some kind soul said, *Let's put these two on the same track?*

I said, "That's a nice story, Ma. Did you see it on the Hallmark Channel?"

"I knew you'd make fun of me. But look at Dad and me. We met because he wandered into the wrong wake. What was that if not fate? Your situation reminds me of people they talked about on our tour of the Tenement Museum. You and Perry were like two immigrants who met in the same building, each one alone, each with baggage from another life, then love grew out of . . . nothing!"

Of course I had to quote her in my farewell TikTok post. "Take heart!" I told my alleged followers. "Look at me, returning to work, to a better job, by which I mean hired by superior people. Incidentally, I'm getting married at almost forty! What had looked like the end of the world, due to that miscarriage of justice I've previously griped about, turned out to be, as my sister the dermatologist puts it, a reconstruction."

I felt obliged to follow that with a fitting recipe, but at the same time one that was faithful to my brand. I found the perfect inedible one, simply titled Wedding Cake. I didn't go through the motions of making it, with its two pounds of butter, two pounds of sugar, two and a half pounds of flour, and—unbelievably—four pounds each of currants and raisins, fourteen eggs, and two cups each of wine and brandy. Then—holy hell—baked for five hours! It made what? Two large *loaves*. "Loaves?" I asked my audience with theatrical disbelief, "Loaves? A wedding cake?"

Wouldn't you know that Meera and Nadeem's daughter, with her parents approving the fortune in ingredients, halved the recipe, using a mere seven eggs and two pounds each of raisins and currants. I'd still never met her, but when I came to the office and saw the result of my most outlandish of recipes tied up with a bow on my desk, I knew immediately what it was and which guardian angel–follower had made it.

* * *

I was working on getting Perry's felony reduced to a misdemeanor, now that I was practicing and studying whatever kind of law a walk-in client needed. His invented career as Duncan's staging consultant was not for the long term. In fact, he was finding it awkward and embarrassing in the short term. Who wants to go into someone's apartment and make their family photos and knickknacks disappear, only to find them restored and displayed on his follow-up visits?

What could *I* do? First, against Perry's wishes and finally with his dubious consent, I dropped in on the small auction house that had fired him for having scruples. The head crook/owner/CEO had retired to Florida, and his younger daughter was now in charge of Prince Auctions. I visited, woman to woman. Was I making a veiled threat when I explained that Perry had been fired by her father for telling the truth, for confronting him about—no offense—his dodgy business practices? But *she* could restore the house's good name by righting that wrong.

She could? How?

I was prepared. "By hiring Mr. Salisbury back. Who, by the way, went on to be senior art handler at Gladstone's, who could've reported your father's business practices to the Auctioneers Ethical Review Board or to the police."

She didn't rise to her father's defense, which encouraged me. She asked what rules or ethics or standards her father had violated. I told her: holding on to money that wasn't his for way too long.

She asked when Perry worked at Prince. When I told her, she said, "I had no idea. I was still in college then."

To our advantage, this new proprietor knew very little about the auction business or about the law or if any review board covered such things as bad money management.

I asked who currently did framing, packing, unpacking, shipping, mounting, cataloging?

"Um. We're working on that. Part-timers."

"And out front, in the gallery?"

"My sister," she said.

"Was that her out in the gallery?"

She answered with an apologetic yes.

I said, "I think my timing is excellent," because that sister was surely far along in a noticeable pregnancy.

"I'd have to discuss this with her. We're partners."

I said, "What if you gave him a trial? Maybe a week? If you find him helpful, he'll stay. And your troubles will be over."

I think implying that Prince Auctions had troubles hit home. She said, "A month's trial. And I'll need a letter of reference from his current employer."

Duncan. No problem.

I called Perry from the sidewalk, a half block from the auction house. "It worked. I spoke with one of the daughters. I don't think she had any idea about the sins of her father. She may have thought I was there in an official capacity, as your lawyer."

"No threats, I hope."

"No threats. Just laid out the facts: Her father fired you when you complained about his holding on to his buyers' money. And being the kind soul that you are, you hadn't turned him in. Okay, I also invented an Auctioneers Ethics Review Board—but only as a test of what she knew. And maybe I elevated you to head handler at Gladstone's. But these women need help! I don't think she knows much about the business, and her sister appears to be ten months pregnant." Before he could question me further I said, "The next step is a letter of recommendation from your current employer."

He didn't seem delighted with his new prospects.

"No?" I asked. "What's wrong? Is it because I told a few white lies?"

"No. It's just . . . like I'm in a remedial program that gets ex-felons hired."

I said, "Wanna bet? Did I say one word about the teapot dome scandal? I certainly did not."

After a long pause, he said, "The letter of recommendation from my current employer? That would be Duncan? Even if he's in real estate?"

"Duncan's a busy man. Should I write it, or should you?"

"I will," Perry said. "I have a growing sense of what they'll need."

"It'll be signed by Duncan, so don't make it sound like an art history major wrote it."

"Or a genius," Perry said.

*　*　*

By the time the front-room Prince sister gave birth, before Perry's employment trial had formally ended, the younger sister was coming into work later and later. She confided that what had looked exciting, even glamorous, from afar, was overwhelming. Producing catalogs for their exhibitions, the exhibitions themselves, storage, photography, the actual auctions, online and off-, money in and money out? Her heart wasn't in it. Perry didn't give himself a title, but after two weeks of more or less taking charge, the Prince sisters declared him officially hired.

Chapter 43

Dream Dresses

There were many three-way prewedding phone calls with our mother, who withstood our teasing like a champ. I said, "Maybe Jack and I will wear the same dress, just like when we were little. Mom? Good with that?"

Sounding hopeful but careful, she asked, "Are you talking about a double wedding?"

I said, "Sorry; not a chance."

Jackleen said, "Different timetables. Jane wants to get it over with."

I said, "I wouldn't put it that way. Perry and I don't want a big production. We just need a judge and a table at a restaurant near city hall."

"A new dress, at least?" my mother asked. "Our treat. That's what the parents of the bride do."

* * *

I ducked into Kleinfeld's late one afternoon, appointment-less, and got the impression that I was the first customer in store history to arrive without a mother, sister, maid of honor, or best friend. I asked for a dress I could try on, buy, and take home that day, since I was getting married in three weeks. Something simple, knee-length, no froufrou.

The sales consultant found her voice to repeat, "In three weeks? And the venue?"

"City hall."

I learned that they did have samples, but alterations would be out of the question. I went through them, bedecked and bejeweled dresses, thousands of dollars each. Weren't samples supposed to be bargains? Halfway down the rack, I said, "They seem so extreme."

She asked what I meant by extreme.

I said, "Big."

"Most of our samples are size tens."

"Not that. I meant . . . so much volume . . . and *stuff*."

She picked up the pace of her hanger-sliding as I considered each gown, but after no interest from me, she stopped. "They're wedding dresses. Dream dresses. Our customers have been imagining themselves walking down the aisle since they were little girls."

I looked at my Fitbit, pretending it was a watch, pretending to be startled. I said, "Thanks so much, but I have to get back to work."

*   *   *

The personal shopper at Saks, recommended by Meera, asked if I'd brought pictures of dresses I loved. I told her no, because I wasn't looking for a wedding dress, per se, just . . . well, a dress to get married in. Maybe something, as my mother had suggested, that used to be called a going-away outfit? Maybe a suit I could wear to work and to court?

The notion of suits seemed to sadden her. Was it a second or third wedding?

I said, "It's a first marriage for both of us."

"Don't you want your partner to choke up when he or she sees you?"

I said, "I'm not walking down the aisle. We're going to city hall. I'd just like something . . . pretty."

"Let's do this together," she said.

I vetoed most of what she pulled off the racks, most too summery, many not my taste, some a fortune. The suits I stopped to consider she vetoed as too MOB.

"MOB?" I repeated.

"Mother of the bride."

She was the one who spotted it, triumphantly, on a sale rack, a pale silvery gray, full skirt, three-quarter sleeves, boatneck, a heavy silk-like fabric. My size. "When would I wear it again, though?" I asked.

"We don't care," she said.

It was the only thing we took back to the dressing room. "Close your eyes," she instructed, slipping it over my head. She zipped me into it and made some professional pulls, tugs, and smoothings.

"Now open," she said.

Was it possible that I was feeling what I'd heard conventional brides who'd been picturing their weddings since childhood felt when the right dress appeared: a moment?

I touched the fabric, which was somewhere between stiff and silky. My shopper explained, "Lined with crinoline for fullness."

I whispered, "I love it. How is it possible it was still here?"

"It was waiting for you," she said.

I said, "I'll take it."

"Flowers? Maybe a wrist corsage?"

I said I could do that. "With a matching boutonniere? I know he'd do that."

She fished the price tag out from my neck and said, "Hmm. Let me take another ten percent off this. Okay?"

I took out my phone and snapped a selfie in the mirror, not a preview for Perry or Jackleen or my mother, lest anyone think I was asking for their opinion. I wanted it for the record, in case we forgot to take photos at city hall.

"Can I see a picture of him?" my shopper asked. "I like to see my brides' intended."

I showed her a selfie Perry had sent from Central Park on his first day out, grinning, a thumbs-up in front of Bethesda Fountain. It was my favorite of the many he'd sent me from the day's outing, which he'd captioned "From My Freedom Trail."

She nodded with conviction and smiled.

"You approve?" I asked.

"He loves you a lot," she said.

*　*　*

Three weeks later, still at The Margate, sleeping apart the night before our wedding, for reasons of tradition and superstition, Perry knocked on my door, late. "Not supposed to see you!" I yelled.

"I know. Slipping something under your door. I'm leaving. Sleep tight."

It was an envelope, and inside was an updated hard copy of the outline that had started it all, the one that had enlisted me as his caterer with benefits. The original had been all-business, its bullet points noting we were single, straight, housebound consenting adults. The edited version was titled "Why I'm marrying Jane E. Morgan." Handwritten above the crossed-out old facts were new phrases, such as "semi-pro headhunting," "regular gourmet meals," "forgiving the unforgivable," "unexpected fun," and "she loves me back."

Also edited was the old "but for only as long as both parties want to participate," and replaced with "as long as we both shall live."

I called him. I said, "To hell with tradition. I'm coming up."

*　*　*

We'd made our appointment through nyc.gov/cupid. My parents, Perry's parents, my sister, and Duncan were present, having come from work, Penn Station, and LaGuardia to city hall on this weekday afternoon. Knowing in advance that we were allowed only one witness, we'd put the names in a hat. Silently hoping it wouldn't be his mother or father, and hoping for a Morgan, I was relieved that the winner was my dad.

After signing in at a kiosk, we waited our turn, couples all around us, some in wedding dresses and tuxes, others in jeans and parkas, suits, dresses straining over baby bumps—all languages, most jovial, a few looking less inclined. There was a wall-size photo of city hall, meant for posing in front of for pictures. If I hadn't been carrying my own bunch of violets, there were flowers for sale.

It was a busy Friday afternoon, as expected. Our names finally appeared on an LED screen, which meant we were to go into a smaller waiting area and finally it was our turn, in yet another room.

We knew the ceremony would be quick. The officiant was a female municipal court judge who smiled indulgently when my dad said proudly and coyly, "My daughter could appear before you one of these days."

"Not as a defendant," I said. "He's trying to tell you I'm an attorney."

That was it for chitchat. The ceremony was short. Who knew that something so by-the-book, so familiar, could produce two choked-up "I do"s and a weeping witness?

Outside the chambers, hugs, more tears, photos, handshakes. Next, a short walk to a restaurant we'd chosen as posh enough for the Salisburys with an elegant but unchallenging menu. Our party of a mere eight didn't qualify for a private room, but the five o'clock reservation served us well, no one else arriving for an hour.

The champagne flowed. I appreciated Mrs. Salisbury's best effort to appear not only happy but something resembling effervescent. She rose to make the first toast, to claim how thrilled she and Calvin were. She wasn't losing a son but gaining a daughter, and—if she might count the blessing of a twin sister in the bargain—*two* daughters! They'd waited a loooong time for this day, for this occasion! How lucky that these two wonderful people were, albeit through unusual and not the happiest of circumstances, united. Lemons into lemonade!

"All's well that ends well," said her husband.

"If I came across at first as a little overprotective—"

"Time and place," her husband murmured. "Give someone else the floor."

"I'm rambling, I know," she said. "I wrote it down, but left it at home. I just wanted to say that when I see how happy our son is . . . well, isn't that what counts?"

My mother didn't say *Sit down, DeAndra*, but by standing up, she accomplished that. "As the other mother here—I just have to say that from the minute we met Perry, we thought, *Please let Jane fall in love with him.*"

I knew what she was saying: *Happiness is a two-way street, DeAndra. Notice how I'm tossing bouquets to your son because it's both their happinesses we're after.*

Perry said, "Sally! Don't stop. You were just getting started on me being an ideal if not highly desirable son-in-law."

That earned him a laugh and a blown kiss. Would his mother notice the son-in-law affection willingly expressed and his addressing her so easily on a first-name basis?

Calvin raised his glass. "We are tickled to welcome Jane to the family. And all the Morgans, too."

It didn't take more than that and much champagne for my parents to forgive and forget what I'd told them about DeAndra's earlier hostilities. The courses kept coming. Mrs. Salisbury told me that she loved my dress. That its vintage style reminded her of Jackie O. And she loved the antique thin rose-gold wedding band I'd chosen to match her granny's engagement ring.

"Now known as *Jane's* engagement ring," Perry reminded her.

We were still there at eight o'clock. We'd chosen the restaurant wisely, for its unthreatening American fare. DeAndra complimented the thoughtful black linen napkins, our darling waiter, her sole amandine, the delicious rolls, and the embossed pats of butter.

Perry and I, having anticipated two sets of parents fighting over the check, had quietly slipped a credit card to the waiter during his round of orders. But too late. Duncan had gotten there first with his platinum card, and his practiced sleight of hand.

Chapter 44

Thank You, Frances FitzRoy

How long would it take me to perform a mental exorcism, freeing our new home of Frances FitzRoy? My parents had stayed at The Margate, postwedding, to help us finish packing, then unpack the next day in Penthouse-2. As my father and Perry were hanging pictures, my mother and I debating what went where on the kitchen shelves, Jackleen arrived with a bouquet of dried sage, lit it, and despite my cynicism, went from room to room in quasi-religious fashion.

My father, the self-described bumpkin, asked the movers enthusiastically if this was the shortest move they'd ever had to make—across Seventh Avenue! Did they even have to repark the truck?

The head guy grunted, "You're in New Yawk. People move to apartments in the same building, sometimes one apartment over."

"Makes sense. Of course," he said.

"We live in Massachusetts," my mother explained.

She and my dad had brought two wedding presents: a soup tureen shaped like a cabbage with accompanying bowls, and a painting I'd always loved, *Harrow from Hospital Hill*, by an artist whose signature my dad had never deciphered. Because I'd been raised with it, I choked up when they brought it; protested that it left the space above the mantel bare, to which my mother scoffed, "Have you *not* been up to our attic? Your father has already picked its replacement. What better resting place than above your new fireplace?"

"Resting place" was too close for comfort. Once again I wondered what ghosts would inhabit this place, and for how long? Even with new names on the deed, even the day after the closing, I was still avoiding the terrace and the planters, those murder weapons, using the winter weather as an excuse.

Jackleen noticed. "You have to get over being spooked by this place. And please don't tell me you're going to avoid the terrace. It's the cherry on top of the ice cream sundae."

"She spied on me from this spot, and then died here."

"Poetic justice—did you ever think of that? Her dying on the very spot where she called 9-1-1."

I hadn't exactly.

"You know what else I think? If Frances FitzRoy hadn't called the police, you'd still be slaving away at that job you didn't know you hated, with partners who dropped you like a hot potato. And without the ankle monitors, when would you have met Perry, who lived on the opposite side of the building, and didn't even use the east elevator? My differential diagnosis is: never. So I personally say, 'Thank you, Frances FitzRoy.'"

I said, "That's very generous of you. But I can only go this far." I raised my coffee cup. "Frances, you didn't have the luckiest life—a secret son who wasn't too happy to find out who gave birth to him, and possibly fed you pesto. Only you know. And now, fornicators and ex-felons live in your beautiful apartment. May you *not* turn over in your grave or burn in hell, as I once or twice may have wished for."

An arm came around my shoulders and squeezed. "That's my girl," said Perry.

Chapter 45

Ladies' Lunch

Another posh restaurant, this one on Central Park South, for the ladies' lunch Jackleen and I had been promising each other for months. I turned down the first table we were led to, asking for more privacy, explaining that we had business to discuss. After the long-considered appetizers were delivered, a fortune each, I said, "I want to pay you back."

"Don't be silly. I invited *you*."

"I don't mean who's treating today. I want to reimburse you for six months of financial support."

"For groceries? Absolutely not. You're not paying me back for buying you food."

I said, "Fresh Direct orders, twice a week for six months? Not just food but wine and paper towels and aluminum foil and feeding Perry an increasing number of meals per week, which, incidentally, he was paying me for."

Jackleen, eyes closed, shaking her head, said, "If you write me a check, I won't cash it."

I had no better argument, no better closing statement, and I didn't want to turn lunch into a debate. I said, "Okay. Life is long. I'll find some sneaky ways to help that won't look like reimbursement."

"Fine! If we get pregnant, you'll be the godmother and backup babysitter."

"And vice versa," I said.

We clinked glasses, our dwindling fertility acknowledged but not spoken. We sighed. Always an efficient pivoter, Jackleen asked, "Work is good?"

"I'm getting there, branching out. Yesterday I went to a real estate closing. Last week I got someone's stupid son out on bail."

"But you like it?"

"Enough. Love my partners."

"And Perry's settling into his job?"

"He runs the place! Well, not officially. The Prince sisters are beyond happy to delegate. The older one is on maternity leave and the younger one is applying to law school."

We moved on to wedding talk—a review of mine, two weeks earlier. First topic, the Salisburys. I said, "Mom wants them to be jumping for joy but it's not who they are. They were absent parents, so I'm not expecting them to be doting in-laws."

"*I* want them to be jumping for joy, too."

I asked if she'd be inviting them to her wedding.

"Should we?"

"They might think, 'This must be how normal families operate. When one sister gets married, the in-laws of the other sister automatically make it onto the guest list.' They might even come."

Jackleen said, "Duncan's mother thinks we should have a small, tasteful wedding, since it's his second marriage. She thinks we should show some restraint."

"Restraint, thine name is not Jackleen," I said.

"Thank you. It's my first wedding. Even Miss Manners would say, 'Go for it.'"

I said, "I know Perry's parents would've liked us to go big, go black-tie, and do it in Cincinnati. Besides, what a disgrace to get married on short notice. They asked Perry if it was a shotgun wedding."

"If only," said Jackleen.

We both ordered pasta. Though we had the same favorite, fettuccini Alfredo, I chose, for variety and sharing, spaghetti Bolognese. No dessert, but two cappuccinos. "We should do this every Saturday," said Jackleen.

When the check came, I got there first, despite her outstretched hand. I said, "Be serious."

"Before we leave," she said, "I want to run something by you."

"Such as?"

"You. In my wedding."

She was looking so apologetic that I asked, "Is it about what I'm wearing?"

"No. It's about breaking a tradition."

"Which one?"

She put her cup down and put her hand over mine. "I want you to walk me down the aisle," she said.

Chapter 46

We Four

Our dad was all-in. He not only wasn't crushed, but thought that my walking Jackleen down the aisle elevated our mother.

I asked how and why it elevated Mom.

"Because we'll walk ahead of you two, leading the way, both of us. And I'll do that dad job at the altar, lifting your veil and kissing you."

My not entirely sincere pushback to Jackleen had been "But the thing about a dad walking the daughter down the aisle is that he's wearing a tux, like every other man in a tux. All eyes are on the bride and her dress."

Jackleen said, "Of course I've thought of that! You'll wear what you were married in. It'll be . . . just right."

I laughed. "Plain . . . pale gray. Not an inch of lace."

She said, "But beautiful."

"I hope you're not doing it to say, 'Look how proud and happy Jane is. She's not worried that we'll be separated by marriage. No, not these two! And you may have heard my sister got herself into serious trouble, but she's back.'"

"What nonsense," Jackleen said.

We sprang it on the event planner at the wedding rehearsal. Not possible. Not done! Were we two brides at a same-sex wedding who didn't have parents? She'd seen dogs, a pair of chihuahuas, for God's sake, walk a bride down the aisle. And mothers, stepfathers, grandparents, uncles, both parents together. But with the father alive and present? It'll make the guests wonder if the bride and her father are estranged.

Jackleen didn't answer. Was she backing down, intimidated by Manhattan's A-list event planner? I said, "Excuse me. I happen to be the bride's attorney as well as her sister and matron of honor. Is there something in your agreement that gives you veto power over the bride? I'm walking her down the aisle because we shared a freaking womb. We used to be one zygote."

Jackleen found her voice again. "Whose decision is this? My employee's? Or mine and our father's?"

"And their mother's," said our mom.

The event planner snapped, "It's my job to anticipate future regrets."

As I was thinking, *What horseshit*, our dad said, "It's settled. I only wish their mother and I were walking *behind* them so I could watch Jane lead Jackleen down the aisle."

"Jack?" I asked.

"Done," she said.

*   *   *

Next to the bride, I was unadorned, wearing lower heels and carrying a single white rose. Our two skirts, mine full and hers sprouting in mermaid fashion, dovetailed perfectly. Even with my eyes front, I could tell by the gasps of delight and approval that Jackleen had been right, that our procession was causing something of a splash. Ahead, a teary Duncan, his daughters in pink dresses and matching pink hair, waited.

After welcoming the guests, the chaplain said, "I feel compelled to say, lest this question imply that the bride is property to be passed on from father to husband, but Jackleen has requested I ask just the same: 'Who giveth this woman to be married to this man?'"

Dad, barely able to speak, answered, "Her mother and I and her *sister* do"—more twindom overkill, for sure, yet making my eyes fill.

Next came the vows, Jackleen's on paper and Duncan's read from his iPhone. On and on they went, detailed and personal, expressing their feelings and failings.

I caught Perry's eye and we smiled. We hadn't written vows. We'd agreed that those were for an audience, which we'd never had and never needed.

Finally, Jackleen and Duncan were pronounced husband and wife, and they kissed to boisterous applause.

* * *

At the Harrow Inn, my father gave the welcoming toast. I'd helped him with it the night before, urging him to cut the lines that gave me unnecessary credit. It was Jackleen's wedding, okay? And remember how the child psychologists wanted us to be treated as separate entities?

"I know that," he said. "We did. We do."

"And he isn't giving you equal time because you're his favorite," said my mother, smiling. "What a crazy notion that would be."

Second to toast was Duncan's older daughter, unsmiling, testifying to how miserable her dad had been during the breakup, discomforting all until her sister joined her. They broke into song, harmonizing beautifully, music borrowed from *Frozen*, lyrics adapted to their happy father and stepmother.

Directed by the band's front man, the bride and groom took to the dance floor, followed by our parents, then Duncan's widowed mother taking a turn with her son. Perry and I were called up next, which meant it was our turn to be subjects for the roving videographer. Imagining a future niece or nephew watching, I said, "I'm Aunt Jane and this is your uncle Perry. We're having a wonderful time. It's our first dance together because . . . long story."

"Mainly, we were stuck at home," he said.

"Where we didn't know each other," I said.

"But luckily, due to a coincidence . . ."

"We met."

"And this person—the matron of honor, my wife? She fixed everything."

"So did he," I said.

The videographer lowered her camera. "Okay, okay, got it: You met, you married, and you lived happily ever after, right? They're about to cut the cake."

We said okay, fine, thanks. But when she'd left I said, "Kind of cynical, don't you think?"

"We exhausted her," Perry said. "She thought we were renewing our vows."

"What a good idea," I said. "Maybe we'll do that in ten years?"

"Or in twenty-five."

"And we'll dance," I said. "Now that I know what a good dancer you are. I'm going to add that to the plus column."

We said that often, referring to the outline, our founding document, now hanging on the wall above our bed. I'd wanted to preserve, protect, and display it; Perry wanted it matted and framed. How had I known, not that many months ago, to say yes to that invitation from left field, delivered clinically, point by point, without a hint of romance or the suggestion of a future; without even a smile? Look where it led—that hunch, that leap of faith! He'd picked a beautiful frame, and every night we slept beneath our story.

Acknowledgments

I took no liberties with the law or the courtroom, relying heavily on the advice of these good-natured attorneys: Bonnie Covey, who led me to Marwa Abdulla, who schooled me in immigration law and offered tips that worked their way into plot points; former criminal lawyer and professor of criminal law Daniel Medwed, who helped me throw the book at Jane and Perry; Judge Michael Ponsor, novelist and U.S. district judge, who ensured that everything was bench-correct; and intellectual property attorney Lawrence Siskind, who gave me license to quote, nearly word for word, recipes from my treasured antique cookbooks: *Hood's Practical Cook's Book for the Average Household*, published by C. J. Hood & Co, Lowell, MA, copyright 1897; and *Good Cooking* by Mrs. S.T. Rorer, published by Curtis Publishing Company of Philadelphia, copyright 1896.

For his help on police matters, book after book, I am indebted to James E. Mulligan, former chief of police in Georgetown, MA, police commissioner in Rockport and Rowley, MA, and surely the nicest-ever graduate of the FBI National Academy.

I salute Millicent Bennett with huge and fondest thanks for her early faith in *Ms. Demeanor*, and for her excellent editorial guidance and her gusto. We voyaged together from Houghton Mifflin, and reached the Harper shore a very committed crew. Her assistant, Liz Velez, is a constant provider of cheerful and speedy help, no matter the question.

I started this novel at the urging of my agent, Suzanne Gluck, whose wisdom, humor, support, and velvet glove I treasure every day. My thanks, too, to Nina Iandolo, her champion assistant, and to WME's Grayson Jernigan, my TikTok advisor.

Stacy Schiff bought my first book at Viking in 1985. Though she left editing to write prizewinning biographies, she's never left my side, and remains a wise and faithful reader, advisor, and dear friend.

I owe everything relating to art and (fictional) auction houses to the very dear, Significant Jonathan Greenberg.

Ellen Kapit, an associate real estate agent in New York City, allowed Duncan's dodgy dealings with great good humor, against her own impeccable standards. Lucky for me, fellow novelist Jillian Medoff was married at city hall in New York City and helped bring Jane and Perry's wedding to the page.

This book is dedicated to the memory of Mameve Medwed, who died on December 26, 2021. For thirty years, she read every page of every book as I polished each chapter. I depended on her approval, her laughter, and her wisdom every day. She was my perfect reader.

About the Author

ELINOR LIPMAN is the award-winning author of sixteen books of fiction and nonfiction. Her first novel, *Then She Found Me*, became a feature film directed by and starring Helen Hunt, with Bette Midler, Colin Firth, and Matthew Broderick. She was an Elizabeth Drew Professor of Creative Writing at Smith College, a finalist in the *New York Times*'s Nicholas Kristof Trump poetry contest, and the author of two *New York Times* Modern Love essays. She divides her time between Manhattan and the Hudson Valley.